My GiGi's House
Finding Hope

Many—
May you blossom
into the Masterpiece
God created you to
be. Meredith

MEREDITH SAGE KENDALL

Carpenter's Son Publishing

My GiGi's House

©2019 by Meredith Sage Kendall

Published by Carpenter's Son Publishing, Franklin, Tennessee

Edited by Lori Martinsek

Cover Illustration by Lauren Hickling

Cover Design by Amber Weigand-Buckley

This is a work of fiction. Names, characters, businesses, places, events, locales, and incidents are either the products of the author's imagination or used in a fictitious manner. Any resemblance to actual persons, living or dead, or actual events is purely coincidental.

This book is not intended as a substitute for the medical advice of physicians. The reader should regularly consult a physician in matters relating to his/her health and particularly with respect to any symptoms that may require diagnosis or medical attention.

ISBN:978-1-949572-47-6

To my amazing husband Rob for being my 180 Person and for seeing my potential even when I couldn't. Thank you for not allowing me to settle, but always pushing me to succeed.

This series has been a long time coming and my prayer is that you, the reader will find your 180 Person, and that above all else you will live a life transformed for the only one worth living for, Jesus.

If you or someone you know is dealing with an unplanned pregnancy, please contact your local pregnancy center. If you are unsure, please call Right to Life at 1-800-848-LOVE

If you are in a domestic abuse situation, please know there is help. Please call 1-800-799-SAFE

If you are finding yourself in an addiction and want help, please call 1-800-662-HELP (4357)

I

Ralynn and Ben were about to celebrate a year together when she started to feel sick every morning before she would go to work. Not thinking too much about it, she decided it was stress and nerves. Things had started getting tense between them, and she seemed to always be walking on eggshells around him now. Besides, there was no way she could be pregnant; she was on the newest form of birth control, and the commercials said no pregnancy was guaranteed.

After about a month of being sick every day, throwing up after eating certain foods, she decided to walk across to the drugstore on her lunch hour and get a pregnancy test. Ralynn knew she could not take it at home, so she locked herself in the bathroom at the pharmacy. It was positive.

As she made up scenarios in her head as to how this could have happened, Ben's threats from the other night began swarming like bees whose nest had just been bothered. Out of nowhere the other night, Ben told her explicitly that under no circumstance did he want kids and that if he ever found out she was pregnant, there would be no need for a doctor to perform the abortion because he would do it for her. Ralynn knew Ben did not make empty threats, and now she was going to have to fix this before he found out.

Trying to compose herself, the beep from her phone alarm went off, telling her that lunch break was over, and she needed to clock back in.

Walking back across the parking lot, Ralynn was surprised when she saw an old friend from high school get out of his car.

"Hey!" She yelled from about fifty feet away. He turned around, and Ralynn could not believe it really was him. *How'd he know?* she thought to herself. He was always there when I needed him the most in high school. Even though Ralynn had not seen him since high school, she was truly in shock that he was there in the parking lot of the restaurant where she worked.

The memories came flooding back faster than she would have liked, both the good and the bad. Back in high school they were inseparable. He had been her rock, her voice of reason, when things were crazy and she was wanting to run away. He would let her hide out at his house when things got really bad at home. Even though they were never an item, just seeing him made Ralynn feel like just maybe there was hope.

"Dave, how are you?" Ralynn leaned in to hug her old friend, but quickly retreated when she saw his female friend getting out of the car. The scowl on her face made Ralynn believe she had just overstepped her bounds.

"I'm fine. I want you to meet my girlfriend, Julia."

Ralynn went to shake her hand, but Julia was not having it. Ralynn turned back to Dave and started catching up as they walked into KT's Sandwich Shoppe. Ralynn was blindsided by the bombardment of questions from Ben: "Who is he? Why is here? Where'd he come from?"

The questions were coming so fast that Ralynn thought Ben might make a scene and ruin her chances for the promotion. Earlier in the day, Tim, the store manager, had asked her to stay a few minutes after her shift so that he could have her finish the paperwork for her new position of assistant manager. Relief that Ben left without incident was short-lived. As her shift continued, the anxiety and fear started to increase. She knew she was going to get it when she got to the house tonight. But she also knew better than to be late or not show up at all, so she mentally prepared herself for the punishment.

The rest of Ralynn's shift was spent mostly in the bathroom, throwing up. She wasn't entirely sure if it was pregnancy or fear induced; either way she was prepared to take the punishment that Ben felt was appropriate.

The paperwork was finished, and Ralynn was genuinely happy for the promotion, work at least before today, was her retreat away from Ben. As Ralynn was walking out to the bus stop, she looked up and saw him. He was parked across the street. Relieved because she had just missed the 7:05 bus, she thought for certain he would pull in and pick her up. To her amazement though, he revved up the engine on his truck, pulled across five lanes of traffic and almost hit her as he misjudged the turn. Squealing tires, yelling expletives, and shaking his fists was all that she saw as he sped away. Ralynn started talking to herself. "If only I had somewhere to go, I would leave him. This is not worth it." But because he had convinced her mother, Rita, that he was some sort of saint, she knew going home was not an option. Plus, the last time she lived at home, her mother's newest boyfriend was not so nice to her, and the last Ralynn had heard, he was still around. Ralynn felt her chances of some sort of normal life would be staying with Ben.

As Ralynn walked the quarter mile to the closest bus stop, she was happy that the rainy weather that had been forecasted had gone around the city. Ralynn was just about to sit down on the bench when the bus came. As she took her regular seat in the front row behind the driver, her anxiety started to get the best of her. She was very thankful for Mr. Henry, as he started to chat about his day and all that he had seen in his seventy-plus years living in this town. Their time together was a little longer this evening as the bus got stopped by the train. Ralynn was wondering why the train was going through the town so late tonight. You could set your clocks by it: 7 a.m. and 7 p.m. The bus got rolling again, and Mr. Henry got off at the first stop. Ralynn watched him jump off the bus with as much excitement as a three-year-old on Christmas morning. She found herself hoping to have just an ounce of his enthusiasm for life on any given day. To Ralynn's disappointment, the safety that the bus provided was coming to an end. Here it was, her stop. For a split second she was wondering if there was any way the driver could hide her away. Maybe she could go home with him. He was always speaking so wonderfully of his wife and their home. As the bus stopped and the doors opened, Ralynn found that her legs were not cooperating. The driver cleared his throat to announce her stop, but Ralynn felt like somehow she had become glued to the seat. Finally getting up from her seat, Ralynn found it more and more difficult to put one foot in front of the other and just about tumbled down the stairs of the bus. As she was walking the block to the house, it started to drizzle. Trying to keep her mind occupied, she started to think back on the day and realized that she had had almost every emotion possible.

She was excited about her promotion and couldn't wait to share it with Ben. Even though he had just left her at work and almost ran her over, she still cared for him and wanted their relationship to work.

II

Walking through the front door, Ralynn was not prepared for the first punch that knocked her flat on the floor. Crawling over to the couch to use it as leverage to pick herself up, Ben started charging toward her spewing statements about how she was seeing that guy behind his back. Realizing now that Ben was even more outraged about the day's events, Ralynn could not believe it when Ben accused her of being late tonight because she was with him. She was trying to make sense of what he was saying because she knew that he had seen her walk out of the restaurant and walk toward the bus stop. Before she could answer or question him, he kept the accusations going. He was accusing her of things she had not done.

In what common sense Ralynn had left from the bizarre events that had taken place in the last five minutes, she realized that Ben had been smoldering all day from seeing her with Dave and Julia. Surveying the room, Ralynn saw the empty twelve-pack of beer cardboard box, and while he was still spewing his allegations, he went to the refrigerator to grab another beer. Trying to make sense with whatever this was that had taken over Ben's body, she started to talk about her new promotion as assistant manager. That fast, the beer can that had been in Ben's hand narrowly missed her face. It ricocheted off the wall and hit her in the back of the head. Somehow it was her fault that beer was now spilling from the can all over the couch. As she was attempting to clean up the mess, a knock on the door made everything stop for a split second.

Ralynn could not believe what started to play out next but it was like everything was in slow motion. She could see and hear what was happening but there was nothing she could do. The pizza had arrived, and Dave, her old friend from the restaurant earlier that day was the one delivering it. Ben was irate and started accusing her of calling Dave to come save her. Being drunk, Ben started to go after Dave. Ralynn was not sure what happened to Dave, but the door slammed shut, the pizza was laying in the middle of the floor, and Ben was lunging toward her, yelling that everything was her fault. Before she could stop him, his hands were around her throat. Barely able to breath she squeaked out, *"Ben you are going to kill me!"*

At that moment, Ralynn started silently praying, *"Lord, you get me out of here alive, I will seek help."*

Ben mysteriously let go and walked to the bedroom. When she was sure that Ben was not coming back to start another round, Ralynn tiptoed to the bathroom to survey the damage. Staring in the mirror she started to cry. She did not even recognize the person she had become. Sliding down the wall, the cool tile felt good on her now-bruising body.

Not sure what she could take for the pain, she decided it was best to just go lay down and try to sleep. If she thought her mom would come get her, she would have left right away. Ralynn knew that Ben trusted Rita, so he would not have suspected anything if she showed up and they had walked outside together. But unfortunately, Ralynn knew how the conversation would go if she were to call. Rita would say how good Ben was for her and then say, *"Well, you made your bed. I guess you will need to lie in it."*

In the middle of the night, Ralynn felt like she was going to throw up again. Making her way to the bathroom, she was not prepared to see how her bruising was making its way up her neck. Sitting on the floor she started to cry and plead with God. *"If You allow me to see the light of day, I will seek help."*

Crawling quietly back in bed, Ralynn found herself thinking that she really didn't know what help would look like, but she did know that most people would be in church. It was the Bible Belt after all, and that's what people living in the South did on Sunday morning, especially in this small town. Then she remembered that while taking the bus to work last week she had counted eighteen churches in the two miles from the bus stop to KT's Sandwich Shop. *"Church. I will start with the first church I come to."*

Never fully falling asleep, Ralynn was grateful when the sun started to peek through the drapes. Ben was still passed out lying next to her, and his chainsaw sounding snore gave her the signal that she could roll out of bed unnoticed. Trying to be as quiet as a mouse, Ralynn was trying to remember what the weather was supposed to be as she rummaged through her closet. She remembered seeing the weather report briefly while at work; it was supposed to be a beautiful spring day with thundershowers in the afternoon. Trying to find something she thought would be appropriate for church and also hide her bruising without bringing attention to it, she came upon a modest skirt that looked like it belonged in the '70s. She quickly took it off the hanger and then grabbed a button down long sleeve brown shirt that matched and ran to the bathroom to change. She was also happy to find a scarf that accented her outfit but in her case was able to hide the bruising. As Ralynn was standing in the living room, grabbing her bag Ben took in a real loud snore that told her he was not waking anytime soon. Ralynn took this as her signal to walk out and live up to the end of the bargain with God.

The morning air was unseasonably cold, and the brisk wind made it feel like winter was about to make another appearance, but there was no turning back. Wishing she had found a warmer coat, she was grateful that she had enough sense about her to grab the large handbag. It still had her work uniform in it, wallet, ID, and her uncashed paycheck.

Turning the corner, the church was coming into view. This very large church was built in the late 1800s. The intricate architecture of the tower looked like it belonged on a castle from medieval times. As Ralynn got an up-close look at the church, it brought back a memory from history class all those years ago in high school. One afternoon a historian, employed by the Mapleton's Heritage Society, came to class. Ms. Ware, the historian, explained that the reason there were cut-outs on the towers of many of the downtown buildings were for protection during the Civil War. Men from the Confederate Army could be stationed up there. Ms. Ware went on to say, "as the story goes, these were the highest points in town. The soldiers had a 360-degree view and could see for miles. Therefore, they were able to give plenty of warning if the enemy was approaching and rally the troops." Ralynn wondered if the people in this church would rally the troops and fight her enemy today.

As Ralynn crossed the street and walked onto the church's property, she could hear people singing. The words; "Amazing Grace how sweet the sound that saved a wretch like me . . ." filled the air, and with each step, the voices in Ralynn's head started screaming, "No one in that building cares about you."

One step.

Two steps.

Now standing on the stoop, her hand was on the enormous handle, which matched the size of the door. Ralynn said a simple prayer that also included a prayer, hoping that these made-for-Goliath, wooden doors could be opened by a 5'4", 125-pound weakling.

Finding it hard to swallow because her throat was dry, Ralynn thought at any moment her air supply would be completely cut off. Ralynn took a big deep breath, and said out loud, "*God help me,*" all the while pulling the door open.

Expecting the door to be much heavier than it was, Ralynn yanked it open with more force than necessary. Thud! The door hit the black wrought-iron rail on the stoop, which startled Ralynn. She was not sure what caused the man who was standing watch over the entry to scowl, but with his stern look, formal dress, and dignified stature, he looked like a soldier from England who was guarding his post at Buckingham Palace.

Ralynn's body started to fill with shame and guilt. She wasn't sure what the trigger was, the man's scowl or that she thought she recognized someone from high school sitting in the pews about a third of the way up. Standing there in what seemed to be an eternity, she started hearing Ben's voice yelling. "*You don't belong in no place like this.*"

From all the commotion, the congregation turned around, and Ralynn's fears were confirmed. Her eyes met with the young man she knew from high school. Now feeling even more shame for being a distraction, Ben's words continued to ring through her ears. Ben had been emotionally tearing her down and lately had repeatedly been saying, "*If you ever went to church, God would strike it with lightning and burn it to the ground.*"

Ralynn turned and bolted down the stairs. Even though it was cold, she was burning up. The tears were flowing and her eyes were stinging, but fear started to paralyze her forward movement. She knew that Ben would have come out of his unconscious state, so going home was not an option. Based upon his behavior in the past when Ralynn had gone to the neighbor's house without his knowledge, she knew he would have already torn the neighborhood up and called her mom.

Ralynn knew standing in the parking lot was not an option either, so she started walking toward the center of town. The weather was starting to take a turn for the worse. The clouds were rolling in. The sky turned so dark that the street lights turned on. You could see the weather front coming, and Ralynn started mumbling that for once the meteorologist was correct, and she was wandering the streets with nowhere to go. Trying to figure out her next move, the smell of fresh baked bread coming from the Italian restaurant reminded her of the day Ben walked into KT's sandwich shop.

KT's was busier than normal for a Monday, and Ralynn was finally able to slow down for a minute. Then he walked in and took her breath away. Based upon the tool belt hanging loosely from his tight-fitting jeans and his yellow hard hat under his bulging bicep muscles, Ralynn took him as a carpenter.

Stammering to utter a "May I help you?" or "Welcome to KT's" Ralynn felt the words tumble back down her throat. Feeling the heat from her cheeks as she started to blush, she turned around as the manager came to her rescue and took the customer's order.

This seemed to satisfy the customer for the time being, but as he sat and ate, Ralynn would peek around the corner. When their eyes met, she wondered if her glances had excited him and stroked his ego. She hoped so. As he was getting up to leave, Ralynn conveniently needed to straighten the dining room. Her skin heated as she felt him slip a napkin into her apron as he was walking out.

Ralynn was so excited to see what was written on the napkin that she forgot about cleaning the rest of the dining room and took off running to the breakroom. She felt her face was going to break she was smiling so hard.

Ben's the name. See you tonight at the park. 8 p.m.

Ralynn not only wasn't able to concentrate for the rest of her shift, she couldn't contain her excitement about meeting this mystery man named Ben either.

They became inseparable, which was good for her because that meant she did not have to spend days off days at home. Ralynn and her mom, Rita, did not see eye to eye. As a matter of fact, if Ralynn had had any other option, she would not have moved back home in the first place. She was naïve when her friend told her she could move in with her. There was nothing in writing saying she had been paying rent nor was her name on the lease. So when the sheriff arrived that day to carry out the eviction, there was nothing Ralynn could do. The manager was at least nice enough to let her get her things out.

Ben became a welcomed excuse. Ben would show up every day just as her shift was ending and take her home. At first, Ralynn was over the top in love with all this attention. Rita told Ralynn one day that she thought he was just a true Southern cowboy and was so excited to see how he was treating her. Rita also would use any opportunity to tell Ralynn that Ben was certainly a step above the others. He was always around and never let Ralynn out of his sight, so when Ben asked Ralynn to move in with him only after two months of dating, Rita was all for the idea. In fact, Rita all but packed Ralynn's bags.

Ralynn's relationship was tolerable with her mother until the day Rita chose a man over Ralynn. They had gone shopping earlier in the day and bought a new bathroom mirror; unfortunately it never made it out of the kitchen where it was put for safekeeping. Ralynn was in her room when she heard the pleading of her mother. She knew better than to intervene; she had done that once and still had a bald spot where the hair never grew back. When the crashing of the glass had stopped and the back door slammed shut, Ralynn knew it was safe to come out. She was not prepared for what she encountered. Rita was sitting in the fetal position, tears streaming down her face. Her clothes torn and soaked in blood and beer. Ralynn pleaded with her mother to kick him out, but within an hour Ralynn, was being banished to her room. He had come back to the house, said he was sorry for getting so angry, and Rita let him stay. From that day on, Ralynn lived in her room and could not wait until she turned eighteen, so she could leave the house for good.

Ralynn didn't know when she first began to use the mirror memory as the measure for judging Ben's altered behavior. *"Things aren't so bad,"* she'd offer as an excuse. *"At least he hasn't thrown me into a mirror."*

Ben would start to make a scene at KT's when Ralynn was not ready to go as soon as he walked in the door. It did not matter that her shift was not over for another five minutes; he wanted her to be in the truck immediately when he pulled in. Ralynn was always apologizing for Ben's behavior. Then with no warning, Ben decided that Ralynn needed to start catching the bus to and from work. Ralynn did not even know how to use the transit system, and without any notice, she had to figure it out. Ralynn was getting pretty good at figuring things out and allowing life to happen as the days went by, though.

Even though things were getting progressively worse at home, she was excelling at work. She had gone from part time to full time in a matter of a few weeks. Then after just a month, they promoted her to team lead. She was really excited about her newest promotion: assistant manager. Ralynn never let anyone know what was really happening at home. She wore a smile even though she was dying on the inside and wanted out. Ben had quit his job, and Ralynn had somehow become the reason for it. His yelling had gotten louder and more frequent, but now, there were outbursts of anger. Things had started to be thrown in Ralynn's direction almost every night when she would come home. She had not realized that Ben was actually watching her from across the street until she got home one night and he confronted her.

"Why were you smiling at him?"

"Who?"

"That customer. You were getting pretty chummy with him. I saw you."

"What? Where were you?"

"It doesn't matter. Just know if I can't have you, then no one will have you."

That night was the first time Ralynn started to fear for her life. His anger had become almost to the boiling point. He had his hands on her arms, holding them so tight that she was black and blue within thirty minutes. Ralynn had thought that work was the only normal part of her life, and now Ben was controlling that, too.

The abuse she suffered was no longer just emotional. It had become physical, and Ralynn had to find creative ways to hide the bruising. She had stopped thinking about what was next in her life; she was just trying to get through today alive. That brought back even more memories of her childhood and the abuse she suffered at the hands of her mother's boyfriends. But why did she not leave? Why did she not move out? Fear. Ben during his episodes of rage would yell out, *"If I can't have you no one will."*

Ralynn chose to stay with Ben and live with his threats because she really wanted to live and did not want to find out if he really would kill her if she left. Ralynn also started to believe that this was all life had to offer. This was the life her mother lived while Ralynn was in the home and was still living today.

III

As the thunder clapped, the clouds let loose a torrential down-pour. Ralynn sought safety in the local coffee shop. She was hoping to use the bathroom and just sit in a corner bench alone while she figured out her next move because going to the church for help did not turn out the way she had hoped. Daydreaming and watching the storm blow in, Ralynn was brought back to reality when a woman with a determined look on her face walked in the door and dropped her purse, Bible, and a notebook on the table next to her. There was no one sitting at any of the other tables, but she chose to sit almost on top of Ralynn.

"Seriously, out of all the seats in this store, you sit right next to me!" she thought. Luckily Ralynn did not speak what she was thinking because she was about to find out that God was answering her prayer from last night.

The lady said, *"I'm sorry, is someone sitting here?"* Ralynn really want-ed to say yes, but something made her stay silent. This lady hadn't even been sitting there long enough to power-on her tablet when her phone rang. Ralynn didn't mean to eavesdrop, but this woman was practically sitting on her, and it was a public place. The longer the phone conversation went, the more emphatic, but with compassion she was speaking to the person on the other line. Ralynn's ears perked up the longer the one-sided exchange took place. Now Ralynn was listening on purpose because her interest was piqued.

"No, it's not okay that he hits you only a couple times a week."

"No, I am not willing to call you out of work, so you can work it out."

"Well dinner is at 6 p.m. on Thursday. You know how to get there if you are interested in learning to do things differently. And if you need a safe place to go, the offer still stands, and I will still be waiting."

Hanging up the phone, the lady turned to Ralynn. She said, "Hi, my name is Shelly Waddell and I apologize for taking that call and not walking out."

Ralynn was still in shock with how direct this woman was with the person on the other end of the conversation, so much so that she didn't hear Shelly introduce herself. Ralynn was trying to act as if she had no desire to take this woman up on the offer she had just given to the person on the phone. Ralynn was also trying to act like she didn't have any problems, but she had made the mistake of turning on her phone and it kept buzzing saying she now had fifty voicemails. The fear started to control Ralynn's emotions, and the tears that had stopped were now flowing even harder. Afraid of making a scene and being an embarrassment to everyone, Ralynn attempted to get out of her seat, but it was like she was superglued to it. There was no standing up. That's when Shelly leaned over and as she was handing Ralynn her card, she said, "My name is Shelly, if you ever want to talk."

Before Ralynn could put up a wall to insulate herself, her mouth opened and said, "I am running from my boyfriend. He beat me up pretty bad last night."

Ralynn moved the scarf over so Shelly could see the bruises around her throat.

Ralynn kept talking and Shelly just listened. Just when Ralynn thought she was done telling this complete stranger her life story, a smell or a sound would trigger another memory so she would keep on talking. By this time, Ralynn was crying uncontrollably, but she didn't care and she wasn't going to run away. There was something different about this woman and she felt safe.

As they sat in their own little world of this locally owned coffee shop, patrons came and went. Ralynn realized Shelly was not fazed at all and just sat there listening intently. Ralynn was surprised that not once did Shelly open her Bible to show her passages that would shame or guilt her into changing her life. Shelly just became an empathic sounding board and showed no judgment. They talked for hours while the stormy weather rolled in. The coffee shop shook a few times when the thunder rumbled in the not-so-far distance, and the lightning filled up the sky with the most amazing light show that could only be attributed to God's handiwork.

The owner of The Coffee Shoppe had just started going through the dining area, giving the thirty-minute warning to closing. Ralynn started to get nervous when she saw Shelly starting to pack up her things. Shelly must have sensed Ralynn's apprehension because without hesitation Shelly put her hand on Ralynn's arm and said, "Honey, I am here to help if you want something different."

It was in that moment that Ralynn felt what she thought was the love of a mother. The tears started again. "I'm sorry, I didn't mean for you to start crying."

Shelly's tone was so comforting and soothing that it caught Ralynn off guard. She had not had anyone talk to her that tenderly to her since her GiGi passed. When she did talk to her mother, it often ended with everything being her fault and she heard that she "deserved what she got" and, "she needed to stop being an embarrassment to the family."

Shelly's hand was still laying on Ralynn's shoulder. To Ralynn that let her know that Shelly wasn't leaving and that she wasn't ashamed of her crying. "Honey, I am sorry but I don't even know your name, but I take it you have nowhere to go, do you?"

"My name is Ralynn."

Shelly then asked the question a little more pointed. "You have nowhere safe to go do you?"

Ralynn hung her head and shook it to say "no." Shelly scooted even closer to Ralynn and put her arm around her. For the first time in a while, Ralynn felt safe with someone touching her. She didn't stiffen up, getting ready to take the next blow. Shelly softly whispered. "It's going to be okay. You will not have to go back."

What seemed like an eternity later to Ralynn but was in reality less than fifteen minutes, Shelly had her phone out. After scrolling through her contacts, she handed Ralynn the phone and said, "I can't make the call for you, but if you are wanting to change your life and start over, there is a safe house you can go to, and I will help you get to the pickup point."

Ralynn was now shaking for the first time, not because she was in fear of her life, but she was afraid of the unknown. She took the phone and pushed talk. Ralynn was surprised, the phone didn't even ring and a lady's voice said, "Are you safe?"

"Yes"

Shelly just sat next to her saying nothing, no judgment, no I told you so, no how dare you let your life get so bad, just a grandmotherly figure, wanting to help the hurting stop. After answering a few questions, the lady on the other end of the phone asked Ralynn to put Shelly back on.

"Hello. Yes, I know where that is. Give us fifteen minutes and we will meet you there."

Shelly hung up the phone. The tone in Shelly's voice was partly asking in nature, but mostly telling to Ralynn to pick up her things, so they could go. Ralynn followed Shelly out to the parking lot, and they got into Shelly's champagne-colored minivan. This van had all the bells and whistles: leather interior with seat warmers for the driver and passenger, which Ralynn quickly realized had been turned on; electric windows; and both side doors were electric sliding with a push of a button. The best part for Shelly, she said, was the moon roof. She loved looking out into the sky after a hard day at work. Pulling out of the parking lot, Shelly told Ralynn that this van was her gift from God. On Shelly's birthday a few years earlier a very kind donor purchased it for the ministry. Shelly took a quick right turn, and they were now driving down the main street headed out of town toward the country. As they drove past the street Ralynn's apartment was on, she had this overwhelming feeling of darkness come over her. Panic. Anxiety. Ralynn thought she was going to have to have Shelly pull over, so she could throw up. Feelings of shame started to overtake Ralynn. Rita's words started to take over Ralynn's thoughts: *"You made your bed; now you lie in it."*

The road got narrow and started having many bends and turns. As the road started to curve, Shelly took a sharp right, down a hill. Then an immediate right into what looked like an abandoned building's driveway but was in reality an old country church. As part of protocol, Shelly went behind the church and turned off her lights.

Ralynn, holding her belly ever so tenderly had decided that there was no way she could go through with this pregnancy after Ben's outrage. She had made the decision that she would call the clinic in the morning to make an appointment for an abortion. She had not told anyone that she was pregnant, and it was going to stay a secret. Ralynn vowed that no one would ever know.

Shelly broke the silence and Ralynn's thoughts by asking, "Hey, you okay? You've been quiet."

"Yeah, I'm good. Thanks for doing this," Ralynn said

Within five minutes, another vehicle pulled into the driveway and followed the same protocol. It was now parked next to them. As soon as the other van parked, the driver got out and walked up to the driver's side of Shelly's van. Rolling down her window, Shelly made the introductions.

"Ms. Stacy, this is Ralynn. And Ralynn this is Ms. Stacy the assistant director of Z-House."

The pleasantries were short and sweet. Ralynn thought that Ms. Stacy belonged in a fashion magazine or on the cover as a model. What was she doing working at a safe house?

As Ralynn was reaching for the door handle to let herself out, Shelly handed her another card. "Ralynn we would love to have you come to dinner on Thursday night. Dinner starts at 6 p.m."

Shelly then explained to Ralynn that her phone is on 24/7, so unless it was an emergency, please do not call or text in the middle of the night because she would answer. Shelly went on to say that she hoped she would hear from Ralynn, asking for directions.

As Ralynn got out of Shelly's van to get into the safe house vehicle, Shelly also got out. She came around to the passenger side and gave Ralynn a hug. Telling Ralynn she loved her made Ralynn freeze. That combination triggered in Ralynn a fear that the beatings would start again, or they had just finished and Ben was trying to settle her down before someone called the police.

As Ralynn's body started to stiffen, Shelly whispered, "I am not him. We are proud of you for taking the first step to be free."

As Shelly released her hug, she said quietly in Ralynn's ear, "I pray we see you on Thursday night."

As Shelly turned to get back in her van, Ralynn saw the tears. This exchange lasted less than a minute but was so powerful for Ralynn. Shelly was someone who didn't know her, but from an afternoon chance encounter, wanted more for her life than she had wanted for herself.

Ralynn climbed into the passenger side of the rundown van, thinking she was ready for a new start. As Ms. Stacy shut her door and started the van, Ralynn's anxiety was rising as her mind started racing with thousands of questions.

What am I doing?

Will I lose my freedom?

Was he really that abusive?

Did I overreact?

Was he really that bad?

Did I deserve the beatings?

How will he make it without me?

How will I make it without him?

What will this place look like?

Will I feel like I am in prison?

Will they take my phone?

Can I keep my job?

What will the rules be like?

Will I feel safe?

Her questions were interrupted when Ms. Stacy announced that they had arrived at the house. As Ralynn surveyed her new surroundings, she had no idea there was a safe house so close to downtown. Ralynn hesitantly got out of the van and walked sheepishly toward the house. With Ms. Stacy's arm around Ralynn's waist, she whispered, *"You're safe here."*

IV

W alking through the door of the safe house, Ralynn was taken back to a time in her life when everything was perfect. The sweet smell of homemade sugar cookies was filling the house and the sound of laughter that was coming from the kitchen made the five-year-old in her want to run past the adults and take her place on the stool next to her GiGi. For just a moment she saw herself in a dark navy-blue shirt with multi-colored flowered shorts, navy-blue knee highs, and white tennis shoes. Her GiGi's smile said it all when she used to walk in the door, and Ralynn asked to help.

GiGi had a special stool for her, and it was always right where she had left it. The old apron that Ralynn wore would be hanging on the inside of the pantry door, waiting patiently to be put back to work. GiGi was a very loving, patient, and religious woman who died unexpectedly right before Ralynn's eighth birthday, and her life was never the same.

Ralynn was quickly brought back to the present with the sound of a pot hitting the floor. No GiGi, no mom, just a bunch of strange women who would instantly become her housemates.

Ms. Stacy began the introductions, "Hey everyone, I would like you to meet Ralynn." Ralynn was greeted with smiles and head nods. In a strange sort of way, she had a sense of belonging.

Just then a young lady came running into the kitchen. She stopped in her tracks when she saw Ralynn. Cautiously she walked over and introduced herself as though they had never met. *"Hi my name is Julia. Can I help you get settled?"*

Ralynn was confused because she was sure she already knew Julia. Ralynn was pretty sure that she had met her the day before in the parking lot at KT's, as she was being introduced as Dave's girlfriend. So she was wondering why Julia was acting like she didn't know her. As Julia guided Ralynn through the living room, Ralynn was getting the hint to not say a word. Julia took her down a hallway to a room on the right and stopped, saying, *"We are here."*

Ralynn was astonished and wanted to make sure she understood. "You mean; I get my own room?"

"Yes, and you have your own bathroom too."

Julia was now acting like a game show hostess and started opening and closing drawers and doors, showing Ralynn that they were fully stocked with anything and everything she would need. Julia led her into the hallway and stopped at a closet. Again, pretending to be on a game show she announced, "And behind door number one, you will find all the make-up—every kind, color and shade. There are also brand new PJs, socks, underwear, and bras—all sizes; just take what you need."

Ralynn was shocked and stood in silence, taking it all in. As the tears started to fall, Julia, broke the silence and quietly said, "You are worth it."

Ralynn was taken back and wanted to know how Julia knew how she was feeling. Ralynn had been beaten down by Ben's words for so long that she had forgotten what it felt like to be given something, just because, expecting nothing in return.

Guiding Ralynn back to the bedroom, Julia sat her down.

"Please don't tell anyone that you saw me with Dave yesterday. I was supposed to be at work. I met Dave a few years ago, and he has always just been a friend. Then we reconnected when he came in the store last month."

"Well, I figured something was up. What will happen if you get caught?"

"I will get kicked out. And I didn't know he was going to introduce me as his girlfriend. He has just been an amazing friend."

"I understand. Thank you for helping me get settled."

"Before I leave, one more thing. Do you have a cellphone?"

Without questioning, Ralynn grabbed her phone out of the pocket of her purse and handed it to Julia. Julia immediately started going through Ralynn's apps explaining that a few months ago, one of the ladies who had just fled her domestic partner had a smart phone and it had apps that were able to find friends. When she connected to the internet here at the house, the apps were activated. Her abuser found her the next day. Julia went on to explain that the cell service was very sketchy at the house, so the management allowed the girls to connect to the Wi-Fi to enable Wi-Fi calling if they have it as an option.

Ralynn was surprised to learn that she had a find friend's app on her phone, and it was set to go active if she had connected to the internet.

Julia told Ralynn to get some sleep, but Ralynn's stomach was not thinking of sleep as it was too busy growling. Looking at her watch, Ralynn realized she not only had missed lunch but she also hadn't eaten since she clocked out of work almost twenty-four hours earlier. About that time, Ms. Stacy must have realized that Ralynn hadn't eaten, because she showed up with a plate of food. Sitting on her bed, she scarfed down the chicken pot pie and homemade apple pie. As soon as the last bite hit her stomach, it all came right back up, though. Luckily, there was a trash can within reach, and she was able to get to the toilet before it was too bad. Quietly and quickly, Ralynn tried to clean everything up. She was so afraid that someone would come to check on her, and that was the last thing she needed to explain. The clinic opened at 8 a.m., and she already had the number hidden in her wallet. With all the emotions she had today, Ralynn really didn't know what she was feeling at that moment, but she heard Julia talking with another lady as they walked passed her room.

"If Ralynn's day was anything like most of ours the day we made the phone call to get picked up, she is probably running on fumes and probably about to pass out. I am pretty sure her adrenaline rush has stopped."

Ralynn overheard the other lady then add, "I wish we could tell her tomorrow will be better. But like most of us, tomorrow is when you start to doubt the decision."

Ralynn stuck her head out the door and got their attention, "What do you mean, why won't tomorrow be better?"

Julia turned around to come back to Ralynn, but the other lady hurried off to her room. Julia started to explain that the regret will set in shortly, and she will start to make excuses that it wasn't that bad. Julia went on to say, "You will start to question everything, but take it from me, don't leave and go back to him."

Julia then rolled up her sleeve and showed Ralynn the scars from where her boyfriend had placed lit cigarettes on her arms. "This is what he did when I went back last time. He told me things were going to be different. They weren't. They actually were worse. So, believe me when I say if he does happen to contact you, don't listen to his lies. Someone doesn't change overnight, and your life is too important."

With that Julia spun on her heels and exited the room.

Now as Ralynn was standing in her new room in her new home, the loneliness started to creep in. The thought of Ben finding her was bittersweet. Would he come and apologize? Would he sweep her off her feet? Oh, how she longed for the fairytale life. Now feeling ready for bed, Ralynn was walking toward the bathroom when she caught a glimpse of herself in the mirror. The voices started again. *"No one will come to your rescue. You aren't worth their time."*

As she pulled the neck of her shirt down, all she could see was black and blue. Ben was always very careful not to leave marks that couldn't be covered by clothing; sometimes it meant Ralynn had to wear a turtleneck or scarf. Just like the ladies said, the adrenaline rush of the day was ending. Ralynn was starting to feel all the bruises she was seeing in the mirror. As she stared at herself in the mirror, she remembered her promise to God, and the last thing she wanted now was for Ben to find her.

After surveying all her damage, she invaded the hall closet for the necessities. The longer Ralynn stayed upright, the more the bruises started to hurt, so she quickly sank down on the bed, hoping to stay awake for just a few more hours. Looking around at the new surroundings, she came upon a large woven basket that had found its home in the seat of the comfy-looking rocking chair. There was a manila envelope sticking out that said "Welcome" on it.

Ralynn reached over to grab it when she had a sudden hot flash followed by nausea. Running to the bathroom, she sat on the tile floor, waiting to see if her system was going to clean itself out again. The coolness of the tile floor felt refreshing, but Ralynn was confused, was she getting sick or was it from the pregnancy? Sitting there all she could think of was *"I can't be sick; I have to work tomorrow."*

Even though the tile floor was keeping away the nausea and hot flashes, Ralynn felt that the bed was going to be a better choice. Crawling out of the bathroom, she climbed into the bed. Lying there, she felt like she was floating on the clouds. The mattress was so comfortable, and the best part was she wasn't being poked in her backside by springs that had broken. Just as she was falling asleep, she rolled onto her side and found security in the fetal position.

Ralynn woke herself up gasping for air. She wasn't totally awake, her heart was racing, but when she opened her eyes and saw the sun peeking through the blinds, she realized it was just a nightmare. His hands were around her throat. She couldn't breathe. Ben was mad because she had left and spent the night at a friend's house. As he was choking her, he kept repeating, *"If I can't have you, no one will."*

Ralynn tried to fall back asleep, but every time she closed her eyes, the image of Ben filled the space. Rolling over, the clock read 7:01, so Ralynn decided to get up and get ready for the day.

The showerhead had multiple settings, and that made Ralynn's body happy. The bruising was now all over her chest, stomach, and arms. As much as the hot water felt awesome, every drop hurt as it hit a bruised spot. That nightmare was so real that the tears were starting all over again. After about thirty minutes of just sitting in the tub and letting the water run, Ralynn finally had the guts to get out of the shower and face the day. Putting the clothes she came in back on was her only option. So she got dressed, did her hair, put some make-up on, and before she made her way to the kitchen, she called the clinic.

They answered immediately. Ralynn told them that she wanted to terminate her pregnancy and had Friday off from work if she could get it done then. They had a 9 a.m. appointment and would see her then. Before they hung up, they had her repeat the address to make sure she had the closest clinic.

"520 Cobbles Way"

V

Ralynn made her way to the kitchen and stood there in silence, taking in all the commotion of the morning. Single moms, kids, babies, and then women who were like her—pregnant. She hadn't told anyone yet, and she wasn't about to. Ralynn had made up her mind, and her appointment was on Friday. Now she just needed to figure out how to get there. The emotions were real and overwhelming. Ralynn went from being excited for new opportunities to feeling paralyzed of starting over. Then panic would set in, thinking:

What if I fail?

What if I get lonely and run back to him?

What if . . . ?

Just then, Ms. Stacy who was still on her shift, broke Ralynn's train of "what if's" to tell her good morning. Ms. Stacy also asked if she would like breakfast.

Julia walked in about that time and offered to make Ralynn a bowl of oatmeal topped with fresh fruit. While she was still trying to decide if she trusted herself to eat and not throw up, Julia told her to sit down, and it would be out in a minute.

Just as Julia put down the oatmeal in front of Ralynn, Ms. Stacy came back into the kitchen and asked Ralynn to come to her office, which was located off the dining room, when she was finished. After the oatmeal with fresh strawberries and blueberries was gone, Julia joked that Ralynn had won the clean plate award and that she could be excused. Ralynn laughed and said, *"Thanks, Mom."*

It was not hard to find Ms. Stacy's office. The house was an open concept, and even though she had sat at the bar in the kitchen for breakfast, the dining area was in full view and Ms. Stacy's office door could be seen from where Ralynn had parked herself.

"Ms. Stacy, can I ask you a question?"

"Sure."

"Why?"

"Why what?"

"Why here? Why do you work here?"

"Well, that's simple. I was sitting where you were many years ago. Not exactly that same chair. But in your circumstances. I was fighting for my life. I was married fresh out of high school. We lived in a very depressed area of the country, and you either were a farmer or you worked in the factory. My husband graduated one day and went to work in the factory the next. He was ready to make money, buy a car, and buy a home, and I was head over heels in love. We bought the American Dream on credit.

Then one day the factory closed, and my husband no longer had a job. The bills started to come in and we had no way to pay for them. He started drinking. I didn't think anything of it. He said it relaxed him. The problem was, he started drinking to escape. Then one night, just about dark, the lights went off. He walked outside and the electric company worker was leaving in his pickup. Somehow that night, everything was my fault.

Now I will tell you I did have a temper, and I may not have always said things in the nicest way possible, but that night, I ended up in the hospital, literally fighting for my life. He found the closest thing he could to throw at me and that happened to be a sledge hammer. I didn't see the warning signs. Or, maybe I didn't want to see the warning signs. At first, I would make excuses for his anger. Then I became the reason for his anger. The day I was taken out in the stretcher was the last day I saw him or my house.

When I was released from the hospital, I had nowhere to go. I had no one to call. It was just me. While I was in the hospital, they told me I was pregnant, but the trauma caused me to miscarry. I vowed that day that I would never ever let another person, especially a man, cause me harm. I scraped enough money together through what friends I still had left and moved to Tennessee. I found out about Z-House and applied for a job. Unfortunately, I was not ready to work here because I needed to heal first, so I became a resident. And next week, I celebrate my tenth anniversary to my amazing husband."

After Ms. Stacy finished her story, Ralynn found herself more open to following the rules, if that meant she could heal, too.

The first day in the home was packed with filling out papers and interviews. Part of the rules for the nonprofit were that they will always rescue a lady who calls in on the dedicated line. After a good night's sleep, they sit you down and ask some very hard questions to make sure you really want a life free from your abuser. It's not a foolproof questionnaire, and they know that, but it at least helps them to understand where you are coming from and whether or not you are being sincere at the time. During one of the interviews, the staff said they would help navigate getting personal items out of the house if wanted.

Ralynn told them anything of value was still at her mom's house. The only thing that was at Ben's was clothing and personal hygiene items, and she didn't think it was worth risking her life or anyone else's for those items. The staff agreed. Ms. Stacy did realize that Ralynn was wearing yesterday's clothes, so after they were done filling out paperwork, Ms. Stacy took her to the clothes closet. Ralynn once again was overwhelmed with the outpouring of gifts she could choose from. The house had very strict rules on what they allowed to be donated. The clothing had to be new or gently worn. No holes, unless they were jeans made that way, and nothing that could be considered sexual or revealing was allowed. The only rule for the ladies was take what you need, and if you find it doesn't fit or you aren't going to wear it after all, put it back.

After Ralynn was freshly dressed, she met back up with Ms. Stacy to finish going over the rules of the house. Ms. Stacy also told Ralynn how the home got its name.

"Its name came from the Old Testament. There was a widow in Zarephath, and the prophet Elijah was directed to ask her for food and water even though there was a famine in the land. She did as she was told. The Bible never tells of her name but what was written about her focused on what she did, rather than on who she was."

Ms. Stacy went on to say that at Z-house, they wanted the women to be remembered for what they did with their future not who they were when they started.

Going over the rules for Z-house, participants needed to understand that the home was a faith-based home. Those who lived here did not need to profess Christianity, but all of the teachings, classes, and partners would come from that point of view. Anyone who lived here would be required to participate in at least one program that was approved by the staff. It was also mandatory that the women sit through budgeting class. Ms. Stacy explained that parenting was also needed if you had a child. She went on to explain that the state brought in a case manager once a month to explain further any rights and obligations, or answer questions we might have and to sign us up for any benefits we may be eligible for. Anyone who lived here also needed to understand that all the classes were through partnerships at this time. The staff was hoping to get classes offered again onsite, but since the economy went south, things have been strained. The staff's main job was to help the women navigate the legal system, help the women find a job, if needed, that was in the approved pick-up area if they didn't have transportation and to get children into the local school or daycare.

Finally finished with paperwork and interviews, Ralynn had a few minutes to herself before she needed to leave for her shift at KT's. Ralynn found herself being pulled to the front porch. The swings were swaying ever so gently in the wind and looked inviting, but with a cup of coffee, a danish in one hand and her new journal that she found in her welcome basket, in the other, Ralynn opted for the oversized chairs. Sitting there in the quiet of the afternoon, Ralynn let her mind just unwind. She closed her eyes, but immediately started having flashbacks of Saturday night. She had never seen Ben so unstable. That night went from bad to worse.

Everything was wrong. Nothing could calm him down. All Ralynn did was ask a simple question. *"Did I do something to make you angry?"* She hadn't realized how much he despised her job—how many things she did wrong in a single day and how much the sight of her made him sick. Then he lunged toward her. Before she could stop him, his hands were around her throat, and she couldn't breathe. Ralynn still didn't know why he let go, but she remembered squeaking out, "Ben you are going to kill me!"

But she did start praying at that moment, *"Lord, if you get me out of here alive, I will seek help."*

That Saturday night was a moment she never wanted to repeat. She truly wanted to live and never desired to find herself in fear like that again.

The slamming of the front screen door jolted Ralynn out of that nightmare. Ms. Stacy had sent Julia out to tell her they would be ready to take her to work in thirty minutes. Ralynn took this time to walk down off the porch and survey her new surroundings. She couldn't believe it; it was so beautiful. The trees hid it well. The driveway looked to be a private dirt road at the beginning. Then as it passed the tree line, it turned into a beautifully paved driveway outlined with brick pavers and antique gas lanterns. There were Bradford Pear trees on both sides, accented with flowering hostas.

The wrap-around porch was painted a bright white, which accented the New England Blue Victorian mansion. There were white rocking chairs lining both sides of the front screen door. On the ends of the porch, hanging from the white beadboard ceiling, were white painted wooden swings, made for just one person. The swings had oversized yellow with blue floral homemade cushions. On both sides of the house, still on the porch, were oversized white wicker chairs with a coffee table in between them. It was perfect for morning coffee.

Just as the perfectly manicured lawn, which reminded Ralynn of a baseball field she had seen on TV, ended, the trees had been cut back to allow for a beautiful prayer garden off to the left, and where the garden ended, a walking trail began. This trail was completely hidden within the trees, so to the passerby, it was just a wooded lot.

Ralynn found herself feeling like she had just been transported into a fairy tale, and she was thankful for her chance meeting yesterday.

VI

The director, Ms. Shaw, drove Ralynn to work that day. Ralynn hadn't had the opportunity to meet her yet, so she was excited to have her to herself for the ride to work.

Ralynn never got a word in, nor did she get to ask any questions. All the way to KT's Ms. Shaw spoke of all the protocols and what to do if he shows up at work and remember not to go outside by herself. Ms. Shaw also let Ralynn know that she thought this was a bad idea, but because they had a working relationship with KT's for years, she was going to allow Ralynn to go to work tonight. But if there was any trouble, she would be unemployed for the time being.

As Ralynn was about to exit the vehicle, hand on the door handle, Ms. Shaw once again reiterated the explicit instructions: "Do not go outside alone at all during your shift. When your shift is over, come out only if one of us is waiting for you. We will be waiting for you right here."

Ms. Shaw pointed to the curb right up next to the sidewalk. Ralynn was so thrilled to have someone on her side for a change, that she didn't even see Ben sitting across the street. Ralynn may have gone her entire shift without noticing him, but as she was sitting down to enjoy her dinner break, there were tires screeching and horns blowing. That combination always made the employees at KT's look out the front window. There he was.

Ben was sitting close enough to the store, but far enough away that as long as Ms. Shaw or whomever came to pick up Ralynn parked right next to the building she would have enough time to get to the vehicle.

Thankfully, Ben stayed across the street all night, and as Ralynn's shift was over, Ms. Shaw pulled in, circled the building and parked up against the sidewalk. Making a run for it and slamming the door as she got in, Ralynn's heart was pounding so loudly, she was pretty sure Ms. Shaw could hear it too. "You alright?" she asked. "You look like you saw a ghost."

Before Ralynn could say a word, she had to fling back open the door, so all her dinner could come back up.

"Honey, where is he?"

Ralynn pointed across the street.

"You okay for me to drive now?"

Ralynn nodded. Ms. Shaw pulled out on to the busy highway. The street that KT's is on never has a lull in the traffic, so Ben couldn't get across the five lanes to follow them. Ralynn watched in the side mirror as Ms. Shaw put more and more distance between he and them.

Ms. Shaw took a different way home that night. She took turns that had nothing to do with getting to the house, but when she was sure, he was not following them she proceeded home.

It was pitch black by the time they reached the property. Ms. Shaw pushed a button on a remote and the gate opened. As soon as they were on the other side, it closed back up. Ralynn was not sure how she missed that detail last night. The gate was nothing fancy. It actually looked like you would have to manually get out and unlock the padlock that was attached to the chunky-link chain.

Ralynn's expression must have said it all because Ms. Shaw said, "Yes, it is made to look simple. Like it's just a pasture so that we don't bring attention to the property. In the spring and the fall, the farmer next door, who is also a supporter, comes and bales the wheat to make it look like it's part of his property."

By the time they were safely inside, Ralynn had finally settled down. Ms. Shaw thought it best for Ralynn to call KT's and ask for the rest of the week off. Seeing that Ben was waiting for her, she agreed to call Tim. Looking at the time, she realized he would still be there so she called right away. To her relief, Tim thought that it was a good idea also and gave her the rest of the week off. As a matter of fact, Tim told her to take all the time she needed.

VII

The first few days flew by for Ralynn. The ladies who lived there were from all walks of life. Some had been there for months and others just days. Wednesday evening, Ralynn was on her way to the kitchen to offer her help when she walked in on Diane and her girls sitting on the floor in the living room. They had been living at Z-house for about two-weeks and were in the middle of a heated exchange. From what Ralynn could gather, friends had invited the girls to ride the bus home after school on Friday and spend the weekend. The girls were crying as their mother kept reiterating the fact that they should be used to the shelter rules by now. They couldn't have friends over, nor spend the night away without their parent, and then they could only stay with immediate family for a maximum of forty-eight hours. Ralynn understood the rules were created to keep everyone safe. The job of those who run the house was to keep everyone safe, and what if an abuser found out that the children were staying away from the property? What if the child called their father while away? This could have awful consequences for all involved, including innocent parties.

Ralynn heard Diane mention to her girls that she knew this shelter was different than the last one, but that they needed to behave and not cause a fuss. She then went on to explain that they should be used to living in shelters, as shelters have been their home for the majority of the past four years. Ralynn kept thinking how grateful she was that she didn't have children with her.

Sitting down to dinner, Diane and the girls sat next to Ralynn. She felt so sorry for these girls. Even though it was a home atmosphere, there were rules, and it wasn't their home.

"Excuse me ladies. May I have your attention?" Ms. Debbie, who was the night manager for this week, was trying to get our attention. "Tonight's dinner is brought to you by First Main Street Baptist. These ladies love cooking for you, so please show them your gratitude and help me welcome them."

The room erupted with applause and whistles. After dinner the church ladies gave a brief devotion on God's answers and how they don't always come from places we would expect.

The Kingdom of Heaven is like a hidden treasure in a field. When the man found it, he hid it again, then he went and sold all he had and bought that field. (Matthew 13:44 NIV)

What if the field looked like the one on the left? (They showed a picture of a field that looked like it was from the desert—all dry and barren.) You may miss the treasure because you are thinking only good things could be found when the field looks like the one on the right. (This picture was a field that had a full harvest. The trees in the background were green and full of life.) God doesn't always give you answers in the places you think they should come from. Start looking for the treasure even when it doesn't make sense.

That was the end of that. Ralynn was confused why there wasn't a discussion or dialogue. Being new, she was just along for the ride, but she really would love to have asked a few questions. The ladies from the church, packed up their things and were out the door as soon as they prayed and said "Amen."

Ralynn thought that was odd but decided it was just the way it was. She was grateful for the food, though. It was amazing tasting.

Excusing herself to her room, Ralynn decided to get out her journal and write down some questions and thoughts:

What is a treasure that I need to be looking for?

God doesn't always give you answers in the places you think they should come from.

Start looking for the treasure even when it doesn't make sense.

What does this mean?

What am I supposed to learn from this?

Ralynn started yawning and thought it would be good to get ready for bed. Everyday so far had brought a new challenge. Today she was ready to call it quits. As much as she felt safe here, she felt something was missing, and she could not put her finger on it. Just as she was going to crawl under the covers, there was a knock on the door. "Come in."

For the next hour, Ralynn listened to Julia talk about how wonderful Dave was. Dave this and Dave that. Ralynn didn't realize the more Julia talked, the more bitter she became. Why couldn't she have reconnected with Dave before Julia? Ralynn kept reminding herself that she and Dave were just buddies from high school. There was nothing ever there. So why was she jealous?

Finding it harder to keep her eyes open, Ralynn asked if they could finish this conversation later. Julia apologized for keeping her up, but she had to talk to someone, and she felt Ralynn would keep her secret. Julia walked out, and Ralynn lay down. Now her mind was racing, so she got her journal back out.

Why am I so jealous of Julia's relationship?

Dave and I have only ever been friends.

Ralynn was startled awake. Her journal went flying as she jumped because something or someone hit her door. Now fully awake she realized there was a huge commotion going on outside her door. The clock read 9 a.m., but Ralynn felt like she had just fallen asleep. Opening her door, Ralynn was surprised to find Diane dragging all her belongings down the hallway. Her girls were lagging behind, begging her not to do this again. "Diane what in the world are you doing?"

Not missing a beat, Diane almost in a high school giddy fashion said, "He loves me. He said he wants things to be different. He's waiting for us. It'll be so wonderful. You should have heard him last night on the phone."

Diane continued with the conversation, telling anyone who would listen that she was headed home and things were going to be terrific. Ralynn knew she was about to step out of bounds but she cornered Diane anyway. "Diane, didn't you just tell me at dinner last night that you were determined that the last time was the last time, and you were never going back?"

Standing her ground, Diane came back with, "You didn't hear his voice last night. He said he was sorry. He also said it'll never happen again."

Watching Diane interact with her girls was scary. Their bags were already packed and in the car. Diane was making promises of material possessions to get the girls coaxed into the car, all the while reassuring them that this time, it would be different. With the car completely loaded, their faces told a different story. Last night they were angry they couldn't spend the night with a friend. Today their anger was a fear of what was about to happen. They were not as excited as their mom was to get back to the 2500 square foot, four-bedroom, three-bath home in the exclusive subdivision.

Ralynn feared for their lives and she started to yell at the vehicle as it was pulling away. "Diane you have a choice, but your girls have to come along for the ride, and it isn't fair. Don't do this."

Ralynn was not sure where her courage to tell someone else not to run back came from when she herself had been having her own pity party. Just the other night in her loneliness, she was making out a list of the pros and cons of going back. Luckily, she had fallen asleep while writing the list. When she woke up, the first thing she saw in the mirror was deep black and blue with a little yellow creeping up her neck. Slamming her fists on the counter, Ralynn yelled out that she would never be put in this situation again. *Ever!*

And now, a mom and her two girls were headed back because he said he was sorry. Ralynn was not sure what she was to feel, but she was angry— angry that no one stopped her and angry that she was allowed to take off with her girls. Ralynn felt she was not the only one who felt something was wrong when the rest of the girls were just kind of somber for most of the morning. As Ralynn was heading out to the front porch, she overheard the staff talking about Diane's girls and the fact that they had already seen so much in their short time on this earth. Ms. Shaw told Ms. Dee to call the churches that had prayer lines and to "Ask for prayer for a mom and her kids who decided to leave and go back. Tell them nothing more and nothing less. God knows the rest."

Taking her seat on what had become her favorite chair on the front porch, Ralynn started to journal.

Day 5

Not sure what exactly happened today. Dianne and the girls walked out. Why didn't anyone stop them? What is going to happen to the girls?

Putting her pen down for a moment, Ralynn closed her eyes and listened to the sounds of nature. There were birds chirping. A dog was barking in the distance ever so incessantly, and then out of nowhere was a meow. The meow was continuing, and it sounded to Ralynn like the cat was real close. Ralynn got up and walked down the stairs trying to locate the animal, and there it was—a grey kitten with light black stripes. She could see it had a white mustache and a white belly as it sat looking up at her from within the boxwoods. Ralynn without thinking, reached down to pick it up. As it was letting out a screech, its left front paw with its tiny claws was connecting with Ralynn's hand.

She pulled her hand back, and the kitten took off under the front porch. Surveying the damage done to her hand, she decided it was best to go in the house and get it cleaned up. Walking in the house, she was met with little Kyra running through the kitchen with her mother Kia following right behind, acting like she was going to get her. Kyra's giggle made something inside Ralynn flutter, but the sight of the blood on her hand made her push her feelings aside and rush to the sink to wash her hand.

As she was cleaning up her mess, she realized it was past lunchtime and maybe that was why her stomach started to gurgle and growl. Going to the refrigerator, she realized there was leftover pot pie. She grabbed a plate and warmed her lunch up in the microwave. Just as the bell went off, telling her it was finished, Kyra walked over and asked for a bite. Ralynn looking around for her mother, didn't see her. "Honey, I am sorry. Where's your momma?"

Just then, Kia walked in from the office area and with no pleasantries, saying, "Kyra, whatcha doin'?"

Her abrasive tone made both Ralynn and Kyra jump. Kyra started to cry, and Ralynn was not sure what to think. Just a few moments ago, the two of them were running through the kitchen chasing each other, and now she was being short with her. What's that about she wondered?

"She wasn't bothering me. I wanted to know if I could make her some pot pie? It's no bother, but I didn't know if she had any allergies or anything."

Kia, still not lightening up, "I'm her mom, and I'll make it."

Ralynn was taken aback but figured she would let it slide. Kia grabbed Kyra's arm and pulled her toward the living room. Ralynn started to speak under her breath, "And that is why I cannot bring a child into this mess. Tomorrow can't get here soon enough."

Ralynn had had enough of the mood in the house that she decided to eat her lunch outside on the front porch where she left her journal.

Getting settled in, she turned back to the page she was writing on.

I will not bring a child here. It is too stressful to be in this situation and have a baby. Tomorrow is the day. Then it will be over, and I won't have to worry about it anymore. I can get on with my life. I can leave here. I will start over with no strings attached.

Her lunch had hit the spot and now she felt like going out and exploring a little bit when her text message alert went off. "Why'd you leave me?"

Before she could even read the first message, her phone pinged again. "I need you. Ray . . . you there?"

Reading his messages Ralynn felt maybe she had made a mistake. Then her phone pinged again. "Bitch, answer me."

And just that fast, her feelings of maybe they could make it work, were gone. She instinctively put her hand over her neck and ran her hand down her arms. There was a chill she couldn't shake. Putting her phone down, she picked up all her things and started to walk back in the house when her phone went off again.

"I'm sorry. I didn't mean to get mad."

With this last text, Ralynn quickened her step. Now almost running she went to find Julia. Not stopping to see if Julia was in or wanted visitors, Ralynn barged into her room. Startled, Julia looked up from her book and was able to move out of the way as Ralynn threw her phone on the bed.

"Fix it. He's texting me. Make it stop."

Julia picked up Ralynn's phone. She did a few things and then handed it back to her, saying, "Next time, knock."

"I'm sorry. I just wanted it to stop." Ralynn was about to leave when she saw Julia wipe her eyes with her sleeve. "What's up?"

Ralynn walked back to the bed and sat down next to Julia. Not sure where the empathy came from, but before she could stop herself, Ralynn had her arm around Julia.

Letting her cry, Ralynn had a flashback of Sunday, when she met Shelly. As they sat in silence, both their phones pinged simultaneously. Ralynn had decided she would not check hers; then Julia picked up her phone.

"Oh . . . do I really want to go?"

"Go where?"

"Oh. Just a thing."

Ralynn's phone pinged again because she had not cleared out the reminder. Picking up her phone, she saw: *Dinner. Shelly's.* Completely forgetting it was Thursday, she had decided to just blow it off, until Julia said,

"You wouldn't want to go to a dinner with me would you?"

"Well I kinda was supposed to go to a dinner thing myself but I don't have a ride, plus I didn't want to leave you like this."

"Well, I kinda promised this lady and a friend I would go. Will you go with me?"

Ralynn nodded, and they headed to the kitchen to ask Ms. Dee or Ms. Shaw for a ride.

Ms. Shaw was in the kitchen, talking with Kia when they walked in. Kia and her daughter, Kyra, had arrived on Monday. Kia was mentioning to Ms. Shaw that she and Kyra were not going to be there for dinner tonight because she had been invited to a dinner.

"Ms. Shaw. Pardon me," Julia interrupted, "But is there any way to get a ride to the dinner meeting?"

Ms. Shaw just looked blankly at Ralynn and Julia. Ralynn nudged Julia and whispered, "I think she is waiting to hear where we want to go."

'Oh, yeah. Her name is Shelly Waddell. She does a class at her ho . . ."

Before Julia could finish, Kia piped up, "I have wanted to go for weeks, and as a matter of fact, I was just telling Ms. Shaw that Kyra and I were not going to be home tonight because we had been invited to dinner. If you all don't mind riding with us, you are more than welcome. Ms. Shaw, is that okay?"

Ms. Shaw agreed that we all could go.

"Let me get Kyra's coat on her, grab the diaper bag, and meet you in the car?"

"That would be great. Thanks, Kia."

Julia started to walk outside to get in the car.

"Thanks, Kia. I need to run to my room real quick and I'll meet you out there."

Ralynn ran to her room to fetch her coat and a wave of nausea hit again. Grabbing some saltines, she prayed it would do the trick. Ralynn's appointment was tomorrow morning, and she knew it was for the best. After watching Diane's girls, Ralynn had decided that there was no way she was going to bring another human into this mess that she had created. Ralynn kept telling herself it would be fine because no one would ever know. Looking in the mirror as she was leaving her bedroom, she looked down at her stomach, gave it a little pat and said, *"I'm sorry little one."*

VIII

T he drive to Shelly's was peaceful and uneventful, but Ralynn couldn't figure Kia out. Right now she was caring and helpful, but earlier she didn't want anything to do with anyone. Sitting there contemplating whether or not to say anything, Kia broke the silence. "I am glad you all are coming. We are here."

The closest parking spot was down the street from the house. As they all piled out of the car, they realized there were no sidewalks. Kyra was not happy. She wanted to walk, but Kia insisted that she be carried. With cars lining both sides of the road, they were having to be careful not to get hit from the traffic.

Walking up the driveway, Ralynn noticed that Shelly's house was nothing to write home about. It was a two-story white brick home. The landscaping was quaint and established, but there was something coming from the house that she hadn't heard in a while.

"Do you hear that?"

"Hear what?"

The laughter was so loud coming from the house. That it could be heard from out on the road. Ralynn realized that she missed laughing, and she too wanted to get in the house to see what was so funny.

Before they hit the blacktopped driveway, the glass-plated brown wooden door opened. Shelly was greeting them from the beautifully crafted front door that didn't fit the construction or style of the house.

"Oh, you must be Julia. I am so glad you decided to join us. Isabella has told me so much about you."

Shelly was giving Julia the motherly hug. As Ralynn was watching Julia's body language, she realized she must be feeling the same way she was on Sunday. Letting Julia out of her death grip, Shelly exclaimed, "Oh, Kia I am so glad you and Kyra were able to make it. I am proud of you for making the call on Monday. Are you settling in at Z-house?"

Kia, being noncommittal in her answers, put Kyra down as soon as she was on the stoop. Kia's attitude changed right before Ralynn's eyes. She seemed excited to come to the house. What has changed? Why is she giving Shelly the cold shoulder? Wow! I cannot believe she just blew past her. It was now Ralynn's turn and as she entered the doorway, Shelly gave her the biggest hug. Ralynn started to freeze in panic, but Kyra grabbed her hand to pull her in the house. Shelly was squealing with excitement.

"I am so glad you are here. I told my husband all about you, and then I told him, but I never got her number. I was hoping that you would choose this as your program to participate in."

Ralynn was given a list of programs to choose from on Monday. She had not made a decision yet. Now she guesses it was made for her. Shelly finally released her motherly death-grip hug. Ralynn was really not okay, because her body told her to expect the worse. But there was something different about Shelly; Ralynn could not put her finger on it, but she just felt it.

With tears in her eyes, Shelly gave Ralynn another hug and whispered, *"I am so proud of you."*

Ralynn trying to change the subject off of her, said, "I really like your front door."

Shelly went on to explain that Jim, her husband, remodeled homes for a living. One of his customers lived in the local Country Club and was getting a new door. The customer told Jim that he could have it if he hauled it off that day. Jim knew that Shelly wanted to get rid of their plain red front door, so he brought it home that day. Shelly was so excited when he came home with that door but even more excited when Jim got it hung. Shelly went on to explain that the joke was that Jim had a habit of starting remodeling projects around the house. He would get it finished just enough and then go onto the next project or get busy at work; Shelly said she was used to it.

As Ralynn was heading upstairs where all the laughter was coming from, she noticed for being so simple outside, the remodel that that was done on the inside was immaculate, with hardwoods and ceramic tile floors. Everything looked to be newly finished. Ralynn commented on the fact that Shelly's home was beautiful and looked brand new.

"Thank you Ralynn. Yes, the remodel is brand new. If you ever come over during the daylight, you will see there is a creek in the backyard. One night, it rained so hard that the creek came out of its banks, and we ended up with three inches of water in the house. So Jim had to take time off of work and fix our house."

Shelly, now trying to get everyone's attention, was thrown for a loop when the pots and pans started clanging together. Shelly turned around and started to laugh. "And most of you know my illustrious husband, Jim." Jim took a bow and the room erupted with even more laughter.

"Ladies I want to introduce to you Kia, Kyra, Julia, and Ralynn. They are living at Z-House and have chosen this dinner meeting to be their program."

Shelly now turning to face us. "Ladies we are sooooooo excited that you have chosen to dine with us. It is our prayer that you will make this your Thursday night home for the next couple of months as we eat and learn how to be the woman God created us to be."

Looking around, Ralynn was trying to count how many moms and kids there were, but the children kept running from the kitchen, to the living room, to the dining room, and kept making the loop. Finally, Jim jumped in the middle of the mix and had all the kids laughing. Shelly gave him a look, and Jim stopped, threw up his arms, and said, "What!"

Shelly just gave him another look, and the moms all started to laugh. The smell of Italian infused the air. Shelly was getting the food out of the oven and set up. Lasagna. Salad. Garlic Bread. Cola.

"Alright, ladies, get your kids plates ready. You older kids grab your plates and head to the living room and find your seat."

Waiting for the line to go down, Ralynn went over to the table to claim a seat but realized the dining table was so large that everyone had a seat. So she proceeded to get back in line. As the kids were getting settled in the living room, Jai was putting her son BJ in the high chair. He was eighteen months old and believed he was five. He was not too happy when his mother put him in the high chair as he was not allowed to sit with the bigger kids. Pitching a fit, Jai was trying her best to quiet BJ down. He was not having it. Just then Shelly walked over with his plate, put it on the tray of the high chair, and before anyone knew what happened, lasagna was landing on the wall and the window. The room froze waiting to see what would happen. Jai was apologetic to Shelly and Jim but started swatting at BJ and yelling at him. Shelly very calmly walked to the kitchen grabbed a washcloth, and then walked back over and started to clean up the lasagna. Jim walked over to BJ and rescued him from his mother's wrath.

"Jai, it's okay. Shelly's got it cleaned up. But, hitting your son is not the answer."

"Jai, I am sorry. I should have waited to put his food down. I knew better than that. Come on, ladies, let's sit down and start eating."

"Well, we won't be a bother anymore. This will be our last week here. I am done with this town. There is a job in Alabama, and I'm going to move there so I can get that job."

"Jai, do you already have the job?" Jim questioned.

"That doesn't matter. I am leaving this town."

"Ok, Jai. Seriously, what is going on?" Shelly asked.

"Nothing"

"Nothing? Really? Your son throws his food. He is eighteen months old, and you start swatting at him. What was that going to accomplish?"

"I dunno."

"Okay, I'll take that answer for the time being. So why are you leaving this town? What happened now?"

Jai, looking at her plate, with her fork in her hand, started playing with her food. Ralynn was not sure exactly what she should be doing, seeing the empty chair she had taken was right next to Jai, so she just started shoveling her lasagna in her mouth. When the first bite hit her stomach, though, she was afraid it might all come back up. She had not thrown up in a day or so and was really afraid her lasagna was going to end up going all over like JB's did. Taking a sip of her cola started to take the edge off, and she felt like she could pay attention to the discussion that was now taking place.

"Jai you have been threatening to leave this town for a long time." Shelly was getting heated and animated as she continued, "And you still have not moved."

Now Shelly got out of her seat and was walking around the table as she was speaking.

"I was going to save this for our class time, but let's just talk about it right now. Ladies, if you want to run away, then remember this. You take you with you wherever you go. So if you want to go to Alabama," looking in Jai's direction, "and think your life is going to be perfect because you went to a new town, remember you took you with you. And until you know who you are and what you want out of life, the same life you have here will be the same life you will end up with there."

Even with Shelly raising her voice, Ralynn felt a presence in the home that she had not felt since her GiGi was alive.

Jim breaking in, said, "Well now that Shelly has gone off on her tangent, let's talk about our week. Isabella, you go first . . . let's hear your high and low for the week."

Isabella excitedly told everyone that her high for that week was that she had gotten a raise at work, but then she started stumbling over her words. Now with uncontrollable sobs Isabella trying to get out her low, took a deep breath and blurted out, "I have an STD."

You could hear a pin drop. Shelly was the first to reach Isabella. She gave her a hug from behind and whispered but could be heard by us at the table, "It's going to be okay. We will get through this."

Giving Isabella her space, Shelly went back to her seat. Isabella finally composed herself after a few moments, "I just knew you would be disappointed in me. I told you I was done with guys until God brought the right one. Well, I guess I wasn't as strong as I thought I was."

Isabella's voice got a little softer: "I lost it a couple of weeks ago with the girls. We had gone to the grocery store, and I let my anger get the best of me. The girls were out of control and I was completely spent. As we were getting out of the car, they started in again, and I let them have it right there in the middle of the driveway. The more I yelled, the harder I found it to stop, and then I didn't care who heard. I just kept screaming and yelling at them, carrying on like a crazed woman. As I was in the middle of my rage, people started coming out of their apartments. That is when Bobby came out and very politely steered the girls away from my foul-mouthed wrath. He took them to the side yard where there were hula-hoops and jump-ropes." Now starting to cry again, Isabella went on. "They looked so happy but I just could not control my mouth, and the words just kept coming."

After taking a long breath, Isabella continued, "Bobby then came back over and took the groceries from my hands and placed his other hand on the small of my back and when he did that I just melted. He started to direct me to the house. It was at that moment that I felt the anger leave, and it was like I was under a spell. He then called for the girls and they obeyed. Right *away*. Now he was in my house, and they listened to him as he gave them instructions. I just stood there memorized by all the calm. I then invited him to stay for dinner. Now here is the bad part, I only knew of him because he had been at my neighbor's house."

At this point in the story Isabella stopped for a breath as she was starting to cry. She put her hand out, as to say, don't say a word then finally said, "I know what you all are thinking and going to say . . . but I waaaaas lllloonnnnnely."

Again you could hear a pin drop. Everyone was waiting to see what Jim and Shelly would do. After what seemed to be an eternity of awkward silence, Shelly walked back over to Isabella and put her arm around her. Shelly said absolutely nothing. There was no judgment. There was no guilt or shame added, but Jim was the first to break the silence.

"Well let's see who else has some news they would like to share." We all kind of chuckled nervously.

"Sorry ladies, but when I get nervous I make jokes."

Then we all started to laugh and it did seem to restart the evening. Looking around, Ralynn realized that the kids were missing but could hear them laughing downstairs; before she could question it, Kia jumped in to tell her high.

"I am proud of myself for making the call and walking away from my boyfriend. He was so abusive, but I didn't see it until I called Ms. Shelly last Sunday. I had asked her to lie for me and call me out of work because I wanted us to work it out. Then she told me that it was not okay for him to hit me even if it was only a couple times a week. You see, I made excuses and told everyone that if I was a better girlfriend he would not get mad and hit me. Shelly also told me that if I needed a safe place that the offer still stood and she would be waiting. So thank you, Ms. Shelly, for taking my call and helping me get to the safe house pick-up. But my low is that I now find myself in a shelter and having to start over. And I am afraid that I might fail."

As Kia was talking, Ralynn was thinking, based upon the conversations she had overheard Kia have, she was not too sure how long Kia was going to stay at Z-House. Kia really liked her freedom. Ralynn could not count how many excuses as to why things would never change for her or her daughter, so to hear her talk tonight, Ralynn was hoping she was having a change of heart.

Shelly quickly responded, "Kia, Jim and I are proud of you for making that call and getting you and Kyra out of that situation."

Now switching her focus to Julia, Kia, and Ralynn, she said, "You all need to see the positive of living at Z-House and not a low. You need to see it as the safe place it is to start over. It is a place to grow and fail successfully."

I guess the look on our faces told Shelly she needed to explain further.

"Let me explain. What you have at Z-House is a place where they will love you well and not just when you succeed but also when you make a mistake. With the women who are in charge over there, you for the most part are allowed to go about life with little say so from them. As you are learning a new way of living without the abuse, if you happen to make a wrong choice, whether that means you get into a relationship or you make a bad parenting choice, they are there to help you pick up the pieces and help you learn from it. They help you then make better choices through their daily guidance, the state workers, the church groups, and even this class. We all work together to help you 'fail successfully,' meaning as long as you are willing to learn from your mistakes or 'failures,' and take advice and try a new way, then you fail successfully because you learned the way it didn't work and are willing to take a different path to become successful. And remember, ladies, success doesn't mean a million dollars in the bank. Success can be freedom from an addiction, freedom from abuse, freedom to make your own choices and not have to depend on a man. But, ladies, what you choose from now on will be the difference maker for your future."

As soon as Shelly stopped to take a breath, Jim took that time to explain that the kids had not been kidnapped but when Isabella was talking, he had texted his oldest daughter, Amber, and she quietly came up and took the kids downstairs to do homework and play. Jim then turned to Julia, "It's your turn to share your high and low for the week."

Julia just sat there, twirling her hair with her fingers. Ralynn thought, *I have seen that look before. It was the look that said, if I talk, I will come unglued and I am trying to keep it together.*

"It's ok Julia you are safe here. But we also don't want to push you if you aren't ready to share."

All of a sudden Ralynn remembered earlier that day, when she had barged in on Julia and she was wiping away tears. She never did tell her what was wrong. *Hmmm. This is strange*, Ralynn thought, she looked so happy the other day when she saw her with Dave. Dave, oh my—the rules. She is seeing someone, and that is against the rules. I wonder if that is what is wrong. But Dave is one of the good guys. Ralynn's thoughts were interrupted when Julia started to cry-talk.

Julia was pushing up her sleeve so you could see her arm. "This is what he did when I went back last time. He told me things were going to be different. They weren't. They actually were worse. Well, the other day, while I was out with a friend who happens to be a boy . . ."

Julia was now trying to stop the sobs but they were coming so fast that it was hard to comprehend what she was saying. *"Heeee fffooollloooooweeed uuuuusssss."*

Oh my Ralynn's heart started to break. She knew what kind of heart Dave had and. . . .

"Hhhhheeeee waaaitted foooorrr my ffrriiennd tooooo leave . . . aaaannnd . . ."

Julia lifted up her shirt so we could see the black and blue marks and the newest cigarette burn marks on her stomach. Now we were all crying.

Through the blur of the tears, Ralynn saw Jim handing out tissues and was wishing someone would say something. Shelly was the first to speak, "Ladies in lieu of everything we have heard tonight, I am thinking what we were going to talk about in class tonight is not what we need to hear. So tonight we are going to talk about the why? Why do we feel this is how we need to be treated, or why do we feel it is okay to be treated this way? Ladies, I want to read you something I wrote after one of our first moms walked out."

She said she wanted to change. She said she would never go back there.

She said she was done with him, but yet she still said he was a good person. Then the next day, she would say, "Nope, I want nothing to do with him." Then out of the same mouth came, "but what if . . ."

She had it all.

A safe place to live.

New people in her life.

A job.

But the pull was too great.

She felt she needed him to be complete. She wanted freedom to go and do. The pull was too great. It was calling her. It was too much.

"Sometimes we lose them back to the streets, to their old friends, or back to abusive relationships. The old way, even with the negative consequences, outweighs the positive that comes with change." Before Shelly continued, Jim started to dance around the room handing out more tissues, and everyone started to laugh.

"Sorry, ladies, but when I get uncomfortable, I make a joke. I will apologize now if you think I am making light or fun of a situation, I am not it is just how I lighten the mood. Okay Shelly as you were."

Shelly gave Jim one of her looks which then made all of us laugh even more.

"Ladies, I know that change is hard. I know that you want to run back to what is familiar, to what is easy. I get that. But what we want you to realize is that you were created for more. The challenge is to realize it and want to do the hard work to create that change in your life for you and for your children, whether they are here now or to come in the future. Until you realize that you were created for more, you will always see yourself with the tainted lens that your past has said you are."

As Shelly was continuing to talk, Jim handed out packets.

"Jim was gracious to make these packets for you. So here we go. Abuse, according to the dictionary, is to use wrongly or improperly; misuse to treat in a harmful, injurious, or offensive way: to speak insultingly, harshly, and unjustly to or about; revile; to commit sexual assault upon, to deceive or mislead. I know that was a mouthful, but what I want you to see is that abuse is not just sexual and physical abuse; there is also emotional, verbal, and spiritual abuse. So before we go into the "why" we stay in relationships that are abusive, let's look at a couple of types of abuse: emotional and verbal. Also remember that abuse in relationships is *not* just between significant others. You can find abuse in work relationships, friendships, and parent-child relationships."

Shelly went on to talk about being in relationships where name calling is a daily part of your relationship. She talked about how when people intentionally use words to harm us or to make us feel bad, then we are in a verbally abusive relationship. When she used the example, "You are a sorry excuse for a human being," Ralynn had a flood of emotions come rushing back. Rita had a live-in boyfriend once who used those words constantly toward both her and her mom. A single tear found its way down her cheek as the memories of that man and the four long weeks he lived with them started to rehaunt her. Ralynn was only eleven when he came into their lives. When he finally left and didn't return for seventy-two hours, Rita had promised that she was done, and it was just going to be the two of them. Ralynn was hoping for some kind of normalcy in her life, you know, like shopping and eating ice cream, but then *he* showed up the next afternoon. He stayed for dinner and didn't leave. The words "You are a sorry excuse for a human being," started by the third day.

"Ralynn, you okay? Ralynn. . . . Earth to Ralynn . . ."

Shelly was trying to get Ralynn's attention, but she didn't respond until Julia put her arm on hers, and she jumped.

"Ralynn, you okay?"

"Ummmmm . . . Yeah . . . I guess . . ."

"Do you want to say something?"

"No, I am just taking it all in."

"So, ladies, let's talk about the bully. A bully attacks to show power. This power is over the person who is believed the weaker person. To be in control in the relationship is not always a bad thing. For example, in our relationship," Shelly was pointing to Jim, "I have control over the checkbook. This is not because I am using it as a control of power; it's just the way we have our relationship. I love numbers. Control in a relationship becomes abuse when you use that power to dominate, oppress, manipulate, rule, or even dictate what the other person in the relationship can and can't do.

"Ladies, in your past relationships, have you found that you were always at fault? Were you always being judged? So let's stop here for just a moment and ask yourself about the relationships you are in right now and your past relationships. Are there relationships you need to walk away from? Are there relationships you need to work on? Are you the abuser, the victim, or both, depending on the situation? Now think about your children and your relationship with your parent or parents, and are there things you need to work on with them? Ladies, I want to ask you all a serious question. Are you continually getting into relationships that are unhealthy?

"Part of your homework will include some soul searching before we get together next week. What do *you* need to change about *you* so that you are not attractive to nor are attracting unhealthy relationships? Now let's look at the why? Why do we abuse, and why do we stay in abusive situations? Have you ever heard: 'Well, they just don't know any better?' Sometime you grow up in a dysfunctional family, and you don't realize that the control, the anger, and the name calling are *not* normal. It is just how you grew up and that's how your parents grew up, so the cycle just continues until someone gets a taste of a different way of doing relationships.

"How do we stop getting into relationships that have the same tune to them? It's really easy! *Not* . . . please hear: there is *no* easy formula or fix; if there was, then there would be some very rich people. This change will only come when *you*" now Shelly was pointing right at every one of us, "see *yourself* worthy of something different. You can read every self-help book in the world but until *you* want something different for *yourself,* you will not have a lasting change. Ladies, I want nothing more than for all of you to become the women that God created you to be. As we finish tonight and for part of your homework, I want you to memorize this verse for yourself. Ephesians 2:10 'For we are God's handiwork, created in Christ Jesus to do good works, which God prepared in advance for us to do.' This came from the NIV. I want you to see that God has a job for you. He created you to do good works, and now we need to start doing them. For the other part of your homework, I want you to take your packets, a journal, and make some time to be quiet and let the Lord speak to you. There are plenty of prompts in your packets to get you started as you just sit, think, and write. Does anyone have any questions before we go? I can hear the kids are getting restless and not sure if you have seen or not, but Sabrina has been peeking around the corner for the past ten minutes."

We all chuckled. As the kids came running up the stairs, Shelly interrupted as everyone was trying to get out the door. "Ladies one other thing before you go. For those who are new, this is Amber, our oldest; Nikki, our middle; and Sabrina, our youngest. They were drafted by their father and me to watch the kids tonight."

Walking back to the car, Ralynn, Julia, and Kia didn't say much. The ride home was just as quiet, until the silence was broken by Kyra who squealed from the backseat with excitement.

"Mama, Mama.'

"Yes, Kyra."

Ralynn wondered how does Kia do it? Having a baby and living in the home? Just then Ralynn heard Kyra say, "Mama, Brinnna says I good gurl!"

"Yes, Kyra, you are a good girl, what were you doing?"

"Colors, Mama, my colors."

Ralynn started to chuckle because Kyra was so proud of herself. That exchange also made Ralynn jealous and mad that life had dealt her these cards.

Just that quick they were pulling onto the property, and Kyra was now snoring so loudly that Ralynn, Julia and Kia couldn't help but laugh. Ralynn wondered if her baby would have been a boy or a girl. She also wondered if it was a girl, would it have had cute dishwater blonde hair with curls like Kyra? Ralynn's anger was starting to rise, but she had already made her decision and that was it. Ralynn also didn't want to have another cryfest, so she thanked Kia for the ride and hurried into the house past everyone sitting in the living room and ran to the safety of her room.

Safely tucked in her room, Ralynn found that sleep was not to be had, so she got out the packet of papers and her journal.

Day 5, part 2

Why do I feel this is how I need to be treated?

Why do I feel it is okay to treated this way?

For we are God's handiwork, created in Christ Jesus to do good works, which God prepared in advance for us to do.

What do *you* need to change about *you* so that you are not attractive to nor attracting unhealthy relationships?

Now let's look at the why? Why do we abuse, and why do we stay in abusive situations?"

This change will only come when *you* see *yourself* worthy of something different

Knowing she had to get up really early in the morning, Ralynn tried to shut off her brain from tonight's teaching, but it wasn't happening, so she kept writing in her journal.

Tomorrow will come, and no one will know.

I will never tell anyone.

It'll be my secret.

It's my choice.

It'll be easier

It'll be for the best.

Ralynn was startled when she heard a baby crying. She didn't realize she had fallen asleep. She was dreaming that she was in an apartment. It was furnished beautifully, and there in the middle of the floor was a baby in an infant carrier. Ralynn was walking toward the baby and could see it was dressed in all pink. The little girl was getting fussy. Just as Ralynn was about to pick her up, she was startled awake with a baby crying.

Rolling over trying to go back to sleep, Ralynn realized that the crying was real, and it was coming from the hallway. Jumping out of bed and flinging open the door, the young mom jumped. Ralynn realized this young mom was holding an infant, and that was where the crying was coming from.

"I'm sorry, I didn't mean to startle you."

"I'm sorry, I didn't mean to wake you."

"That's okay. My name is Ralynn."

"My name is Sally, and this is Jessie."

"Nice to meet you. Get some sleep and we will see you later."

Ralynn crawled back into bed, but she could not shake the dream, and now she smelled baby.

IX

Looking over at the clock, it read 7 a.m., and panic started to creep in. Ralynn was determined to get to this appointment. She was excited because in just a few short hours, she would no longer have to worry about bringing another human into the mix of her life.

As Ralynn's feet hit the floor, the plush carpet made it feel like she was walking on cottony clouds, and for whatever reason, she found herself thanking the church for all the amazing gifts she had been given. A double bed had a very nice pillow top to lay her head. A dresser in which all the drawers actually opened and closed. And as she grabbed the hand towel to wash her face, she was so thankful for how soft and fluffy they were. She loved wrapping up in the towels after a long, hot shower. All the items right down to the accent pillows, comforter, sheets, and area rugs all matched. They were a cheery yellow, periwinkle blue, and seafoam green. Ralynn just knew they were expensive and brand new. Then it hit her, "They did it just for *me*."

Now standing in the bathroom, Ralynn caught a glimpse of herself in the mirror, and she didn't recognize the reflection. She looked healthy. She had a smile. She looked happy on the outside but was still dying on the inside.

The knock on the door startled her. "Come in."

Ms. Shaw had sent one of the girls to tell Ralynn that the van was ready to go to town. Grabbing her purse, she hurriedly entered the hallway and plowed into Sally and Jessie.

Rushing through the kitchen Ms. Shaw, quickly questioned Ralynn about not eating. Ralynn just nodded, smiled, and grabbed a granola bar on her way to the van. Ralynn knew if she had said a word, she would have another breakdown. Meeting Sally in person this morning was more than Ralynn could handle. Ralynn saw sheer terror in Sally's expression. She looked extremely exhausted, and Jessie just kept crying.

Sitting in the safety of the van, Ralynn could smell newborn baby permeating her skin again. Ralynn kept thinking, *Innocence. Helplessness. Yet ever so trusting of the person holding him.*

Jessie had no clue whether or not the person holding and caring for him was able to just put one foot in front of the other or was completely at peace and in a great place. Ralynn, trying to change the subject in her head, started staring out the window. It was during this ride, taking in the sights, sounds, and smells that she realized why fall was actually her favorite time of the year. Fall had the smells, the colors, bonfires, hot apple cider, and pumpkin pie. All spring had was muddy, wet roads. Because this year had been colder than usual, the trees and flowers had not yet all bloomed.

Now that Ralynn had figured out that issue in her life, she started asking herself harder questions. *What happened? Where did I go wrong?*

Ralynn was deep in thought when the van came to a screeching halt in the middle of the road. Ms. Dee, the new program director, had to slam on the brakes in order to not hit the cow that was meandering down the middle of the road. Ms. Dee, being new to the area and from around Chicago, started questioning us as to what the protocol was when there was a cow walking down the road.

Ms. Dee decided someone needed to know, so she opted for 911. The 911 desk had already had multiple calls and had an officer on the way. Ms. Dee started to cautiously pass the cow that kept walking like it had no cares in the world.

Ralynn was grateful for the distraction but it didn't last long. Ms. Dee was pulling into the parking lot and started in with Z-House's spiel about pick up and phone numbers. In unison all the ladies said, "Thanks, Mom."

As Ralynn opened her door to get out, reality hit her that in less than an hour she would be at her appointment. Even though she was excited that starting tomorrow, she would be able to start thinking about her future, she found herself also questioning if there wasn't a different way.

Exiting the vehicle, Ralynn's phone started to beep telling her that the driver was only two minutes away. The sun had not made an appearance in a couple of days and actually it was starting to drizzle. Based upon Ralynn's experience, she knew this was not a good combination for driving during rush hour, but she pushed back the anxiety and started walking toward the corner where The Coffee Shoppe sits. As Ralynn turned and started toward her pick-up point in the middle of town, she literally ran into Shelly. Shelly instinctively reached out to catch Ralynn before she actually fell.

"Hey. Hi, how are you?"

"I'm good."

"It was so good to have you come last night. You want to grab a cup of coffee?"

"I have to go, I . . . I . . . have doctor's appointment."

Ralynn was not sure if a look on her face gave her away, or the fact that she was distracted. Did Shelly really know where Ralynn was headed? Shelly got the last words in with "Know we love you and we will help you, you just have to let us in."

Ralynn started to do her walk/run so that she would not miss her ride. Getting to the pickup just in time, she jumped in the back seat and blurted out the address to the clinic in Middleton. Middleton was a city about thirty minutes north of Mapleton. Ralynn was not sure why she thought if she said the address really fast that it would take away some of the dirtiness she felt was associated with the clinic. Now belted into the backseat, a wave of emotion hit Ralynn. The words of Shelly were ringing in her ears. *"Know we love you, and will help you. You just have to let us in."*

Trying to think of anything but her appointment, Ralynn started asking herself, why is it called the Square, when it's a circle? She had heard it also referenced as the Squircle which made Ralynn snicker. As they were driving past KT's, Ralynn longed to be at work, but then she thought she was going to throw up. There was Ben, parked, waiting for her. Shelly's words were on constant repeat in Ralynn's head: *"Just let us in. We will help you."*

The driver took a left to get on the interstate going north, but was met with bright red brake lights for as far as the eye could see. Ralynn, assessing the situation, let out a huff and under her breath said, *"Seriously, I am going to miss my appointment."*

Ralynn realized the driver must have heard her sigh and statement because in a very patient voice, he responded with, "Don't worry. I will get you to your appointment."

The GPS was now saying alternate route found, press to accept. The GPS had them driving through neighborhoods, school zones, and roads that were still two-lanes. Some of the roads had hills as high as the first drop on a roller coaster and sharp turns that mimicked all the rides Ralynn remembered going on as a child at the local fair. The backroads were a welcomed distraction. The driver finally took a left hand turn onto a road that at least Ralynn recognized the name of. She also felt they must be getting closer to the city because the buildings started to have a different feel. They were no longer beautiful red brick buildings with historical architectural archways but were grey buildings, and everything looked the same: Gray. Cold. No life, and the stoplights were spaced less than a block a part.

As GPS was announcing the arrival to 520 Cobbles Way, it brought Ralynn back to the reality of what she was about to do. The driver pulled into the parking lot of the ugliest dingiest building on the block. Ralynn questioned him in her mind, *Are you sure?*

She knew this was the building, she could see the address as plain as day on the building. Ralynn pulled out her money to pay the bill but the driver looked at her and said,

"Ma'am, this one is on me. Take the money to buy your baby his first set of diapers. My name is Chris, and I am the pastor of First Church of Middleton. I know what happens here at this clinic. Actually, one of the ministries of the church is to come here and talk to the women as they come out. Some have changed their minds, while others come out and feel immediate shame and guilt. Our members become someone they can grieve with. Whatever the situation, we just let the young ladies talk. When they are done, we give them our card and tell them that we are here if they want to do something different. If it's okay with you, I don't have anywhere to be for a while, so I will wait right here and take you back wherever you want to go when you are done."

The emotions were coming so fast. The tears were welling up in Ralynn's eyes, and in fear of having Niagara Falls start, she just nodded.

The door to the clinic was only 100 feet from the car. With each step Ralynn felt sicker and sicker. She felt like there was a weight on her like she had never felt. The only way to describe it was that with each step, she felt another story was being added to her load. By the time she reached the door, Ralynn felt like she was dragging an entire eight-story office building on a sled tied to her waist. The handle to the front door felt hot to the touch as Ralynn placed her hand on it to pull it open. As she yanked it open to walk in, Ralynn thought her entire dinner from last night was about to come up.

The office was beautifully decorated with mauve furniture, and all the décor was very complimentary. Relief for a moment swept over Ralynn as she smelled lavender being omitted from the oil diffuser by the front window.

"May I help you?" A young, twenty-something Latino woman said.

"I . . . am. . . ."

"Are you here to see the doctor?"

"Yes."

"Have you been here before?"

"No, this is my first visit."

"Are you sure you are pregnant?"

"I did a home test."

"Please fill out these papers."

Ralynn took a seat in the first chair she came to. Even though the waiting room was beautiful and inviting, Ralynn's stomach was churning. The nausea was setting in, and before she could make it to the bathroom, let alone the trash can, up came last night's dinner.

Feeling embarrassed, Ralynn tried to clean up her mess. The young lady at the window, very politely told Ralynn not to worry about it and that they would get someone to clean it up. Even though she told Ralynn not to worry, Ralynn still found herself trying to clean it up. All of a sudden the door opened and a lady walked out, saying, "Please follow me."

Ralynn, without thinking, got up and followed the lady to the back. There was no small talk. Ralynn felt like she was being led to her slaughter. The nurse handed Ralynn a cup to pee in. Ralynn doing as she was instructed and then found her way to the exam room. Within fifteen minutes, without fanfare or congratulations that you are going to have a baby, all business, the nurse walked in and told Ralynn she was pregnant. The nurse still with no warmth in her voice made the statement to Ralynn, "You are here to terminate the pregnancy."

Ralynn not sure if that was a statement or a question, just sat there on the table. She was then told that the counselor would be in to see her shortly. The exam room Ralynn found herself sitting in was not inviting, like the waiting room. The walls were grey and sterile. There were two chairs. One was aging and could have used a new cover. The other was an old wooden school chair type. While Ralynn was surveying her surroundings, a knock on the door startled her. The doctor came in and sat down with her file in hand and a pamphlet. The man took a seat and introduced himself as Dr. Downs. He told Ralynn that he was here to counsel her and tell her what would happen on her next visit. The words next visit, hit Ralynn like a brick wall.

"Excuse me? What do you mean next visit?"

With a very matter of fact in his tone, he explained that there was a new state law and it required women to wait forty-eight hours for an abortion.

After those words, Ralynn really couldn't remember what exactly the doctor said next, but she felt the walls closing in. Ralynn couldn't breathe and needed to get out of there and fast. She ran out the front door, and the pastor was sitting, waiting just like he said he would be. But now, Ralynn was surprised because Shelly was standing waiting by the vehicle also.

Ralynn felt her knees buckling, and Shelly whipped around just in time to catch her. They both fell to the ground as Ralynn was uncontrollably sobbing. Ralynn was not sure if they were there five minutes or three hours, but they didn't move, and Shelly never said a word.

Ralynn felt like she was being held by a mom who was holding her daughter after she had been dumped by her first love in middle school. Shelly just allowed Ralynn the freedom to weep. Ralynn was now more conflicted than ever. She had never had anyone drive forty-five minutes in morning traffic, let alone to another town for her. Ralynn could not believe that Shelly, who had nothing to gain and everything to lose, did this for her, just because. Ralynn was not sure when Chris left, but by the time they got in Shelly's van, the sun was brightly shining overhead.

They did not talk much during the drive back to Mapleton. Knowing the protocol, Shelly had called Ms. Shaw to arrange a pick-up for Ralynn.

Finally breaking the silence, Shelly said, "You will not go through this alone. We will be there to navigate the system with you, whether you choose to become a mom or adoption. We will be there for you."

Knowing that Shelly meant what she said, Ralynn just smiled as she got out of the van to take her seat in Z-House's van. Sitting in the back seat, Ralynn had a bird's eye view of Ms. Shaw and Shelly. She could not hear what they were saying, but they were not hiding their tears.

The drive back to Z-House was very quiet, and Ralynn was grateful that for the next thirty-six hours she was allowed to lay around and think. Even though she was allowed this freedom, the love she felt in the house was amazing. Over the weekend, many of the ladies and staff stopped by her room and offered their support and ear.

As Ralynn was getting ready for bed on Sunday evening there was a knock on her door.

"Come in."

It was Sally, and she had Jessie with her.

"Ralynn, can I talk to you for a minute."

"Sure, what's up?"

Sally walked around the bed and took a seat in the chair in the corner. Ralynn realized that she was crying.

"Sally, are you okay?"

She just shook her head. Ralynn just let her be for a moment, figuring she would talk when she was ready.

"Ralynn, I know you don't know me, and I just got here . . . but I wanted to share my story if you want to hear it?"

"Sure, if you want to share."

"I had an abortion last year. My boyfriend told me that if I really loved him then I would 'take care of it.' I went to the place like the one on Cobbles Way. It was the scariest thing I have ever done. I was so alone. I was 'in love,' or at least I thought I was, but he made me go alone. Who does that? I was so mad. I was hurting afterward, and he told me to get over myself and get back to work."

Sally was getting angrier and angrier. The more she talked the louder and animated she became. "*Ralynn . . . I am so glad that they made you wait.*"

Then all of a sudden Sally got quiet, looked down at Jessie, and started to mumble.

"Sally, you okay?"

Attempting to speak, Sally handed Jessie to Ralynn. Ralynn awkwardly accepted him. Sally was finally able to speak.

"Ralynn, meet my angel. Meet my miracle."

Ralynn wasn't exactly sure what Sally was trying to say.

"Ralynn, the abortion wasn't successful."

Now Ralynn was crying realizing she was holding a miracle.

"Ralynn that is why I am here. I have been in hiding in another state. When Jessie was born, I could not stay in that home anymore if I wanted to keep my baby. I found Z-House online and am here to have a new start. I know that I just got here. But know what a gift you have in this place— the support and the love. You don't have to worry about where you will go when the baby comes. You get to stay here. And not having the abortion, you don't have to go through the guilt like I did. Then when I found out I was still pregnant . . . Wow! All the emotions I had. Nine months of not knowing if I did any damage. Nine months of worrying. Nine months of guilt. Nine months of shame. Then Jessie entered this world, and I cannot imagine life without him. I know it will not be easy, but I am ready to try something different than what I have done most of my life—getting into bad relationships."

Ralynn was in shock. Sally was a few years younger but seemed to already have a better outlook on life. Sally took Jessie and as she started to walk out, Ralynn being grateful for the talk, thanked her.

X

Monday morning had come and Ralynn had not once thought about calling the clinic to make that appointment. She wasn't sure what was next for her, but she knew for sure that abortion was not an option. As she was getting ready, she found an envelope with a card in it. As she opened it, a slip of paper fell out. It floated to the floor and landed under the corner of her bed. Picking it up, she was trying to figure out what it was. It was about four inches by three inches, and it was black and white. Looking at it closer, she saw the name Sally in the corner in white lettering. Then in the middle of the paper was a white circle with the word "boy." Ralynn, still not understanding, opened the card.

"You didn't answer when I came back. I knocked but didn't want to bother you. This was a game changer for me. This is Jessie's first picture. When I was not feeling well, and all my tests came back negative, they did an ultrasound and that was when I found out the abortion was not successful and I was going to be a mom. This first picture, if I had seen this picture first, I would never had considered an abortion. Look at him. He is a he— not a blob and not a mass, like a tumor. He was and is a baby. I wanted to share this with you, and I can't wait until you get your baby's first picture."

Ralynn was now ugly crying and holding her tummy. She was apologizing to her little one and now longed to have its first picture.

Realizing it was getting late, Ralynn composed herself and walked out to the kitchen. When Ms. Shaw saw her, she told her that they would leave in an hour to go get an order of protection against Ben. Over the weekend, Ralynn had remembered to tell Ms. Shaw that Ben had been waiting at KT's when they drove by on Friday, and she also showed her the texts from last week.

By 11 a.m., Ralynn was physically and mentally exhausted. She was not prepared for the process. Having to relive details and events was not something she was prepared for mentally, but the icing on the cake came as Ralynn had finished with the officer who took her statements. As he handed Ralynn, her copies he said, "I'm sorry Miss but until he is served, there is not much we can do. If he does happen to come by your work and start to bother you, call 911."

Knowing Ben's obsessive behavior, Ralynn knew that he would be waiting for her at work tonight. Before she walked out of the station, she relayed that information to the officer. He said that they would try to get an officer over there to serve it. Walking out of the station, Ralynn found herself fuming that, as the victim, she felt like Ben's life mattered more and that she would be a sitting duck. She needed a job. She was going to have a baby.

Taking longer than expected at the station, Ms. Shaw went ahead and took Ralynn to work early. Ralynn was excited that she was able to get into the front door of KT's without incident. Ben was not sitting in his normal spot, and that gave Ralynn a glimmer of hope that maybe he had given up. Half way through her shift, her hope was smashed. Ben had found his front row spot across the street, waiting.

Ralynn was able to see him clearly from her vantage point at the cash register. She was relieved when an officer in an unmarked car pulled in and parked right next to Ben. She saw the officer get out and hand Ben an envelope.

Letting her guard down because Ben had been served, Ralynn got busy taking care of customers, so she did not see the officer leave nor hear the door open.

A mom and her children were in line ordering when Ralynn heard commotion. She looked up and saw that Ben was not happy. He was shoving his way past customers and yelling obscenities. The children that had been ordering with their mom were now crying. Customers were getting upset and telling him to leave. Ben was angrily telling customers to shut up because this was a personal matter.

Thankfully, as quick as it started was as quick as it finished. Ben was now on the floor, with handcuffs being slapped on. The officers were finally escorting him out of the restaurant, but unfortunately he was still threatening Ralynn with his words. *"If I can't have you, bitch, no one can!"*

Watching this unfold before her eyes, Ralynn could not believe it when the officer was very calmly telling Ben he had the right to remain silent, and that he might want to exercise that right because judges in Mapleton don't take kindly to people threatening to kill people.

What Ralynn didn't know was there was an officer watching, and as soon as Ben touched her that officer was in the restaurant. The officers had served men before and, based upon her accounts earlier, they knew they needed to have officers stationed and ready.

Ralynn was not too sure who called Ms. Shaw, but as soon as Ben was tucked safely in the back of the black and white, she walked in and told Ralynn that it was time to look for another job. Ralynn simply nodded and started to walk out to the van. As she headed to the door, Tim, her boss asked her to come back to the office for a moment.

"Ralynn, you have been an amazing employee, and I wish it had worked out. If you need a reference, I will give you a glowing review. Ralynn, take care of yourself. Your life and the life of that little one you are carrying is too important."

Ralynn was shocked, she hadn't told anyone at work. How'd he know?

"Ralynn, your secret is safe. I won't tell anyone. And no one told me. I saw how you covered your stomach when Ben was swinging. Also you have been glowing for a few weeks now. Plus, I am a husband and a dad. My wife has taught me a few things."

Ralynn did her nervous chuckle and said, "Thank you for everything."

Walking out of the office, Ms. Shaw was waiting for her by the door. The ride back to Z-House was a quiet one, but Ralynn found herself starting to fume at the fact that she was the one who had to quit her job. She was the one who had to go into hiding. What in the world? Why is she being punished for wanting to be free of him? She just wanted Ben out of her life, but now she was having his baby.

Ms. Shaw broke Ralynn's thought process. "Ralynn why don't you call Shelly and see if she can meet with you tomorrow? It'll be good to talk through tonight with someone besides one of us."

Looking at the time, she decided to text Shelly.

"Hey"

"Hey"

"Can you meet me tomorrow? Need to talk."

"You okay?"

"No."

"Jim wants to know if I should wear a waterproof shirt or just bring tissues."

"LOL, waterproof."

"Sure. Ten a.m., our place."

"Thanks"

Pulling into the house, Ralynn was not sure what to expect. It seemed that she had so much drama in her life right now, much more than anyone else.

"You know you are not the only one going through things."

"How do you do that? How'd you know what I was thinking?"

"And I know you think you are creating so much drama, but we have had much worse. So walk in. Keep your head up, and we will get through this."

The ladies were just finishing with their devotions as Ralynn walked into the family room. As she was excusing herself to her room, a lady from the church approached her.

"Ralynn, you don't know me, but I am Chris's wife, Tina. When he found out I was coming tonight to talk to the ladies, he was hoping I would get to meet you. He didn't tell me anything about you, just that he happened to be your driver the other day. I pray you are doing well, and if you ever need anything, here is my card. We would love for you to join us on a Sunday if you want."

Ralynn took the card and excused herself to her room. She was spent. All the events of the day had her unsure whether she was coming or going.

Even though she was tucked safely in her bed, the emotions of what happened at the restaurant or what could have happened escaped and there was no putting them away. One minute, Ralynn was crying; the next, she was screaming into her pillow. She even laid there kicking her legs and feet in anger. In a huff, she was pounding her fists into the mattress. Just when she thought she was done, another wave of emotions would start. Looking at the clock, and seeing it was 3 a.m., she started screaming, "No, you don't."

A flashback of Ben leaving the restaurant entered her mind and his words were taunting her. *"If I can't have you, then no one would."*

XI

Ralynn actually was the first to arrive. The Coffee Shoppe was extremely busy that morning, and Ralynn found the first seat available. Looking around the room, Ralynn started to daydream about all their lives and how perfect they were. The women she saw that morning had perfect hair, makeup, and nails. Their lives were perfect. Their marriages were perfect. Everyone but her had a perfect life.

Shelly clearing her throat and sliding the chair out, brought Ralynn back to the present and her reality. Shelly had also stopped at the counter and ordered their drinks.

"Thank you, Shelly, for meeting me and for the drink."

"What's up? Your text was cryptic, but this is as waterproof of a shirt I have, so I hope it will do."

Ralynn was thankful for laughter, but it was all external; her internal self was crying.

"So, you are the one who called the meeting . . ."

"Yes. Thank you. I . . ."

"So, how about I start? What were you thinking about when I walked up?"

"How perfect everyone looked. How their lives were perfect, and none of them had any worries."

Shelly chuckled, "Really? Is that what you see?"

"Yes."

Shelly scanned the room and without pointing anyone out, she said,

"What if I told you in here right now you had a lady on the brink of divorce? You have a lady who just found out she lost a baby. You have another couple of women who are walking together because they lost their husbands in freak accidents. And those are just the ones I know because they hit the news."

Stopping for a moment to take a drink of her decaf peppermint mocha, Shelly continued: "Just because people look happy on the outside doesn't tell you anything about what they are going through on the inside. Take you, for instance. You may not remember me, but you waited on me weeks ago. I came in for lunch. You were so cheerful and excited to be training someone. You seemed to genuinely love your job. If anyone was looking from a distance for just a short time, they would say the same thing about you. She has the perfect life and no worries."

"Okay, point taken."

"So why are we really here?"

Ralynn went through everything that had happened in the past twenty-four hours. She started with the police station and ended with Ben getting arrested and how she lost her job. She talked about it not being fair that she has to be in hiding and Ben gets to walk around free.

"Did he not get arrested?"

"Yes, but Ms. Shaw called before she dropped me off and he's scheduled to make bond this afternoon."

"Well, that doesn't sound good. What can I do to help?"

"I dunno. Ms. Shaw just told me to call you."

"Well, if it is okay with you, I want to share a story with you."

That's fine.

"I found myself in an unplanned pregnancy in college. I wasn't feeling well, so I went to the clinic. The nurse did a pregnancy test, and the very next statement was, would you like the number to the clinic to get that taken care of?"

Ralynn could not hold back her shock, she let out a loud, "Nooooooo." Quieting down a little, she asked, "What did you do?"

"Thankfully, abortion was not an option for me. So I called my mom. I couldn't even get out the words, but she knew. I then called my boyfriend who had moved over 1000 miles away and told him. And last Thursday, you met the boyfriend, and you met the little girl who wasn't planned."

"You would never know."

74

"It wasn't easy. We have had our ups and downs. And more downs than I like to admit. But we committed to working it out, and here we are today. I tell you this: it doesn't matter where you start from. It's where you end up that counts."

Ralynn was fidgeting with her cup and a single tear drop hit the table. "I am afraid of not doing it right."

"I get that. And I wish I could tell you that I have done everything right, but . . . I would be lying. What I can tell you, is that you are very fortunate to have a group of women who want to see you succeed. That is one of the first things you need in your life."

"What's that?"

"Accountability. People who will hold you accountable, not just by talking to you, but by also modeling the same behavior."

"So are you going to be one of those people?"

"Ralynn, I will be a part of your life as long as you will have me. I have a rule though."

"What's that?"

"I will not chase after you if you choose to run away. I will be ready though, to accept you back when you are done running."

"Now I know why Ms. Shaw wanted me to talk with you. I feel like I have people who really want to see me succeed. Thank you."

As they got up from the table, Ralynn was the one who gave Shelly a hug.

As Ralynn was waiting for the van to come get her, she felt like a ton of bricks had been lifted. Ralynn also realized that Shelly truly wanted all of the women she was working with to succeed in life, and that her hugs, the ones Ralynn had been afraid to receive, were just an extension of her genuine love for all of them.

XII

Ralynn did not like to be idle, so by Wednesday, she was out interviewing for a new job. Ralynn was so excited because the first interview landed her a job, but as she exited the building there he was. Just far enough away to not violate the order of protection but close enough to let Ralynn know she could not get away from him. Ralynn turned around and walked back into the store. She politely declined their offer and asked to use the restroom. Nervously but safely tucked away in the restroom, she waited until Ms. Shaw showed up to take her back to Z-House.

The drive home once again took longer than usual because Ben started to follow them. Ralynn was thankful when she found out that Ms. Shaw had the police on speed dial and they were able to pull him over. Ralynn was grateful that Ms. Shaw waited to make sure Ben was stopped before they drove toward the property. Ralynn did not realize how tense she was until the sight of the driveway triggered relief.

She walked straight into the living room and slumped down on the blue leather couch, feeling like the tidal wave of tears were about to hit again. Ms. Dee must have seen it coming because she came over and sat a little closer to Ralynn than she wanted but most definitely needed because as soon as Ms. Dee's arm touched Ralynn's shoulder, the floodgates opened.

Finally, able to see through the blur of the tears, Ralynn realized that a majority of the women were sitting around her. The tears started back up though when Ralynn noticed that Kia's daughter had come in and laid her favorite teddy bear blanket on her lap.

One by one, the ladies gave Ralynn a hug and told her to keep her chin up. For the first time, Ralynn really felt like she was part of a new family. Even though they all came from different walks of life, they all had the same reason for bringing them together. Everyone at Z-House was running from a domestic partner who thought it was okay to hurt them.

Ralynn sat for a while longer in the living room and could hear the ladies in the kitchen making dinner. Before Ms. Dee got up to leave, she leaned in and told Ralynn that they would help her figure out a way to pay her bills, but for the time being, for her safety, she should not work.

Ralynn's waves of emotion ranged from anger to thankfulness but most of all grateful to be safe and loved.

Just as Ralynn got up to join the ladies in the kitchen, the door opened and in walked a group of ladies from First Christ Church.

"Hey ladies. How's it going?"

"Hey, Cheerful Sadie."

Sadie's smile got even larger. The girls nicknamed her that a few months ago. Sadie was always a welcome distraction at the house. Ralynn had only heard of her; now she was going to get to meet her and see what all the fuss was about. Sadie's arms were full of baking supplies, so Ralynn ran over to help. The group of ladies from First Christ Church had brought pizza dough they purchased from the local pizzeria.

"Ladies, your job is to work together to make a great-looking and great-tasting pizza. And the team that wins, gets to pick two things each from our treasure chest."

Smack talking started, and the teams were formed, but before the competition got started, Ms. Sadie asked us to name the ingredients found in pizza dough.

"Flour."

"Correct."

"Eggs."

"Could be, but not in this recipe."

"Some form of liquid."

"Correct, water and oil. So those are the main ingredients, and then depending upon your style and taste, there is sugar, salt, and so on . . . but how does it rise?"

"Yeast."

"Correct. It needs yeast. Do you all know that in comparison for a batch of dough, the amount of yeast is the smallest thing? In Galatians 5:7–10, and this is from the New Living Translation, it says: 'You were running the race so well. Who has held you back from following the truth? It certainly isn't God, for He is the one who called you to freedom. This false teaching is like a little yeast that spreads through the whole batch of dough! I am trusting the Lord to keep you from believing false teachings. God will judge that person, whoever he is, who has been confusing you.' So ladies, let's make our pizzas, and while they are baking we will break down that scripture. So on your mark . . . get set . . . *Go!*"

The kitchen looked like World War III had hit it. There was flour everywhere. Pizza sauce had somehow made it into Ralynn's hair. Kyra was running around the kitchen, squealing like a normal toddler, and somehow Jessie, who was swaddled and laying contently in what looked to be a hammock attached to Sally, slept through the whole thing. The pizzas were finally in the ovens. Opting to clean up afterward, everyone took a seat at the dining table and Sadie opened up her Bible again and reread the Scripture.

"All right, ladies, now that we read it again, I want to look at the part about yeast. We have already talked about the yeast in the pizza being the smallest ingredient. What would have happened if the yeast would not have been mixed throughout the whole batch of dough? It would not rise, and we would have a flat pizza." Just then Ms. Dee had gotten the pizzas out of the oven and brought them over to show us. "Looking at these amazing masterpieces you all made; it looks like the yeast worked. The crust is fluffy, and they look yummy. But what does that have to do with God and our lives?

"The Scripture says, 'This false teaching is like a little yeast that spreads through the whole batch of dough!' I am trusting the Lord to keep you from believing false teachings. God will judge that person, whoever he is, who has been confusing you. Ladies, yes, this Scripture is talking about false teaching of God's Word, but it also is anything or anyone you are listening to that tells you anything that does not line up with what God says and says about you. God does not say you are worthless. He says you are His masterpiece. God does not say you are ugly; God says you were created in His image. Do you see where I am going with this? False teaching, or in our case, believing what people say about us that is not according to what God says, even as little as the yeast in this pizza dough, can create a mess in our lives when we believe it. Let's pray and then we can eat.

"Daddy, we ask right now that You will touch each one of these women. May they see the truth. May they be ready to run the race You have for them. May they search for Your truth and quit allowing the false teaching to infiltrate their lives and keep them in bondage to thinking this is all life has to offer. In Jesus's name, Amen."

Before we could eat, Sadie called for Ms. Dee.

"Ms. Dee, can you please judge the pizzas? We need a winner based upon appearance and taste."

Ms. Dee jumped at the opportunity to judge, but when it came down to it, she decided that one team had the best looking and the other had the best flavors. So Ms. Sadie allowed all of the ladies two things from the treasure chest.

The treasure chest consisted of fun things that we really didn't need but would like to have. This week it had hair ties, hair bows, fun socks, perfume, note cards, and puzzle books just to name a few things. But then Sadie surprised the girls with signed copies of a local author's book. The author had personalized her message for each girl at Z-House.

Ralynn was overwhelmed with the whole day, and now that the adrenaline rush from the competition was wearing off, she was ready to climb in bed, but she first had to do her chores. This week, it was to clean the kitchen after dinner. She was grateful that Julia jumped in to help because they really had made a mess. The other girls had asked if she wanted their help, but they all had kids who really needed to get to bed, so she declined.

XIII

Thursday was finally here, and Ralynn couldn't wait until it was time for dinner. Kia had been in a better mood this week; she was still making excuses as to why she shouldn't be living in a place like this, but she had no other options, so she would get by until she could do something different. Thankfully, Ralynn did not have to ask for a ride; Kia had already offered to drive again.

Julia had started to make excuses as to why she could not come over the weekend, so Ralynn spent the morning telling her why she needed to come. Then Ralynn pulled the "I'll tell them you are seeing Dave if you don't come."

Ralynn was not sure why she did that, but Julie agreed to come one more time. As it was getting time to leave Kyra, Kia's daughter, running as fast as her little legs would take her, came running into Ralynn's room, grinning from ear to ear.

"Hurry Ms. Rawyn, we be late to see my frends."

Ralynn squatted down so that she was eye level with Kyra.

"Now we don't want to keep your friends waiting, do we?"

Ralynn grabbed her purse as fast as she could because now little Miss Kyra was standing in the door with her little hand on her hip, tapping her foot.

Driving to class didn't seem quite as far this time. Ralynn was anxious about getting there, but at the same time excited to see what they would be learning. Pulling up to the house, there were cars lining both sides of the road. Before Kia even put the car in park, Kyra was in the backseat yelling in her little girl voice,

"Huray, huray, I be late. Leeeetttttts gooooooo. Get me outta here."

Kia, Ralynn, and Julia started to snicker, but quickly realized their laughter was nothing compared to the belly laughs they heard coming from the house.

Walking in the front door and up the stairs, Ralynn saw a freedom in the way everyone was acting. There were no fears of laughing too loud, and there was no fear of being told to knock it off. But just that fast, Ralynn was caught in a memory of growing up. She had talked too loud and next thing she remembered was being sent to her room. Her mother scolded her while explaining that she needed to learn that when "he" was asleep that you had to be very quiet. He needed his beauty sleep, and we would not like the consequences if he was awakened.

Ralynn was brought back to the present with a loud squeal. Jim was chasing the boys down the hallway with a towel he had rolled perfectly. The boys had their towels in tow, but were running away instead.

"Jim, I told you not to teach them how to have a towel fight."

"Shelly, you take all the fun out of having kids around."

Shelly stood there just glaring at Jim. Ralynn, watching the whole exchange, wondered what would happen next.

"Okay, boys, let's go. Shelly is making us put our toys away."

"Jim . . ."

"What? You!"

Jim with the boys following behind walked up to Shelly and gave her their towels, one by one. Jim leading the train, made sure that everyone knew that Shelly wouldn't let them have any fun. Shelly in return got the last laugh. She took the towel that Jim had rolled and snapped Jim in his backend. For the next five minutes, everyone was laughing hysterically as Jim was now chasing Shelly around the house. Shelly was yelling at Jim to stop, but he continued and kept repeating that she had started it. Ralynn loved how Jim and Shelly were still in love, and the laughter in their home was a relief to her. She hoped that one day she too would create fond memories to replace the ones that were taking up space today. Everything came to a screeching halt, though, when Isabella dropped the lid to the four-quart cast iron pot. Isabella and Kia had been left to finish the macaroni and cheese while Shelly and Jim ran around the house.

Isabella was trying to talk, but she was bent over laughing so hard.

Finding Hope

"Ms. Shelly, that is *not* how you make macaroni and cheese!"

Ralynn still trying to comprehend what was happening, Isabella walked to the refrigerator and took out the remaining one and half pounds of the cheese block. Grabbing the knife that Shelly had laid down on the counter, Isabella started cutting the cheese into bite-sized cubes and plopping them into the pot of macaroni. Now Jai was in on the fun and started stirring like she was making a magic potion. Placing the final product on the table and pointing to Ms. Shelly, Isabella said, "Now this is how you make macaroni and cheese."

The laughter started again, but everyone really busted out laughing when Jim said, "Shelly, I really hope you took notes because this looks amazing."

Sitting down for dinner the ladies started sharing their Highs and Lows of the week and day.

When it was Ralynn's turn, she started sharing about her week. All of it!

She shared about the appointment at the abortion clinic. The divine appointment with the driver, Chris, who happened to be a pastor of a local church. Ralynn then talked about how Chris knew Shelly, so he called her, and she came right away. Ralynn got up from her seat and walked over to Shelly gave her a hug from behind and whispered in her ear, *"Thank you again."*

Shelly squeezed Ralynn's arm in response, as to say you are welcome. As Ralynn had finished talking, Alecia started sharing.

"Some of you know I come from a very religious family."

Getting up from her seat Alecia went to the other room where the children were eating and brought her daughter, Gabriella, over to Ralynn who was still standing by Shelly's seat and said, "I would love to introduce you to Gabriella. Shelly, you don't know this but you saved her life four years ago. You may not remember, but you were having a cookout in the park. My boys knew Jai's older boys, and you all invited us to join you. That week, you spoke on the sanctity of life and what may have been done in the dark, God still knew. You also read Psalm 139 and Ephesians 2:10. What you did not know was that on Friday, I had an appointment that I never went to, and I need to tell you thank you."

By now Jim was passing out the tissues because there were no dry eyes. There was no judgment. There was no condemnation. But Jim, being Jim, started making his jokes. When moments got awkward, Jim would start making jokes.

"Alecia, next time warn me so I can take stock up on tissues first."

Jim knew how to lighten a mood but also knew when to walk out and let the ladies have their cryfest. Jim grabbed his Bible and started reading Psalm 139:

For You created my inmost being; You knit me together in my mother's womb. I praise You because I am fearfully and wonderfully made; Your works are wonderful, I know that full well. My frame was not hidden from You when I was made in the secret place, when I was woven together in the depths of the earth. Your eyes saw my unformed body; all the days ordained for me were written in Your book before one of them came to be. (NIV)

Jim then turned to Ephesians 2:10 and started reading:

For we are God's handiwork, created in Christ Jesus to do good works, which God prepared in advance for us to do. (NIV)

When he was finished reading Alecia chimed in, "God makes no junk."

As the women started telling Ralynn how proud they were of her, all she could say was, "I am grateful that the law changed and that I had to wait for forty-eight hours. I can't tell you I would have been strong enough to say no or stop. I cannot believe I actually told all of you everything. I learned at a very young age to keep things in and to isolate myself. I also learned that what I had to say, no one wanted to hear. Thank you for listening. Thank you for caring."

As the stories that night continued on. Shelly started to talk. "Ladies, I can hear in your voices and conversation that there is still a lot of hurt. And I feel that you may be plagued with shame and guilt. If I am counting right, there are eighteen children living in heaven tonight represented at this table."

Shelly took a breath and was ready to speak when Julia raised her hand and with a strained voice, squeaked out, "No, there are nineteen."

Class kind of went into slow motion as Julia started to speak. It made sense to Ralynn why she was making excuses as to why she didn't want to come tonight.

"Ralynn," Julia was now looking right at her. "Ralynn, do you remember the first day I met you?"

Ralynn nodded.

"Dave and I are not boyfriend and girlfriend. He is just a good friend, and he had just picked me up from the clinic. I was hungry because I had not eaten for thirty-six hours. He. Didn't. Know. He. Didn't. Know. What. I. Had. Done. Iiiiii. . . . Mmmmm . . . sssssssoooooo . . . I. Just. Want. To. Die."

The more Julia spoke, the more she cried. The more she cried, the more the rest of the room cried, including Shelly and Jim. *Where were Jim's jokes when we needed them?* Ralynn thought to herself. Instead Jim was allowing Julia her time to grieve.

What seemed to be an eternity was finally interrupted with Shelly cautiously starting to speak.

"Ladies, first I want to say that I am sorry I was not there for you. I am sorry that someone was not there for you. I am sorry that you felt this was your option and that you have not felt you had a safe place to grieve, share, and be released of shame and guilt. What I do want to share is this: you all have a choice tonight to make. Will you allow these actions of your past to keep you in bondage and not allow you to have a productive future? Please hear me. I am not making light of anything you all have gone through.

"What I want you to see is that you have been given a tomorrow, and you can make it say whatever you wish. It is a clean slate. We all have things in our past that we wish we would have done different or not at all. It is what you do with those experiences that create your tomorrow. Ladies, these choices you made were what we call actions. These actions are part of your story, but now you have two choices! Do you allow your past and past mistakes to dictate the future you will have, or do you learn from your past and past mistakes and start your new book or what we like to call, your *second edition*?"

A new book? What new book? Ralynn's brain started in again. Trying to break down what Shelly had said and what she was meaning. Ralynn new she had heard of a new chapter but a new book?

"Let me explain. Ya'll, a new chapter, says you are still wanting to write that story from the book of life you have been living. A second edition, or new book, means the pages are blank, and you can start writing a new ending, one that is full of hope. The challenge will come when you allow the demons of your past to start writing on those new pages as well. So, ladies, in the realm of what we have been talking about tonight, let me ask you this question: what happened in your past to make you who you are today? As we go through life, we allow an incident or an event to start us on a path of what I like to call 'letting life happen.' The challenge becomes when this event is overshadowed with guilt, shame, embarrassment or even the inability to tell anyone it happened, so we live in a silent hell."

Shelly let those words sink in for a minute before she continued.

"Shame is who I am, and because of what I have done, I feel less than or hopeless. This can also be affected by words that have been spoken over us, especially if we are in unhealthy relationships. With shame being in control, we can find ourselves feeling helpless or depressed. We can find ourselves even medicating the pain through addictive behaviors, not just drugs or alcohol but also shopping, pornography, or even unhealthy relationships."

You could hear a pin drop as Shelly was talking. Ralynn, glancing around the room was not sure what anyone else was feeling but she felt like Shelly was speaking right to her. Ralynn couldn't wait to get back to Z-House and talk about everything with Julia and Kia.

"Guilt."

With that word, Shelly had Ralynn's attention again.

"Guilt is what I have done. The challenge is when we allow ourselves to continually think because we did something bad, we need to stay in a place of 'not being worthy.' This then creates many sabotaging behaviors, which means we deliberately destruct something. Guess what, ladies? We do this in relationships especially when we do not feel we deserve something different. We can talk ourselves into believing we deserve to be in an abusive relationship."

Again, Shelly had the room in complete silence, and Ralynn felt like Shelly was only speaking to her. How does she do that?

"Ladies, if you are sitting there thinking 'how does she do that? She is talking right at me'—if any of this resonates with you, it's because God wants you to hear something. Now remember that abuse is not just physical or sexual; it is also verbal, emotional, and spiritual. And all these abuses have their own effects on our lives. Because of guilt and not forgiving ourselves for something in our past, we talk ourselves into thinking this is the best that life has to offer.

"So how do we forgive ourselves for an event or action that keeps our self-esteem and even self-confidence in the low position? By not forgiving ourselves we can find ourselves being only attracted to unhealthy relationships. Not forgiving ourselves for something and allowing others to continue to remind us of our wrongdoing can also cause us to find ourselves in a state of helplessness, depression, or even medicating our pain through addictive behaviors."

Shelly took a drink of her water letting what she just said, sink in.

"I see you all are being extremely quiet. Does anyone want to share what they are thinking?

Jai was the first to start in. "Shelly I hear what you are saying but . . ."

"But what?"

"I . . . don't know what."

"Yes, this is all overwhelming. I understand. So let me ask you this. Who wants to start doing something different? If I asked, are you sick and tired of being sick and tired, who would raise their hand?"

Everyone's hands went up.

"Exactly. So what I need you to do is take what we just talked about and ask God this question: 'What do You want me to take from this and change in myself?' And next week we will start our group talking through your answers. So, unless anyone has anything else, we will see you next week."

Ralynn could not get back to the house soon enough. Everything that Shelly had talked about was buzzing in her head, and she wanted to take time to journal. She was also hoping that Kia and Julia would want to talk but didn't want to seem pushy, so she told Kia thank you for driving and went straight to her room.

As she was getting ready for bed, there was a knock on her door.

"Come in."

"Ralynn can we talk?"

"Sure come on in."

Just as Ralynn and Julia were getting settled, there was a knock on the door.

"Come in."

"Ra . . . oh, I'm sorry I didn't know you had someone in your room."

"That's okay. Come on in. The more the merrier."

Just as Kia was about to take a seat at the desk, Sally peeked her head in.

"Whatcha all doin'?"

"Just talkin'." Julia chimed in.

"Can I join?"

"Sure," Kia said.

Now that her room was more than full, she didn't know where to start. She really wanted to talk about what they had just learned, but she felt that Sally would be left out.

Ralynn hoping that someone would start the conversation threw out the question,

"So what are we going to talk about?"

Julia and Kia simultaneously started to speak. They were speaking over each other. Then they both stopped. Then they both started again. Sally was the first to laugh, which then made all of them start to laugh.

"So it seems that what we talked about tonight really hit home, so let's start there. Julia, you start."

Immediately the tears started, and Ralynn was fumbling around looking for the tissues.

Not being able to say a word, Julia touched Kia's arm as if to say, "You can start."

For the first time Ralynn saw Kia let out a little emotion as she started to share her story.

"I am not sure what I am doing. I have never not had a boyfriend. From the time I can remember, I always had to have a boyfriend. I don't know why. I just did. Most of them were okay. They didn't hurt me or anything at least physically or sexually. But when Shelly was talking about abuse also being in the form of verbal and emotional, I thought I was going to throw up. How does she do that? How does she know what we have been through?"

Ralynn was not sure Kia wanted an answer because she kept right on talking.

"My last boyfriend who isn't even Kyra's dad, was the one who was physically abusive. He told me that it was my fault that he hit me. Then I almost lost my job because of him. Listening tonight to Shelly, I guess I realized I had been beaten so low in my self-esteem and confidence that I believed I got what I deserved. I wish I could go home. My mom was so loving. My dad had a heart of gold. They worked all the time and they bought me anything and everything. We had the best vacations. I did well in school but had no desire to go to college or make a career. I didn't want to be like them, working all the time and missing everything I did.

"The summer after I graduated, I fell in love with this guy. He was older and had a job and a car. He told me that I didn't need to work. I could just live with him. I knew it was wrong. I at least had some moral compass, but he was so sweet. He paid attention to me. We did things as a couple. He filled a space in my heart that I didn't know was needing filled. He never hurt me physically, but, boy, when he got mad, things went flying, and most of his words were directed at me. Then, by morning, he apologized, and it was like nothing ever happened. I really thought we would get married. He said we would. Then one day, he came home and told me to move out, that I had to go. I begged and pleaded for him to let me stay. The look in his eyes told me I had overstayed my welcome. I grabbed a bag and left quickly. I went home. My mom and dad never said a word about it, but our relationship was never the same. I was treated more like a guest than a daughter.

"Then I met Kyra's dad. Again, he was so kind and gentle. When we first got together we did things as a couple, but then after six months, he asked me to move in with him. Mom and Dad were at work like always, and I'm not sure they even knew I had moved out, until I came back six months later with a broken arm. Again nothing major happened, he just came home one day and told me it was time for me to move on. I went to leave, and out of nowhere, he threw me into the wall. Trying to brace for the impact, I put my arm out.

"Embarrassed but hurt more than anything, I didn't go to the doctor right away. When I did finally go to the doctor, he said I fell just right and snapped the bone. I was in a cast for six weeks. That's also when I found out I was pregnant with Kyra. My parents again never said a word. I was welcomed into their home again, more as a guest than their daughter. When they found out I was pregnant, then things started to change. My mom started to take time off of work to make sure I had the best doctors that money could buy. Kyra had all she could ever need or want. I thought things were going to change, but then they wanted to control everything, I was starting to suffocate."

When Kia stopped for a moment to regain her emotion, Ralynn noticed the time, it was now 11 p.m. She was excited that Kia was talking, but she didn't know if she should let this night keep going or put a stop to it. Before she could say anything, Kia started back in.

"I know they love me in their own way, but something was missing. Kyra was about to turn three, and I was getting lonely again. I loved being Kyra's mom, but I needed a relationship for me. My mom agreed to babysit for me, so I could go out. That's when I met Bobby."

"Wait, you mean Isabella's Bobby?"

"Yes, I didn't know he was out seeing other people. He invited me to move in, and I jumped at the chance to get out of my parents' house. He adored Kyra and was really kind to her. He even agreed to babysit, so I could get a job if I wanted. He is and was a smooth talker. His spin on things always made it seem that I was going insane. His hitting me started one night after I had put Kyra to bed. He didn't like the fact that the neighbor lady had come into the house. I had invited her over for coffee because I was getting lonely and wanted someone to talk to. Bobby stated that he was the only one that I needed to talk to.

"I seriously thought he was at work all the times he was gone; I didn't know he was down the street in the next neighborhood getting chummy with the women. For a couple of weeks, he would just slap me across the face. He said it was for good measure, just in case I was thinking of doing anything stupid. I really had no idea what he was talking about. Then the next morning, it was like nothing had happened. One morning, he even prepared breakfast for me. I met Isabella on one of my walks, and we struck up a conversation. She gave me Ms. Shelly's number, and I finally had the nerve to call her. I still was not going to leave because I didn't see a big deal.

"Then on Sunday night a couple weeks ago, I was in the kitchen cooking. I had just hung up the phone with Ms. Shelly, and Kyra started to cry. Before I could reach her, he was lunging at her, telling her that she had better shut up, or he would shut her up. I scooped her up and ran to her room. Bobby followed and was banging on the doors. I thought he was going to bust down the door. I huddled in the corner, Kyra was screaming, I reached for my phone, but it wasn't there. I am not sure who called 911 but the welcome relief was short lived. He lied and told the officer that we had left out the back door, so the officer took his word for it and left. I had never been so scared because he then came to the door, told me I had until the count of ten to open up the door, or he would break it down.

"He then accused me of calling 911, but just as he was grabbing for me, there was a bang on the door. The officer was requesting entry, or he was going to break the door down. The next few minutes are a blur, but Bobby was arrested, and the officer asked me if I wanted to leave. I told them as long as they kept Bobby until tomorrow afternoon, I would be gone by then. He agreed to do a twenty-four-hour cool-down hold. I spent that night packing and when 7 a.m. rolled around, I was on the phone with Z-House. Because I had a car, they met me at the pick-up point and allowed me to follow them here."

Ralynn was the first to speak up.

"I am so glad you made the call and are here. Does Isabella know yet? Wow . . . wait a minute. If Isabella has an STD . . ."

"I am going to call my doctor tomorrow. And no she doesn't know. I am not sure how to tell her or if I should tell her."

"Maybe we could call Shelly tomorrow and see what she thinks?"

"Yeah. Maybe. I'll think about it. It's not like either of us are seeing him any more—at least. I don't think so."

Ralynn realized that their little talk has now gone deeper into a dilemma, and her gut instinct was saying that Isabella needed to know. Her girls need to be protected.

Finally, Ralynn broke the silence.

"It is midnight and I am thinking we should call Shelly in the morning. She will know how to handle this."

"I agree," Julia stated flatly.

"Me too, and I don't even know who you are talking about." With Sally chiming in, they all started to laugh.

"Okay, I need to get some sleep. This baby," as Ralynn patted her tummy, "needs her beauty sleep."

"Do you know it's a girl?" Julia asked with excitement.

"No, we are still waiting on insurance before I can go to the doctor."

XIV

Morning came faster than Ralynn had wanted it to. She could hear the hustle and bustle of the morning. Trying to drown out the noise by pulling the covers over her head didn't work. Coming to the conclusion it was useless, Ralynn was just putting her feet on the floor when Kia knocked on the door.

"Ralynn, do you think it's too early to call Shelly?"

Picking up her phone to look at the time, she realized she had already missed a text from Shelly.

"Nope," turning her phone, so Kia could see the text. "It looks like Isabella has already beat you to it."

"What?"

"All it says is please have both you and Kia call me when you wake up. Isabella wants to meet with us today."

"Text her."

"Can I get out of bed first?"

"No." Kia was laughing. "Of course. I'll meet you out on the front porch."

Shelly texted: Hey you up?

Yes.

Can you and Kia meet for lunch today?

Sure. Time and place?

11:30 at the chicken sandwich restaurant.

See you then.

Ralynn finished getting ready for the day and went out to meet Kia on the front porch.

"Where's Kyra?"

"She's in watching a show with Sally and Jessie."

"That's nice."

"So, they want to meet at 11:30; is that good for you?"

"Sure, can we leave around 11? I need to stop at the bank."

"By the way we are meeting at the chicken sandwich restaurant."

Just as Kia was getting up to go back in, Kyra walked out the door in a huff.

"What's wrong, baby?"

"Show. Over."

"Okay, let's go play. We are going to go away for lunch today with Ms. Ralynn. And there is a playland."

Ralynn had brought her journal and packets of paper with her to the front porch, hoping for some quiet time. The birds were chirping. There was a dog barking off in the distance, and then she heard the cat meowing under the porch.

"Oh no, you don't, I learned my lesson. See," showing her hand as if someone was standing there, "See, I have scabs to show where you got me last time. Not again."

Realizing she was talking to no one, Ralynn started to chuckle. She opened her journal and grabbed the packet from class. Thumbing through the papers, she found the prompt Shelly wanted them to use: What do You (God) want me to take from this and change in myself?

Sitting in her favorite chair, feet pulled up under her, Ralynn started to let her mind go as she journaled.

Change in myself?

What do I need to change?

Relationships—I need healthy relationships

I want to be a good mom.

How do I be a good mom?

I want to do something with my life, but what?

How do I change?

Self-esteem

Self-confidence

No more abuse

No more abusive boyfriends

I need to stand on my own. How?

God, I don't know how to do this, but Shelly told me to ask You to show me what I need to take from this class and change about me. I wrote down things, so I don't know if You agree or if You will talk to me or what? I have never really had this type of conversation with You. I think all I have ever done is ask You to get me out of a jam, so I am not sure what I need to do now. So . . . so I guess I will wait for You to tell me.

Shelly also asked us to write down this verse: '"For we are God's hand-iwork, created in Christ Jesus to do good works, which God prepared in advance for us to do." God what does that even mean? Thank you for listening to me.

The ding on Ralynn's phone went off at the same time Kyra came out to tell her it was time to go.

Ralynn was not sure why she was anxious about this meeting, but she could not get a sickening feeling out of her spirit that something was wrong, really wrong.

By the time Kia was done at the bank, they had all of five minutes to make it to lunch on time. Ralynn was getting antsy about being late, so she got out her phone to text Shelly:

Shelly?

Yes?

Running about ten minutes late. Bank took longer than Kia thought.

Okay, be careful. See you when you get here.

"Why did you text Shelly? We aren't going to be that late."

"Because it's the right thing to do. She was expecting us at 11:30, and now we won't be there until 11:40 or 11:45. It would be rude to make her wonder and wait. Do you not call if you are running late?

"No. People know it's okay to be fifteen minutes late."

"My GiGi always told me that if I was going to be even a minute late, as soon as I realized it, to let the other person know because people's time was worth me being courteous."

Ralynn could not believe that someone who seemed to grow up in a very well to do family, did not learn that is was rude to be late and even ruder to be late and not call. By the time they finally arrived at the restaurant, they were twenty minutes late. Ralynn started to apologize profusely to Shelly. Kia, on the other hand, was very nonchalant about the whole thing. Shelly was very kind about the whole event and thanked Ralynn for texting.

Isabella was sitting there playing on her phone. Ralynn didn't know if what she was doing was something important or whether it was a defense mechanism because she really did not want to be here. She finally acknowledged that Ralynn and Kia had shown up. After everyone had ordered and Kyra took off to the playland, Shelly started the meeting.

"Kia, I am so glad you could meet us today. Do you know why Isabella wanted to meet?"

"I think I do."

"Would you like to hear from her?"

Kia just nodded, and Ralynn wasn't sure she was ready to hear everything.

"Isabella, why don't you share what is on your heart."

Isabella finally put away her phone and blurted out, "I knew that Bobby was your boyfriend when I slept with him. I didn't mean to slip and tell his name. But now that I did, I am glad it is out in the open. You don't deserve him. He told me how awful you were to him. And how dare you have him arrested?"

"What?"

Ralynn thought Kia was about to come unglued and go crazy on Isabella.

Kia continued, "You mean you are still seeing him?"

Isabella just sat there staring at Kia. Ralynn could not believe what she was hearing. Wasn't it Isabella who gave Kia Shelly's card? What? Keep your boyfriend's girlfriend close, so you can keep track of him? Ralynn was not ready for what came out of Isabella's mouth next.

"We are still going together and matter of fact, I am having his baby."

As those words hung in the air, a welcome interruption came; the food arrived. Ralynn excused herself and went into the playland to grab Kyra. She was not happy that she had to join the table to eat; she would have rather played the afternoon away. Ralynn was not happy that she was having to sit at the table, either; she would have much rather watched Kyra play. Getting back to the table, not much had changed. The food had been passed out, and Shelly was getting a high-chair for Kyra.

"I big gurl. I sit thr."

"Kyra, I know you are a big girl, but there is no room for you to sit here, I need you to be a big girl and sit at the head of the table. Can you do that for me?"

Ralynn only hoped that she would be half as good with her baby as Shelly is with kids. Kyra took her seat proudly and started to eat, but not before she told us all we had to pray. Kyra bowed her head, folded her hands, and then looked to make sure everyone had their heads bowed.

"meendneend. Meendedne. Amen!"

Ralynn snickered a little as Kyra said amen. Shelly praised her for her prayer and Kia, under her breath, looked at Kyra and said

"Where'd you learn that?"

Shelly smiling said, "Did Nikki teach you that?"

Kyra, shoving a chicken nugget in her mouth, just smiled.

The conversation while Kyra was at the table changed to be more superficial, but as soon as she was done and back in the playland, the claws came back out.

"Isabella, you have no clue what you are talking about."

"I know enough. Bobby told me all about it."

"You are going to believe him over me? I thought I was your friend."

"Well, today I need to choose. So I choose Bobby. Ms. Shelly, thank you for everything, but I choose Bobby, and that means I won't be back to class."

As soon as Isabella finished choosing, she excused herself and left. Ralynn was still in shock then Kia started to make a scene, yelling at Kyra to get her shoes on immediately because they needed to leave. Trying to comprehend all that was going on, Ralynn just sat there and didn't realize that Kia had just left her at the restaurant.

Sitting in silence for about ten minutes, Shelly was the first to speak.

"Ralynn, are you okay?"

"Yeah, I think so. What just happened? Why did Isabella do that to Kia? I thought they were friends."

"You know how we talked about medicating our hurt with things, like addictions. Well, unfortunately, Isabella has an addiction to being needed. She has to be in a relationship, no matter the expense. I was hoping that she wanted to meet to apologize, not create a bigger issue. Right now, all we can do is pray for her. We will be there for her when she is ready to put her life together—for her and not anyone else. And we will pray that she and her girls come out of this relationship in one piece and without too many bruises or broken bones. This is the part of my job I hate. When I see something more in someone than they see in themselves, it hurts when they walk away and make choices that are going to create a worse situation for them."

"Ummm, Shelly, Kia left me. How am I going to get back to Z-House?"

"Well, I can take you home after I get done running my errands. Do you want to ride along?"

"Sure. Should I call Ms. Shaw?"

"That would be great. You let them know I will bring you back later, and I will get us refills to go."

XV

Ralynn finally made it back to Z-House after eating dinner with the Waddell's. She loved spending time with them. She also found herself longing for a man who would treat her like Jim treats Shelly.

Ralynn walked in the house and went straight to Kia's room. She was afraid at what she might find when she got there. To her disappointment and relief, Kia and Kyra's things were still in the room, but they were not there. After further investigation, Ralynn found out that they had not returned from lunch yet. Ralynn was now worried. Retrieving her phone from her purse she called Kia's number. It went straight to voicemail.

"Kia, I am not sure where you are, but it's not worth it. Please call me when you get this."

Ralynn found herself pacing the floor. She kept looking at her phone like it would magically have a text or voicemail from Kia. Finally, around 10 p.m., Kia and Kyra tried sneaking in, but Ralynn and Ms. Dee were sitting at the bar in the kitchen, waiting. Kyra was almost asleep when the wind caught the screen door and slammed it shut. Startled, she started to cry. Ralynn went over to help Kia and take Kyra, but Kia assured Ralynn that she was fine and that they just needed to go get some sleep. Ms. Dee, on the other hand, was not having the excuses. Motioning for Kia to take a seat, Ms. Dee handed Kia a document.

"Kia, is this your signature?"

"Yes!"

"Kia, do you know what you signed?"

"Yes!"

"And do you know why I am standing here, waiting for your return?"

"Yes!"

"Do you have anything to say for yourself?"

"No!"

Ralynn was trying her hardest to figure Kia out. At this moment, Ralynn knew that Kia could be asked to leave and not return, and she didn't seem to care.

"Kia, unless you can give me a good reason why you broke many of these rules today, you and Kyra will have to leave within the next twenty-four hours. You have not given us any trouble, and I know you had a rough day. First thing in the morning, I want you in my office, so we can decide how to handle this."

With a little less brashness, Kia told Ms. Dee thank you. Grabbing Kyra from Ralynn, she took off toward her room. As she did, Ralynn thought she saw a tear falling. Relieved that they weren't getting kicked out that night, Ralynn was trying to figure out if she should go talk to her or leave her alone.

Ralynn's spirit told her to follow, so she did.

"Kia, can I come in?"

"Sure."

"I can't even imagine what you are or aren't feeling. Can I help?"

"Ralynn, I am not sure anyone can help. Isabella and I have been friends for a very long time, and for her to choose him over me and not even worry about her girls, that's just . . . Well, it's stupid."

About this time, Ralynn felt lost. She also felt she was about to pass out from all the adrenaline rushes she had had.

"Kia, I need to get some sleep. I hope you can work it out and stay here. I would love to see you graduate the program and do something amazing for yourself and for Kyra."

"Good night, and I'll see you in the morning."

Sitting at the breakfast table, the quietness was short lived. There was a commotion at the front door. Ms. Dee was the first to go running through the kitchen, followed by Ms. Shaw. Ralynn's curiosity got the best of her, so she too got up and went to the front door.

She could not believe what she was seeing. It was Diane's girls. They were dragging the same heavy luggage up the stairs that they had reluctantly dragged down the hallway just a few weeks earlier. Their beautiful, long hair looked like it had not been combed in days, and their clothes were torn. With tear-stained cheeks, they fell into Ms. Dee's arms, and new tears just started flowing. Ralynn, taking in all that was unfolding right there on the front porch, was trying to comprehend what had happened when a flash of sun reflecting from something caught her attention. Dianne was trying to navigate the steps with her crutch. Hobbling up the steps, one at a time, trying to balance with her left leg in a cast and her right arm in a sling. Diane's face was so swollen that Ralynn had to take a double take to make sure it really was her.

At the sight of Diane and her girls, Ralynn thought she was going to throw up. Running back into the kitchen, Ralynn ran right into Julia.

"What's up? You okay?"

Ralynn didn't say a word but kept running to her room.

"Ralynn, what happened? You okay?"

Before Ralynn could say a word, Diane and the girls were dragging their luggage past her door. Julia stopped and stared. She too had no words.

Ralynn took a few minutes to take in the past twenty-four hours and under her breath asked the following questions, not realizing Julia was ready to give an answer.

"What was going on? Why is all this happening?"

"You know there was a full moon out last night."

Ralynn didn't know if Julia was trying to be funny or if she was serious.

"You know people get weird during full moons."

Ralynn just shot Julia a look instead of commenting.

"Well they do." And with that Julia walked out of Ralynn's room.

Sitting on her bed, trying to reel in her emotions, there was a knock on her door. Wanting to ignore it, she sat there quietly. Whoever was on the other side of the door was not going to let up. Their knocking got harder and more persistent. Ralynn got up and answered the door.

"What?"

Ralynn startled Kyra when she pulled open the door.

"Oh, Kyra, I am so sorry. I didn't mean to startle you."

"Ralynn, can we come in?"

"Sure, you both okay?"

"I'm not sure. I just need to talk before I go talk with Ms. Dee."

"Okay," Ralynn was motioning for Kia and Kyra to come in and sit down. "Let's talk."

For the next hour, Ralynn listened as Kia talked. Kia talked more about her past and the fact that Isabella become her best friend. She did not understand how Isabella could choose Bobby after she knew what he had done to her.

"Doesn't she care about her girls? Why would she sleep with him in the first place? She knew I was living with him. She knew we were a couple. At least I thought we were a couple."

The more Kia talked the angrier she got.

"Kia, can I ask you a question?"

"Sure."

"Why are you only mad at Isabella? Why aren't you mad at Bobby? He was the one who was not being faithful. He was the one who was not being honest. So, why aren't you mad at him?"

Ralynn thought she had overstepped the boundaries because Kia just sat there, not answering. Then the tears started. Ralynn had not seen Kia get this emotional over anything. She found that Kia's first response was to get angry and shut down. The more Kia cried, the more Ralynn wondered if she should call someone or go get Ms. Dee. Neither was needed because just like that, the tears were done—shut off just like a water spigot. Kia got up off the bed and almost robotically headed for the door, never answering the question.

Ralynn sat there momentarily playing what had just happened over and over in her head but not coming up with any answers only more questions, Ralynn decided her brain needed a break, and the baby probably did, too. Curling up on the bed, Ralynn meant to lay down for just a moment, but when she finally woke up it was dinner time.

Not feeling too well, Ralynn decided to forgo dinner and just go back to bed.

XVI

It was finally Thursday and time for group. Ralynn was excited that Kia had worked everything out with Z-House to stay. The drive to Shelly's was a quiet one, but Ralynn didn't mind; she was just excited that Kia and Kyra were still coming to Shelly's. Based upon Shelly's reaction when they walked in the door, Ralynn was sure Shelly thought Kia would never come back.

"Oh Kia, I am so, so happy you are here. I wanted to call you many times this week, but when you never returned my texts from last week, I figured you didn't want to talk with me."

"I am sorry I didn't text you back. I was in a bad spot. But you are right; I need to be thankful for Z-House and a new beginning."

Dinner was not as lively tonight, and Shelly had taken the kids downstairs to be with Nikki and Sabrina. As the ladies heard Shelly coming back up the stairs, they started their transition into the living room. Shelly started in immediately with telling us once again that these classes were a safe environment for people to talk and to learn. Shelly mentioned that there will be young ladies who will come and go. Those who leave are welcome to come back as long as they have not created an unfriendly environment by talking about others in the community. Shelly also pointed to Jim, who was still cleaning up the kitchen, and told all in attendance that they did not have all the answers but would walk with each of the ladies to help them become all that God created them to be. At this point, Jim walked around the corner, wiping his hands and said, "She may not have all the answers, but I do."

Shelly rolled her eyes and smirked, this made all the ladies chuckle. The way they interacted made Ralynn long to have that same relationship. Loving. Gentle. Kind. Ralynn found herself wondering if she would ever find someone like that.

"Have you ever heard sticks and stones may break my bones but words will never hurt me?"

Not sure where Shelly was going with this, Ralynn was all ears now. Her mother used to quote that nursery rhyme when the newest live-in boyfriend was spouting off hurtful words. Shelly went on to explain that once words were spoken, they couldn't be taken back. Shelly talked about the fact that she knew parenting was hard and that as parents we get frustrated, but remember words hurt and your children should not be the ones who suffer because you had a bad day.

"In Proverbs it says: 'Don't befriend angry people or associate with hot-tempered people, or you will learn to be like them and endanger your soul.' Ladies, much of parenting is caught, not taught. I want you to think about your friends and family that may fit the mold of the Proverb I just read. Now to break it down, let's look at our past. Where did we come from? Jim has handed you out a piece of paper. I want you to write on this piece of paper, your mom's name and your dad's name. Also, if your parents are divorced or were never married, and the one you lived with had multiple partners that stayed for a while, write their names down next to the parent that they cohabitated with. Now that you have done that, here comes the difficult part."

Ralynn was not sure where Shelly was going with this, but it was difficult enough to write down all her mother's boyfriends' names.

"Now I want you to write down adjectives that described those you have written on your paper so far."

Ralynn was grateful when Jai, who still had not moved to Alabama but threatened to leave again just a few minutes prior to group starting, asked Shelly for clarification. Shelly told us that we needed to think about words that would describe each person. Words like strict, religious, spiritual, addict, alcoholic, smoker, dropout, college-educated, workaholic, caring, kind, mean, or abusive. After she listed them for us, she told us this was by no means an exhaustive list but was just to get us started. Shelly gave us fifteen minutes to work on it and get a refill on our drinks or more dessert. Ralynn was just getting into a grove when Shelly called everyone back into the living room.

"Now let's add one more name. Yours."

You could hear a pin drop. Why does she want us to add our names? Ralynn's question was quickly answered.

"Ladies, you are a product of all those people you put on that list whether you are biologically theirs or they influenced your life. Remember I told you a little while ago, most of parenting is caught not taught? Well, part of parenting is teaching you how to interact with the world and how to grow from being a child into an adult. So what did you learn? Good and bad! Circle every word you wrote down for others that describes you."

Simultaneously the group let out an "*Ugh!*"

Shelly chuckled and said, "Don't quit on me yet. I need you to see that everyone we allow to influence us and now, if you have children, are creating in them an imprint. This imprint can be good, or it can be bad. You have heard me say YOU stands for 'Your Own Uniqueness.' This is where it comes from. All those words you circled—they become who you are. Now here is the scary part: if you stay on the same path you are on today and your children take this class when they are twenty, what will they say about you? If this scares you or you don't like who you have become, you have a choice. You can change. You can direct the narrative right now as to what your children will say about you. I will not tell you it will be easy. It will take lots of hard work, and it will require a new attitude, but it can be accomplished. Who is ready to change?"

Ralynn wanted to raise her hand but the weight of shame and guilt had her paralyzed. All she could do was sit there and soak in everything Shelly was saying.

"Before I go on to the next point of today's lesson, I want to talk about the fact that if you still have relationships with your parents or anyone else you felt led to write on that paper, and they are living a life of dysfunction, as an adult, you have a choice to make. Don't be disrespectful, but start standing up for the change you want to have."

Just when Ralynn thought Shelly was done, she brought up anger. Shelly wanted a show of hands by those who were getting angry because she had brought up the past hurts and pains. Everyone raised their hands.

"Good, let's talk about anger."

What? Ralynn thought Shelly had gone off the deep end, but then it all made sense the more she talked. Shelly explained that anger is a natural emotion just like being happy. The challenge with anger is that it can have really bad consequences when we don't control it. With all emotions, we need to control them and not allow them to control us. Shelly then asked the group, "What happens if we allow anger to control us?"

Shelly waited to respond as everyone gave their answers.

Slamming doors.

Swearing.

Throwing things.

Hitting things.

Hitting people.

After these responses, Shelly asked a simple question,

"What about exaggerating."

Again Ralynn was trying to figure out what did exaggerating have to do with anger. She once again did not have to wait long because Shelly was already explaining how when we get angry we need to make sure we don't exaggerate what happened in order to make ourselves to be the bigger victim. *Okay, I see that*, Ralynn was thinking to herself, *but again what does that have to do with the price of tea in China?*

As Ralynn was about to ask Shelly what that had to do with anger, Shelly asked the group what we thought would happen when you and the one you were in the fight with and exaggerated the story wanted to become friends again? Without really waiting for an answer, Shelly continued on that it can actually make things worse when you try to make amends, so remember to stick to the facts and let the chips fall where they may.

Realizing how late it was, Shelly ended the night by telling us not to run ahead, thinking that if we moved or started a new job, our lives would immediately be better. Shelly then again referenced the word YOU.

"Ladies remember that you take *you* wherever *you* go and until you walk through the process of changing *you*, you will end right back up where you started or even worse."

As we were getting ready to leave Shelly got our attention to tell us one more thing. She wanted to remind us of our homework this week. She wanted us to finish taking inventory of the characteristics and habits of everyone we wrote down and maybe even add more people to the list like aunts, uncles, and grandparents. Then we are to write both positive and negative words to describe them. She also handed us a packet of papers that would help explain it further if we needed reminding this week. Shelly asked us to pray over the characteristics. She wanted us to pray and ask God to show us how these characteristics have affected us. She also wanted us to ask God to show us the truth. She gave us instructions for asking God to show us specifically if: this was a word that described us and if it was a word we wanted to describe us.

Shelly went on to say, "If it is not a word that you want people using to describe you, especially your children when they grow up, then pray that God will allow you to see the truth, the hard truth, and to show you what steps you can do to change."

By the time Ralynn got home, she was spent. She was not sure if it was the pregnancy or the fact that class tonight brought back memories that she thought were gone. Ralynn decided it was best to turn in early. She was also hoping she would be able to sleep all night.

XVII

As the sunlight was peeking through the drapes, Ralynn realized she had not once awakened during the night. Even though she was forever grateful for the full night sleep, she didn't feel rested, but why? Still lying in bed, she noticed that the comforter somehow had completely turned itself topside down and the tag was no longer hanging off the end of the bed but was slapping her in the face.

"What in the world did I do in my sleep?" Ralynn thought to herself.

As she propped herself up, she noticed her arms were sore. Sitting up she started rubbing her arms and remembered having a dream. It was actually a nightmare, but she couldn't wake up enough to get out of it.

Shaking off the remnants of the nightmare, Ralynn decided to forgo the shower. Throwing on sweatpants and a sweatshirt, she proceeded to the kitchen for breakfast.

"Ralynn you okay?"

"Yeah, why?"

"You were crying last night. I knocked but you didn't answer, so I figured you didn't want to talk."

"Julia, I didn't hear you knock. Sorry."

Grabbing a muffin and a cup of coffee, Ralynn went back to her room. She wanted to be alone to figure out what happened in her sleep. She grabbed her journal and the paperwork that Shelly had given them as they were walking out the door.

Anger

Standing up for yourself

Choice to walk away from relationships.

"God, help me to do this homework. Help me to look at these words. Help me to be honest with myself."

Ralynn started to read through the extra packet. She knew it was the same as they had gone over, but she remembered Shelly saying it had additional information and more explanation.

Ralynn got to the first question: Who influenced your life as you were growing up?

As she read those words, Ralynn could feel the anger start to rise. Going back to her journal, she started to write as the thoughts and memories came.

Why did my dad leave?

Was I not good enough?

Why did my mom have only negative things to say about him?

Did he love me?

Was it really my fault? Were my mom's troubles really my fault? Why did she say they were?

Wanting to get her mind off that, Ralynn went back to reading the packet of papers. Off to the side, there was an asterisk; reading it made her anger start to rise. She remembered Shelly stating this fact last night also. Ralynn didn't want to admit that her mom's multiple live-ins had anything to do with influencing her.

Armed with her pen, Ralynn started to write with an aggressiveness. The more she wrote names of men and words to describe them, the angrier she got.

Abusive

Alcoholic

Addictions

Codependent

Promiscuous

Kind

Religious

Spiritual

Caring

Enabler

Finding Hope

Critical

Smothering

Fighter

Argumentative

Ralynn found the more adjectives she wrote down for one boyfriend of her mom's; the next boyfriend had the same adjectives plus a couple more that were usually worse. She was trying desperately to come up with positive adjectives for Rita's boyfriends, and that's when a memory came flooding back of Joel. Joel never moved in. He was sweet and gentle. Ralynn's memory started to playback when he was around. They would go out on real dates in a car. Joel would pay and always included Ralynn in the evenings. Ralynn could feel her face starting to turn a smile, remembering all the good times, but then she remembered the last date they had with Joel. He walked her and Rita up to the door. Ralynn could feel his hand in hers as he shook it, and told her how wonderful it was to share his evening with her. Ralynn still seeing the memory as if it had happened yesterday and started to cry. Joel then turned to Rita, gave her a kiss on the cheek and told her she was worth more, but until she saw it, he couldn't do this anymore. Ralynn remembered crying as he pulled out of the driveway.

Shaking her head, Ralynn was determined to finish the assignment. Pushing that memory away, she went on to the next question: Who have you become?

Ralynn felt like a ton of bricks had just landed on her chest. Rita had a different boyfriend every other month or so, and they usually moved in after a couple of days of dating because she was in love. As Ralynn had been writing a few of the names of Rita's live-ins, she remembered that the arguing would start in the middle of the night when they thought she was asleep. As the days went on, the arguing turned into physical fights. Ralynn would hear the door slam shut, and if it stayed quiet for more than a minute, she would escape from her room. Ralynn started remembering one of the times she had found Rita in the fetal position, rocking back and forth on the kitchen floor. Her night clothes were torn. Her eyes were starting to turn black and blue. There was blood flowing from the many cuts, as she was laying in broken glass. Ralynn vowed that day this man would never touch her mom again. Ralynn was so naïve to think she had any say because by 3 p.m., he was meandering in the front door, telling her mom that he was sorry he got so angry. He said he really did love her, and if she would just do what he asked the first time none of this would have happened.

Rubbing the tears from her eyes, Ralynn now grasped the hard fact that she had become her mother when it came to men and relationships. Ralynn also started to comprehend all that she had been reading and rereading and the gravity of the situation. Ralynn's spirit started to yearn for a different ending, but how?

"Lord, help me to change me. Help me to be the best mom possible for my little one. I do not want to be a repeat of my mom."

Finishing up her packet of paperwork, Ralynn was still trying to remember what her nightmare was about. Before she put up her journal she made one more entry.

"Lord, I am not sure what my nightmare was about. I thank you, I think, that I can't remember. Lord, if I need to remember, then let me. If I don't, then let me forget about it."

It was Friday night, and this week there was a group from a local civic group that wanted to treat Z-House to pizza and craft night. Ralynn was excited about the pizza but not so much about the craft night. As the clock in the living room started to chime, by the sixth and last chime, a group of women who seemed to be in their mid-twenties to early thirties started to pile into the kitchen. Each one was carrying something: Pizza, soda, cookies, chocolate, poster board, markers, crayons, and glue sticks. Then a lady walked in with a box of magazines and right behind her came a lady with ribbon, sheets of stickers, and scissors—not just regular scissors but scissors that made designs. Ralynn was getting intrigued, but the smell of pizza and seeing all the chocolate didn't hurt the situation, either.

That night, Ralynn almost forgot that she was living in a home for women who were running away from an abusive partner and felt like she could belong to a group like this one. They talked the night away while making what they called a vision board. Looking through magazines, the ladies found things that represented what they wanted their futures to look like. By the time Ralynn was done with her board, she had a picture represent-ing a career and a two-story house with a white picket fence. She decided that she wanted to get married one day, so she found a picture that represented a family with three kids and a dog. Before the night was finished, the group had all of the women talk about their boards. Ralynn was excited to see that Sally and Julia both had made boards that represented a future where life was different than today. Diane's board was lacking, but Ralynn was excited that she had at least participated. Kia, on the other hand, excused herself to her room without even starting a board, and that saddened Ralynn.

The weekend was quiet around the house and for that, Ralynn was grateful. She was still feeling tired after her nightmare on Thursday night. She was hoping that God would let her forget it, but she just could not get over the feeling that she was in trouble.

XVIII

Shelly asked the group, "What happened in your past to make you who you are today," as Jim passed out this week's packet. Shelly's question started Ralynn's brain to find memories she thought were tucked away forever. She was fifteen, and her mother's newest boyfriend brought over his brother while Rita wasn't home. He cornered her in her bedroom. By the time Rita decided to make her way back to the house, Ralynn was sitting on the floor in her room in the fetal position. Her clothes were torn, and the room was destroyed from the struggle. He was just too much for little Ralynn. Then to make matters worse, somehow it was Ralynn's fault. Now having to write what happened, to make her who she was, all she could write was, "If my mom doesn't care. If my mom doesn't love me. If this is my example, then I guess this is who I will become."

The tapping of the marker on the whiteboard brought Ralynn back to the present, and for that she was grateful. She had not thought of that boy for years, and she really wanted to leave those memories where they were, locked in a hidden compartment that no one would ever know about.

Shelly started to tell the group her story. She had grown up with an abusive stepfather and found that she lived up to the expectations of his words that he spoke over her. Whore. Bitch. Never amounting to anything. Even though she was smart in school, she had very low self-esteem. Shelly also talked about the fact that her biological father quit coming to get her, and she felt abandoned. All this created an addiction in Shelly, not to alcohol, but to boys. She always had to have a boyfriend. She explained to the ladies that it did not matter how they treated her, she just did not want to be alone.

Flipping over the page in the packet, Ralynn found the cycle that Shelly was talking about. The event in Shelly's life was growing up being told she would never amount to anything. Because there was no other adult telling her otherwise, her opinion of herself became extremely low. Shelly would describe herself to the ladies as a doormat. This started her on a pattern of living up to everyone else's expectations of her. And her life started to live it out in her actions.

"Okay, ladies, start writing down the events of your life that started you on this cycle that I like to call letting life happen. You will see prompts next to the diagram in your packets, if you are having a hard time starting."

Before Ralynn could get into a rhythm, Shelly started talking again.

"Ladies, I want you to think about this over the next few days. If you want to get together, call me, and we will walk through these cycles together. We have found that from what you learned last week and what we are going over this week, it's foundational to help you start to heal."

Before Shelly could start in again, Ralynn blurted out, "Wait a minute." Ralynn was confused. Here was a successful woman by the world's standards, and she had a rotten childhood. What in the world? What happened, and why did she turn out different than me?

"Ralynn, you okay? Do you want to say something?"

"Yeah, what happened? Why did your life turn out different than mine?"

Shelly went on to explain that the only reason her life turned out differently was because she had a very special person come into her life. This person saw more in her than she saw in herself. This person became her "180 Person," or in today's society, they would be called a life coach. At this time, Jim beaming from ear to ear approached Shelly and gave her a peck on the cheek and said, "I love you too."

Shelly went on to explain that Jim was her 180 Person. He pulled her out of her pit and helped her see that life had more to offer than letting life happen. He wanted to help her make life happen. Shelly went on to explain that it was not always easy because she would fall back in when she allowed herself to stay a victim of her past. But because she had Jim walking with her as a coach, he would help her to learn new ways to do life.

As Shelly was wrapping up her story, she went on to tell us that she was serious about walking with us if we wanted something different. She explained that on the next page we would see how if we flip the script and put the word expectation on top of the cycle, we would start "making life happen."

Seeing the cycles and prompts, Ralynn was getting excited to get back to Z-House and get started unpacking everything that was in this week's lesson. But before Shelly was done, she wanted the ladies to understand that until they know who they are and what they like and what they want to be, they would continue to live up to everyone else's expectations of them. Shelly also used the movie *Runaway Bride* as an example.

Shelly proceeded to tell us about the fact that Julia Roberts's character (Maggie) was always changing her mind about how she liked her eggs prepared, depending upon her newest fiancés' preference. If he likes his eggs scrambled, then that was her favorite, too. Fried? Then that was her favorite, too. Shelly explained it might just be eggs, but she didn't know what she liked.

Shelly then reiterated that we need to know who we are before we can let anyone or anything define us. She also reminded us that also went for what we wanted in life, which is our expectation.

Ralynn was not sure if any of the other girls got it that night; she was hoping so, but the light bulbs were going off in Ralynn's brain. For the first time in a long time Ralynn felt that she could actually do something different and worthwhile with her life, and bringing a child into this world was not the end of the world. Before Ralynn left that night she made sure she was on Shelly's schedule for next week. She needed a 180 Person in her life because she was not going to let her past become the future for her baby.

Getting back to the house, Ralynn found that Julia was just as excited to talk. Kia was still on the fence, but they invited her anyway. Declining their offer, she took Kyra and headed to bed. Sally, who happened to be grabbing Jessie a bottle when they walked in, asked what they were talking about. Ralynn wanting to share with Sally what they had learned, told her to grab a journal, and meet at the kitchen table in fifteen minutes. Ralynn started to show Sally everything in her packet and explain what it all meant, including Shelly's story. Then all of a sudden, in mid-sentence, Ralynn shoved her chair back and took off running. Within a minute she was running back with her vision board in hand.

"Oh my! This is exactly what Shelly was talking about tonight."

Sally and Julia were sitting there with a look of astonishment. It was like the lightbulbs all turned on at the same time. "These are the expectations that Shelly was talking about. And think where her life started."

For the next hour and a half, Julia, Sally, and Ralynn didn't talk so much about where they had been but where they wanted to go. They all decided that if Shelly could do something different with her life and not allow her past to become her future, then they owed it to themselves to try a different way. Sally also got Shelly's number and said she was going to try and meet with her this week.

For the first time in a week, Ralynn felt a little lighter and the feeling that something bad was going to happen was not forefront in her mind.

Ralynn found that she slept extremely well, even though her mind was swirling with all the new information she had. She also felt like she really needed to go back and finish last weeks' packet before she even started journaling about last night's class. The weather was turning a little warmer, so Ralynn decided to venture out to the front porch. Getting situated in what had become her favorite chair, Ralynn laid out the packet from the week before, opened her journal, and picked up where she had left off.

Anger needs to be controlled by me, not the other way around

Thinking back to all her mother's live-ins, Ralynn started to see a pattern. All she witnessed was how not to control your anger. Their actions usually caused harm to Rita and her or their personal belongings.

Forgiving: Why do I need to forgive them?

Going back and reading the extra packet of paperwork, Ralynn felt a tightness in her chest, and she did not know why. She read: The true seed of anger is in unforgiveness.

"What is she talking about?" Ralynn asked out loud even though no one was out there with her. As she continued to read, it said, "To forgive means to cease to feel resentment against; to pardon an offense or an offender. What if that offender is you?" Continuing on, the next question was, "Have you done so much to yourself that you can't even quit feeling resentment against yourself?"

Birds were chirping, and Ralynn heard the sound of vehicles off in the distance. Kids were running around outside and laughing with their parents not far behind. Ralynn was grateful for the distraction.

She started reminiscing of a time when she was running around at her Gi-

Gi's house. It was a time when she had no care in the world, and life was great. A squeal from one of the toddlers brought her back. The tears started to flow as she started to comprehend that her problems were much deeper than just running from Ben.

Ralynn went back to her journal. She remembered that Shelly had told them during class to just sit quietly allow God to speak to their heart about what they were reading.

God, it's me, and I am not sure what I am feeling. Looking at my past is hard. This book is hard. Ben is just one. There have been many: J, M, C, D.

Why do I always have to have a boyfriend?

Why do I always pick losers?

Why do I let them treat me this way?

As I look at those who influenced me growing up, the only sane one died when I was young.

Why did you have to take her away?

What did she do wrong?

How do I even forgive my mom?

Why should I forgive her? She was never around when her boyfriends took advantage of me. I did try to tell her; she didn't believe me. I could not wait to get out of that house.

Now I am still getting hurt, but at least I chose them.

How do I change?

How do I forgive myself?

Can I even forgive myself?

Feeling tired from pouring out her heart on the paper, Ralynn got up and went into the kitchen to see what was happening. She was excited to know that this was a slow weekend, with no extra groups or visitors. Even though she knew that it was through donations that Z-House existed, and what better way to get donations than to have people involved in the house and to invite groups to tour the facility, Ralynn had been secretly praying she could just lay low this weekend. As excited as Ralynn was that this weekend had been a slow weekend, as she sat in the living room, she found that the home had a different feel.

She knew that weekends were hard for those who didn't have a vehicle, especially if they were used to their freedom. She also knew that some of the women were having to transition to other jobs due to no daycares being open on the weekend. The one thing Ralynn was still trying to wrap her head around was the church vans. In just the four short weeks, she noticed that the van that was the fullest was the one bringing those who were offering gifts and lunch. Ralynn could not understand that, but because she didn't grow up in church, she just thought that was how it was.

Ralynn also gathered that some of the ladies who had arrived just a few weeks before she did were already itching to have a different life. It seemed to Ralynn that they just didn't know how to change. They were walking through every day with no goal for tomorrow, let alone next week or next year. The ladies would say they were just trying to figure out the next hour. As much as Ralynn understood what they were talking about, she also knew from just the few lessons at Shelly's that they were missing purpose in their lives. Ralynn was not too happy with the hard lessons and the hard look in the mirror she was having to do, but she definitely wanted a new expectation out of her life, and she thought maybe that might be the missing piece—they didn't know what new expectation they wanted for their lives.

Ralynn transitioned to the kitchen table and got her journal back out.

Expectation:

What new expectation do I want?

What expectation am I living up to because I saw it growing up and didn't think I was worth more than that?

"Wow," Ralynn thought to herself. "Shelly is really smart. She made me look at where I came from and who I became, and asked whether I am ready to change?"

I am ready to change, God. Help me?

I learned at a very young age that I was not valued. I learned that if you wanted someone to love you, then they beat you. They say they are sorry, and you let them do it again. I learned that to say I love you was a way to be let back in the house or to get the beatings to stop. I learned that you had no say in the relationship and what happened, happened, and it was usually your fault.

I want for myself to . . .

Ralynn's thoughts were interrupted when Ms. Dee asked if she could come help with dinner. Taking her journal and things to her room, she passed Sally and Jessie in the hallway. Sally looked exhausted. Jessie had not been sleeping well, and Ralynn thought Sally was on the verge of a break-down. Ralynn's natural instincts took over and asked if she could take Jessie, so she could go to go take a nap. Sally was grateful for the offer, and at first she declined but then turned back around, crying, and handed Jessie to Ralynn.

Now with a baby in her arms, Ralynn tried to comprehend why she offered to help. She used to love caring for the younger kids in the neighborhood, but then life happened, and she no longer had any joy to help anyone but herself.

"That's not true Ralynn, you love helping customers. You love teaching and training at work."

Ralynn started to look around wondering where that voice came from, but there was no one there. But the words made her smile.

"The voice was right. I do love helping others. I just need to figure out how to help myself. Shelly told us we need to know who we are before we can help anyone else."

Realizing she was talking out loud, she started laughing and thought, now who is losing it? Looking down at Jessie, her heart almost stopped, reality hit that in just a few short months, she would be responsible for her own little human just like him.

Walking back to the kitchen, Ralynn could see Ms. Dee smiling at her. Her nod told Ralynn that she was excused from cooking and could go take care of little Jessie.

Sitting on the floor in the living room, Ralynn was enjoying watching Jessie lay there and play with his toys. Being alone was interrupted when Ruby, who had been at Z-House for about two months came in and sat down. Her defeated look said a lot, but just in case anyone was wondering, Ruby spoke up. Ralynn, being the only one in the living room at the time, sat and listened as she expressed her frustration.

"When will I feel whole again? I want to do something different? But how? How do I change? When will things go my way?"

Jessie started to get fussy, so Ralynn excused herself. While preparing his bottle, Ralynn couldn't help but wish Ruby would have taken up her offer to go to Shelly's. Ruby politely declined because she said she was a spiritual person but wasn't interested in going to a Christian class.

Ralynn knew that Ruby went to work every day, but she also knew that with no foundation for a life without the abuse, she would not find true freedom.

As Ralynn was sitting there, feeding Jessie and looking around at all the women, she realized that many of the women could not get to classes without transportation, and there were others who were not ready to venture out of the house except for work.

Before Ralynn could shut off her thought pattern, she decided she was going to ask Shelly if she could take what she was learning and teach the girls here. Even though Ralynn was shaking her head, like where did that come from, she could feel a smile come across her face.

XIX

Ralynn got a ride into town on Tuesday with Ms. Dee. After listening once again to the protocol, Ralynn hurried to The Coffee Shoppe. The thought of teaching had not left her, so she had called Shelly to request a meeting. Walking through the front door, Ralynn was thinking how different this place looked today versus the first time she walked in. Today, feeling a lot more confident in herself and her future, she found herself thanking God for that chance meeting. Taking in her surroundings, she realized that the Coffee Shoppe was actually an old country farmhouse that had been rehabbed. As she rounded the corner, she found Shelly sitting in the same spot she had found Ralynn sitting just over a month ago. With what Ralynn wanted to talk to Shelly about, she thought it was fitting that Shelly had chosen that table. As she approached the table and was about to sit down, Ralynn noticed an extremely large leather purse under the table. Shelly was on the phone, but motioned for Ralynn to sit down. As Ralynn was trying to motion about the purse, a young lady Ralynn guessed was in her mid-twenties, wearing a white t-shirt and navy blue sweat pants, came back to retrieve it. Her eyes were all puffy from what Ralynn could only assume, based upon her talks with Shelly, were from crying. Shelly started to get up as she was ending her phone conversation. She went straight for Ralynn and gave her a hug. In just a few short weeks, Ralynn was getting more and more used to Shelly's hugs. Shelly then invited the young lady to sit down also.

Shelly introduced Ralynn to Jules. Shelly went on to tell Ralynn that she was excited that she had requested to meet because she already had an appointment with Jules. Shelly went on to say that she felt that Jules and her could benefit from each other's stories. Jules was a single mom with her own baggage but wanted to change. Shaking hands just seemed too formal and stuffy, so Ralynn gave her a hug and whispered,

"I am here, Shelly is here, and if you come to group, the rest of the girls will be there for you also."

With that Jules started crying again.

"Jules, if you want to share your story with Ralynn, we have time."

"Do you really want to hear my troubles?"

"Sure, if you want to share."

"Well, I am already living back at home with my parents. He was not abusive, but he was sleeping with three other women. When I confronted him, he called me old-fashioned and that I needed to get with the twenty-first century because everyone was doing it."

In the midst of her tears, Jules talked about growing up going to church a little but mostly attended youth group functions, and even though her mom and dad were married, they were workaholics and left her to care for her for her brother and three sisters.

"I finally found freedom in college. I'll admit I went a little wild. I was quickly introduced to alcohol and pot, but that didn't take care of the fear and loneliness. I needed someone to love me. I was introduced to Thomas and, boy, was he a smooth talker. Thomas was only a few years older . . ."

Jules stopped, and Ralynn realized that Shelly was giving Jules that look that she does when she knows there is more to the story and you aren't opening up.

"Fine, Thomas was ten years older than me. But it wasn't my fault. He swept me off my feet. Things were great for a while, but then my money ran out, and the pot was no longer giving me the high I needed to forget my troubles. Thomas introduced me to painkillers. He also taught me how to fake being in pain to get the ER to give me a shot and a prescription for Lortabs."

Ralynn could not believe Jules was being so open and honest about this in a public place. And the more she talked, the louder she got. Starting back in with her story, Jules's demeanor changed.

"The Lortabs made my mental pain go away. I liked how it made me feel, which was nothing. This went on for about six months, and I remember it like it was yesterday. Thomas asked me if I had had a cycle recently. I couldn't remember."

The tears were starting again, and Ralynn was pretty sure she was not going to like the ending to this story.

"He had a pregnancy test in his hands, and made me take it right away. It . . . was. . . . positive . . ."

Now Julie was sobbing. Taking a few moments to compose herself, she finally was able to tell the rest of the story.

"Things started to fly. He was on the phone making the appointment for an abortion. I ran out of the house and back to my dorm. I called my mom, and within three hours, my dorm was packed up, and we were headed home."

Jules further explained that they never talked about the white elephant in the room, and things changed only a little bit for the better. Her daughter, Liza, was born last year, and her parents absolutely love her. Ralynn was getting jealous that Jules had a loving family and didn't seem that she ever had to run from someone trying to kill her. As Jules continued with the story though, Ralynn started to feel sorry for her.

"I had stopped cold turkey doing the Lortabs until . . . just . . . recently."

Now Niagara Falls had started. "I, I, They . . . found. . . . me . . . I . . . waaaaassss . . . Unnnnnn . . ."

Then all of a sudden Jules blurted out, "I OD'd."

Allowing her time, Jules finally said that when she was revived, her daughter had the pill bottle in her little hands because she had been lying next to her on the bed.

"Now my mom and dad have custody of my daughter."

Ralynn's heart broke for Jules and Liza. That afternoon, Ralynn never actually talked to Shelly about what she had called her for, but Ralynn started to see a bigger purpose for her life. Losing track of time, Ralynn had to excuse herself to catch a ride back to Z-House. All the way home, Ralynn kept thinking what a class at Z-House would look like?

As the week went by, Ralynn could not get the crazy idea out of her head of starting a class at Z-House, so she decided to get a tall glass of lemonade and head out to her favorite spot on the front porch with her journal. The breeze had just a slight chill, but the sun felt amazing. Sitting in the chair she had claimed as her own, she sat quietly and asked God to talk to her and give her the idea of what His plan would be for the class at Z-House.

Opening up her journal the words just started to flow: Dinner would be provided by church ladies, the church ladies would eat with us, the ladies would stay and babysit or participate.

The more Ralynn wrote, the more excited she became and could not wait until tomorrow, so she could ask Shelly's opinion.

XX

Arriving at Shelly and Jim's was now part of her new routine, and she could not wait to ask Shelly her thoughts on teaching. The laughter, smiling, and hugging did not bother Ralynn nor surprise her anymore. Tonight's dinner was being prepared by Jim. He made his award-winning chili. Jim told the story about the ministry entering Mapleton's chili cook-off and how he had won first place both years for "People's Choice." Jim was so proud of that recipe, and he made sure everyone knew it was a secret, and no one could have it. Thinking he was joking, Ralynn quickly realized it didn't matter how many compliments he received, he was not budging on giving up the recipe. Jim did make enough for everyone to take home leftovers, though. As dinner was finished, Shelly walked in with a homemade Texas sheet cake. Ralynn had heard the ladies begging Shelly to make it, but now she would get the opportunity to taste it for herself. It was Jai's birthday this month, and she loved this cake. Shelly made such a huge cake that everyone got leftovers of that also.

Ralynn was surprised that Shelly got right into class without some sort of segue.

"How many choices do you think you make in a day? How many of those choices do you think are positive? How many of those choices are negative? Did you know that all choices have consequences? Those consequences will either be good or bad, depending on the choice you made."

Shelly went on to explain that just because this was the way it had always been done, we could choose to make a different choice in order to have a different outcome. Ralynn again, taking notes as fast as she could, started to think about the choices she made in her life that got her where she was today. She had been blaming her mother for the life she had today. But as Shelly was explaining, Ralynn started to have an "aha" moment that she needed to start making different choices. Instead of continuing to make choices based upon the knowledge she learned from Rita, her mother, she needed to get people in her life who would start to show her a different way.

Shelly had used an analogy from a book called *Good to Great* by Jim Collins. In it, he uses this idea of a bus, and on this bus you have many people. The challenge will be to make sure you have the right people in the right seats on this bus so that your business will be successful. Shelly told the ladies that for this lesson, she is not talking about business but life. Shelly then asked a very important question.

"Who is on your bus? Who are the people that you listen to and take advice from? Do you follow their lead?"

Shelly went on and told us that we needed to write down the names of the people who were still on our bus that were toxic, which meant deadly or dysfunctional relationships, not working as they should be. Shelly then told us to slam on the brakes and throw them off. She also told us that if we have a boyfriend and are not engaged to be married—she meant ring on the finger and having a real relationship in which we *both* were being faithful to each other—she told us to throw him off the bus too, and we were not allowed to pick him back up. Shelly got on a roll and told us that we needed to save ourselves for who God wanted us to be with. With so much passion that Ralynn thought Shelly was going to cry, Shelly went on with: "Ladies, you are worth more than a one-night stand and being one girl in many."

Shelly had her finger pointing at all of us, going around the circle, speaking with conviction. "You all need to see yourself worthy to be all that God called you to be."

Ralynn noticed that Shelly's pointing lingered a little longer in Jules's direction. Ralynn was hoping that she wasn't getting overwhelmed. Shelly had been elated when Jules showed up with Liza in tow. Jules had to get it cleared with the judge to be able to bring Liza to the dinner. Thankfully, Jules mentioned to the judge that the classes she wanted to attend were at Ms. Shelly's, and the judge allowed it. Now Ralynn was hoping that Jules wasn't regretting getting approval to be in class.

Clearing her throat, Ralynn realized Shelly had started talking again. Looking back down at her papers, Ralynn found her bus to be empty and wondering what she was supposed to do next. She didn't have to wonder too long.

"Starting something new is never easy, but I can tell you the end result will be worth it, and as my husband Jim always says, 'Let's make the best version of ourselves.'"

Ralynn was not sure what anyone else was writing, but she knew that she didn't want to stay in the cycle she was on anymore, so as Shelly was talking about who they were to be picking up and putting on their bus, she was trying to think of names. Luckily, Shelly let her off the hook when she told the group that they may not know the actual names of the people, but we needed to look for pastors, business owners, case managers, counselors, and so forth to ride with us on this new adventure. Shelly called this new bus our Board of Directors, but she did warn us that the only way it would work is if we trusted them to have our best interest at heart. We also needed to take their advice seriously.

Shelly told us that if we were going to ask our Board for advice but then turn around and do our own thing, two things would happen. The first would be we would lose our board of directors, and second, we would end up right where we started or worse. Shelly went on to explain that even though we say we want something different, we will go back to what is familiar if we don't get new, successful people in our lives. Shelly also told us that success didn't mean money necessarily; it could be that that person has already overcome abuse, addiction, or anything else, and they were living a productive life.

Ralynn loved how Shelly was very passionate about wanting the women to succeed. So it was only fitting how fired up she got when she started asking about our goals in life now that we had a new expectation in life. Shelly asked where everyone wanted to be in ten years. Based upon the rumbling that started, Ralynn knew that everyone felt the same way she did. "Ten years is a long way away; I just want to make it to . . ." Ralynn's thoughts were interrupted as Shelly asked, "When you were younger what did you want to do when you grew up?"

Ralynn tried to hide the tears, but there were too many of them too quickly. That question triggered a memory of her GiGi. Her GiGi always told her that she would grow up and have a career where she was helping people.

Where did that dream go? Ralynn answering her own question under her breath, *"I can't even help myself how am I supposed to help others?"*

Now in her own world, Ralynn started to doodle on the lines: help others who are like me.

Ralynn still did not put them on specific lines like Shelly asked because truthfully, Ralynn did not want it to take ten years; she wanted to start tomorrow.

During the rest of the class, Shelly explained that most people do not reach their goals because they are not written down. Shelly also talked about the fact that most goals are scary, and people don't realize that they need to break them down and make them simple.

"Ladies, how do you eat an elephant?"

Where did that come from? Shelly did not wait for a response but finished the punchline herself,

"One bite at a time. You see ladies your ten-year goal is an elephant. So break it down to a five-year goal, from there make it a two-year goal, a one-year goal, and finally, a six-month goal. And ladies, you know how at the end of every session we talk about weekly goals? Well, these goals now need to start reflecting where you want to be in six months in order to reach your year goal, and so on."

Shelly finished the class by explaining that goals and timelines can change. The first question she had us ask ourselves was, "Is it your goal or someone else's goal for you?"

Shelly told a story about a young mom who went to college to get a degree in business management. The mom hated every moment of it. Shelly finally had sat down with her, and they talked about college and why business management. Shelly said that the young mom's response was, "I was told I could make lots of money and my family said I would be good."

Shelly then went on to tell us, "Make sure it is your goal and no one else's goal for you."

Class was over, and Ralynn really wanted to talk to Shelly but Kyra had fallen asleep in Nikki's lap during group, and Jim was ready to carry her to the car. For whatever reason, Kia was more anxious than usual and wanted to leave in a hurry. Kyra was so out of it that she didn't even wake up as Jim carried her out to the car and put her in her car seat. Ralynn asked Kia if she would wait just a minute, so she could go back in and talk with Shelly.

"Shelly," she jumped when Ralynn said her name.

"Oh my, you scared me. What is it? You okay?"

"Shelly, you know there are many women at the shelter, who have not gotten involved in a group yet. Some don't feel they can leave the safety of the house. If it is okay with you and okay with Ms. Shaw, can I use my worksheets to start working with the women at the house?

"Oh Ralynn, I think that you would be an awesome facilitator, and when Ms. Shaw gives you the green light, you let me know, and I will give you everything you will need for each woman living at the shelter."

In the excitement, Ralynn hugged Shelly. Ralynn was so excited about having a purpose in life, and she could hear the words of her GiGi: *"Helping others—you should get a career helping people."*

The ride home was unusually quiet because Kyra stayed asleep. Ralynn really wanted to break the silence and make sure Kia was okay but felt it would be better left alone for tonight.

By the time they had gotten back to Z-House, Ms. Shaw had already left for the night. Ralynn was still on an adrenaline high. She did not realize that having a purpose in life could change things that fast in her thinking. Being just a little too excited, Ralynn found that sleep was not an option. While sitting in her room putting on paper her goals for the next ten years, Ruby walked by with her head down and she was mumbling, "When will I feel whole again?"

Taking a chance, Ralynn invited Ruby to come sit on her bed and talk. Ruby and Ralynn sat for the next three hours, talking about life. Ruby even asked Ralynn what she was working on. Ralynn knew better than to explain everything to Ruby, so she explained to her about the weekly goal sheets. Ralynn, not meaning to, started to talk like Shelly. She asked Ruby if she ever had a goal in her life. Ralynn found out that like her, she said she did want things in life but never knew how to make it happen.

Ralynn went on to explain that we have to write down our goals. Getting out her papers, Ralynn found an empty goals diagram. Ralynn told Ruby that the example was given about getting a job.

"Your ultimate goal is to get the job, but how? In these boxes you break it down into bite-sized pieces. You need to get your references ready.

You need to make sure you have the correct clothes to wear. You need to actually go get the applications or, as Ms. Shelly, our teacher, says, 'get on the computer to do online applications and not play on your social media sites.' Then you need to actually turn in the applications, filled out correctly. You need to make sure you have reliable transportation and reliable babysitting."

Ralynn started to fill out a blank sheet so that Ruby could see it in writing. She couldn't believe it, but Ruby let a smile peek through. It was at that point that Ralynn grasped the fact that just like she needed Ms. Shelly to start the ball rolling for her, she may have just been the much-needed nudge to show Ruby the first step. Ruby needed someone to believe in her, to show her the first step, and then to walk with her. Ralynn found herself praying that Ms. Shaw would see the advantage of having the classes here and started thinking how many of the women would thrive if they could see there was hope in doing things in a different way.

XXI

At 9 a.m., bright and early, Ralynn was standing in the doorway of Ms. Shaw's office.

Looking up over her readers, Ms. Shaw asked, "May I help you?"

"I hope so,"

Ralynn handed the paperwork to Ms. Shaw. In her excitement last night, Ralynn had written out everything. She had a calendar with the eight weeks all planned. There were slots for all the churches that supported the house to get involved with dinners, babysitting, and even the need for women to stick around and participate in the class with the women. Ralynn, stating her case, said she knew it would be a lot of traffic to the house on that night but felt they could ask the ladies to carpool as much as possible.

As Ms. Shaw put the paper down, she took off her readers, Ralynn stood there with anticipation. "Ralynn, come in and sit down."

Ralynn felt her dreams start to shatter. She could feel it. Another "you are not good enough." "It'll never work." All the words she had come to hear in her head.

"Ralynn, as amazing as your offer is, and I can see how much thought and work you put into the proposal . . ."

Ms. Shaw took a breath, and Ralynn could feel the emotions start to rise within her. She wanted to turn back the clock and never even walk in with a request like this.

"Ralynn, we as an organization made it a rule that classes would never be conducted by a person who lived here. I am sorry. It sounds amazing, but as a structured class and inviting people in, that just will not work."

Ralynn felt the waterfall starting, but held it together. "I understand. Thank you for your time."

Ralynn got up to leave when Ms. Shaw stopped her and said,

"But . . . if you can get Shelly to come teach . . . that would be different."

Ralynn felt like a knife was tearing her heart out. She politely excused herself and went to her room. She heard the why. She understood in her head the why. But her heart was breaking; she really thought she had found her purpose.

She texted: Hey Shelly. Can you talk?

What's up?

Can I call you?

Sure.

Ralynn called Shelly to explain what had happened and that Ms. Shaw said sure as long as Shelly taught the classes. To Ralynn's surprise, Shelly said she would teach as long as Ralynn would set everything up. Shelly also went on to help Ralynn understand that as much as we may not like rules, such as this one, there was a reason for it to be made. Telling Ralynn to trust the process and make the best of the class the way they needed it to be taught, didn't sit to well, but she understood. Shelly also made Ralynn understand that teaching full time didn't need to be her priority, but getting ready to have a baby was. Ralynn's head knew that, but it still hurt to have to change gears as she really thought her purpose was to help people.

Walking back to Ms. Shaw's office after she had a good cry.

"Ms. Shaw, can I come in?"

"Sure. Have a seat."

"I talked with Shelly, and she is in, as long as I help with logistics."

"How much is this going to cost?"

"Ms. Shelly told me that she would give us all the material."

Ralynn could not believe the next words out of Ms. Shaw's mouth—"Then I say let's try it. When do you and Shelly want to get started?"

Ms. Shaw went on to explain to Ralynn that there had been a few women's groups that wanted to be more involved more than once-a-month dinners or doing the care packages. Ms. Shaw said she would call them today and invite them to come out to lunch next week. Then Ms. Shaw told Ralynn her job would be to pitch the idea to the ladies. In her excitement,

Ralynn almost hugged Ms. Shaw but refrained and just shook her hand. Tearing out of the office, she dialed Shelly's number to tell her the good news.

Not having a job, and trying to pass time on the weekends, Ralynn went back and read and journaled all that she was learning. She wanted to be the best teacher's assistant as possible. As she was pouring herself into the words and writing her own story, the alarm on her phone pinged. It was a reminder that she had court tomorrow morning: 9 a.m. Monday morning.

Ben had violated the order of protection, so he was arrested, and the court date was finally coming up. Ralynn had not thought about him in a long time, but for whatever reason, that ping, coupled with the word *court*, as a reminder, made Ralynn feel like she was about to throw up. She ran to the toilet, but nothing was coming up. Slumped down on the cool floor, she sat there for a few minutes until she was sure nothing was coming back up.

Realizing this was a triggered response from the fear of Ben, she texted Shelly for prayer.

"Shelly, please pray. Triggered. Court tomorrow."

Shelly texted back: "Oh Daddy, we thank you for Ralynn and her strength. You are here, and she knows that. She knows You are her Daddy. She longs to be free from Ben's manipulative ways. May she be strong in court tomorrow, and may the sight of Ben not create in her a loneliness but a freedom to do life as You have created her to have.

Ralynn started to cry as she read that. "How does she know when I am feeling weak?" Ralynn finally texted back, "Thanks!"

At the same time, Shelly texted, "I can go with you if you want."

With tears freely falling and all she could text was, "Yes!"

Not knowing what to expect, Ralynn allowed fear to rob her of the rest of the day. As she was moping around her, phone pinged. This time it was Shelly.

"Don't let satan rob you of your joy. God has this. I don't know what tomorrow will bring, but I do know the One who does, and He has asked us to pray about it and leave it at His feet. See you in the morning."

Thankful for the prayer, Ralynn started to read her journal and the papers from class. Choice! Everything is a *choice*! Thumbing through the papers, Ralynn found a quote that made her stop. *"Did you know that today is the tomorrow you worried about yesterday? So why worry?*

The scripture that was attached to that quote was in Matthew 6. Ralynn found herself getting out her journal.

Did you know that today is the tomorrow you worried about yesterday? So why worry?

> Therefore I tell you, do not worry about your life, what you will eat or drink; or about your body, what you will wear. Is not life more than food, and the body more than clothes? Look at the birds of the air; they do not sow or reap or store away in barns, and yet your heavenly Father feeds them. Are you not much more valuable than they? Can any one of you by worrying add a single hour to your life? (Matthew 6:25–27 NIV)

As she was writing and reading, she felt a peace come over her, and she liked that feeling, but as soon as she started thinking about tomorrow, she lost that feeling and started to worry again. Luckily, there was a knock on the door; it was Julia. Dinner was ready and the women from First United Church had brought it and were going to bring the devotion tonight.

Closing up her journal, she got to the table just in time for the prayer. Feeling that there was something off, Ralynn found herself on alert. The food was amazing. It was a homemade chicken pot pie, but the ladies from the church group just sat there like a bump on a log. Ralynn was not sure if they were scared or really didn't know what to say, but it was creepy seeing they chose to do nothing. Just when Ralynn thought it couldn't get any worse, Kyra spilled her drink all over one of the ladies' plate of food. The woman, jumped up and started yelling. "How dare you? Are you not watching your child? That was just irresponsible!"

Sitting in awe, Ralynn could not believe what she was witnessing. Finally, Ms. Shaw, who happened to be working late, came in and escorted the woman out to the front porch. After dinner was over, the woman came back in and took a seat on the couch next to Kia, the mom whom she had scolded just minutes earlier. The tension was thick already, and Ralynn was hoping that nothing else would go wrong, but it did. The leader stood up and proceeded to tell the ladies that they needed to forgive their husbands or boyfriends for beating them and that they needed to go back and make the relationship work. She also went on to say that the children needed their fathers even if they were abusive.

Ralynn could not believe her ears, and she wasn't sure what made her stand up and confront the woman, but she had had just enough of this group.

"Ma'am, I do not mean any disrespect, but these ladies and I are done listening to you and your group. How dare you come in here and tell us we need to forgive our abusers and to go back to them. And I will not go back to someone who is constantly beating me, so my child will have a father. Ma'am, I thought I was going to die that night, and I am carrying his child, but there is *no way* I will ever go back to him. I value my life too much and also the life of my child."

Following Ralynn's lead, the rest of the group got up and went to their rooms. In tears, she texted Shelly and told her everything that had happened. Shelly's text wasn't what she had hoped to get, but made her stop and think.

"We do need to forgive our abusers. We do not need to put ourselves in harm's way, but if we don't forgive them, we allow them to have a hold on us. We forgive, so we can find freedom. Remember the prayer a couple of weeks ago? Go back and look at it. Goodnight, and I will see you tomorrow."

Before she got ready for bed, Ralynn went to check on Kia and Kyra. She knew Kia was already on the fence about church and religion, and after tonight she wouldn't blame her if she never wanted to have anything to do with either. Luckily, Kia was not as mad as Ralynn about the situation and told her she would still be her ride for Thursday night dinners at Shelly's.

Still angry herself, Ralynn went back to the papers and checked out the prayer again.

From this day forward I choose to forgive [Name]. I forgive [him/her] for: [list everything you can think of that caused the offense]. From this day forward, I choose to lose sight of this offense, and if I am ever reminded of the offense, I will choose to dismiss that memory as an old, resolved conflict I no longer choose to revisit. Today I choose to simply forget the incident and move on with or without rebuilding that relationship.

After praying through that a few times and mentioning everyone Ralynn could think of by name, she reread it and this time put her name in there, and put her relationship with Ben as the offense.

From this day forward, I choose to forgive myself. I forgive myself for getting into a relationship with Ben, for allowing him to treat me as a punching bag, and for thinking so low of myself that I felt I deserved to be treated that way. From this day forward, I choose to lose sight of this offense and feeling I deserved to be treated less than what You, Lord, desire for my life. If I am ever reminded of the offense, I will choose to dismiss that memory as an old, resolved conflict I no longer choose to revisit. I choose today to see myself worthy of more. Today I choose to simply forget the incident and move on with or without rebuilding that relationship.

Just as she was finishing the prayer, a peace came over her like she had felt earlier. She decided she wanted that peace to last, but how?

XXII

Ralynn was up bright and early because she did not want to miss a second of court. The paper stated she needed to be there by 9 a.m., so Ms. Debbie had agreed to come in on her day off to drive her. Ralynn was also grateful that Shelly was going to be there for support.

Ralynn's belly was starting to take shape, and the last thing she needed was Ben to have another excuse to be a part of her life, so she looked in the clothing closet for an outfit that would hide her condition. She quickly found a very flowing but flattering shirt to wear with a pair of dressy stretch pants. Looking at herself in the mirror, she was pleased that you could not tell she was pregnant. Ready to move on, she wanted anything to do with Ben behind her. She was also a little apprehensive as she really did not know what to expect from the court hearing today.

The knock on her bedroom door interrupted her thoughts; it was Ms. Debbie telling her they needed to leave in order to find a parking space in downtown Mapleton. Ralynn has noticed that since the city had won all these awards for being a great small historic town to visit, people from all over spent their vacations here and downtown had become a madhouse. Ralynn hoping to get the day over without any complications, was excited to see a parking spot open up in front of the courthouse. *"Now to parallel park."*

Come to find out walking up the steps and in the front doors was the easiest part of her day. Ralynn was so thankful that Shelly was there. Everyone seemed to know her, and it made the day go faster as it seemed to be a hurry-up-and-wait game all day. Ben's case had still not been called by the time they adjourned for lunch. There was a burger joint across the street, so they opted to eat close so that Shelly did not lose her parking spot. Ms. Debbie had already left, when she realized court was possibly going to be an all-day affair.

Patting her tummy as she took the last bite of blueberry cobbler a la mode, Ralynn said, "Wow, I guess I was hungry."

"I would say so. I have never seen someone inhale a half-pound burger, sweet potato fries, and a blueberry cobbler a la mode."

Laughing as they got up from the table, Shelly looked at her watch and motioned to Ralynn that they had less than two minutes before court reconvened.

Opening the doors to the courtroom, they hear Ben's name be called. Ralynn's heart stopped. Shelly caught her as her knees buckled. How can one person have so much control over someone else? At this point Ralynn really thought Shelly had ESP because she leaned over and whispered, "Because you allow them to."

"What? No, I don't."

Ralynn argued, using her eyes to talk because she was pretty sure she was about to lose her entire lunch if she tried to speak. In his, "you are not going to like the consequences voice," the judge was now calling Ben's name. He was not in the courtroom. Ralynn's heart didn't know if she should be jumping up and down for joy or scared that he was still out there and hadn't come to face the court.

The judge looked over to his assistant and issued a bench warrant and said to revoke Ben's bond. The judge was just about to hit his gavel on his bench to tell us court was adjourned when the back doors flew open with so much force that the sheriff deputy, who was guarding the front door grabbed for his gun. Ben stumbled in, slurring his speech, and yelling some excuse as to why he was late. Ralynn could not believe what happened next. One-minute Ben was storming the bench, and the next minute he was in handcuffs, face down on the ground. The deputy picked Ben up to stand before the judge.

"Are you Ben Williams?"

Ben shook his head. The deputy who was holding him up explained to Ben that he needed to speak and not shake his head.

"Yeah."

"Yes, sir, is the proper response," stated the judge. "You are late, and I have already put out a warrant for your arrest and revoked your bond. Bailiff, take him to the back and have him locked up. We will see him at a later date."

While Ben started yelling profanities at the judge, another deputy came from around the corner and took Ben through a side door. Even though the door slammed shut, you could still hear Ben yelling and shouting swear words. Ralynn could not believe it when she heard Ben starting to threaten the judge. Actually, the whole courtroom heard Ben threaten the judge, and before we all could respond, Ben was back in front of the judge.

"Mr. Williams, you have just added a nice stay in our local hotel we like to call the county jail. I am going to let you sit there for a while and cool off. I am pretty sure you did not mean the words you were just spouting off back there, but I am not taking any chances. Mr. Williams, unless you want me to add more time to your sentence that you have not even been given, I suggest you become the model inmate and learn some manners. Deputy, you may take him back to the back."

Ralynn was not sure what the deputy said, but Ben had started to open his mouth again and quickly decided against it.

Happy that court was finally over, Ralynn found herself running to the bathroom to throw up her entire lunch. Not entirely positive she was finished, she opted to sit in the stall for a couple of minutes to regroup.

"You are not going to control me, Ben Williams!"

She did not hear the door open, so she was not aware that Shelly had been standing outside the stall waiting for her.

"You are right. You have a choice whether or not to allow him to have control over you anymore."

Ralynn didn't understand the toll the day was taking on her body. The baby was not liking whatever was going on, either. Ralynn started to cramp and get nauseated. She also thought she was about to pass out. Holding onto the wall because the room was spinning was the last thing she remembered.

The slamming of the ambulance doors jarred her awake. *"What? Where am I? What happened?"*

Ralynn could see out the back of the ambulance as they drove down the highway. She saw a familiar face and vehicle following with their hazards on. She was not sure if Shelly could see her or not, but seeing her following and looking worried was a sight that made Ralynn feel like she was worth someone caring about. The hospital was only a short fifteen-minute ride, but Ralynn thought they would never get there. She was ready to get off the gurney and go home, but the emergency room doctors had another idea; they were sending her to the maternity ward to be checked out.

Ralynn was trying to find out what happened to Shelly when she appeared out of nowhere. Ralynn started to cry, but this time they were happy tears because someone cared.

The orderly came and wheeled Ralynn up to the sixth floor. As they got off the elevator, the nurses were ready to take over and get her into a room. Within the first fifteen minutes she had to pee in a cup. She got her vitals taken. She was now hooked up to a few machines, and an IV had been started. Then they hooked up a machine to measure the baby and make sure that he or she was okay, too. Then the nurse turned a knob on one of the machines, messed with the disk that was belted around Ralynn's tummy, and said, "There it is. It is nice and strong." Turning toward Ralynn, the nurse said, "You've got a fighter in there. Hear that heartbeat. Nice and strong."

All of sudden, Ralynn was overtaken with emotion. She was hearing her baby's heartbeat for the first time. *What a sweet sound! This baby is going to rely on me for everything. I'm not sure I can do this.* Then she felt something move, and she heard the heartbeat get louder.

"There you go, get closer, so we can hear you better." The nurse was talking, then she turned her attention back to Ralynn,

"Who is your OBGYN?"

"I don't have one yet."

That answer started a firestorm of other questions. Ralynn felt that the look on Shelly's face meant that she was disappointed in her, but it was quite the opposite.

"Oh, my Ralynn, I am so sorry. I thought Z-House had gotten everything worked out?"

Without missing a beat though, Shelly piped in that they should call Dr. Smith. As fate would have it, he had just delivered a baby a few doors down, so he stopped in to check on Ralynn and the baby.

After a few more tests, the baby's heartbeat stayed strong and the bag of fluids had finished. Dr. Smith felt it was safe enough to let Ralynn return home but did tell her that she was dehydrated and needed to start drinking more water and less soft drinks and coffee. He also gave her strict orders to follow up with her OBGYN and do what they said. It was at that moment Ralynn realized that Dr. Smith did not get the memo that she did not have a doctor as of yet. Grateful that she did not get read the riot act for not seeing the doctor yet, she decided she would need to follow up on her medical insurance. She had been trying to get it taken care of since she arrived at Z-House. She was hopeful that this ER visit would expedite the process.

XXIII

Walking out of the hospital, Ralynn's stomach let out a loud grumble. Shelly must have heard the noise because without even asking she drove straight to the pizzeria. Jim had been working a few hours a week for a friend who needed help, and tonight he had gotten called in. Listening to the greeting they received when they walked in, you would have thought they had been gone for years, not just a few hours. They were welcomed and greeted with excitement. One of the workers that night had been a previous graduate of the program, and Jim was giving her a chance to gain leadership skills so that she could get a job with a bigger restaurant that was looking for a manager. She ran over and gave Ralynn a hug.

"He told us what happened. I am so happy you are okay. What can I get-cha for dinner?"

The company and food were a welcome relief from the day. Ralynn fell in love with the pizza and wondered if she could take the leftovers home. Just as she was finishing her fourth piece of pizza, Ms. Dee pulled in to take her back to Z-House. Reluctantly she left but found herself wanting to be a part of this family more and more.

The adrenaline rush had finally worn off and Ralynn found herself barely able to stay awake for the ride home. When they were finally pulling into the driveway, Ralynn thanked Ms. Dee for everything and went straight to her room.

Ralynn was startled awake when Julia knocked on the door to make sure she was okay.

Monday had taken so much out of Ralynn that she decided a pair of sweat-pants and a t-shirt was about all she could muster to put on. Out of habit, she went for a cup of coffee. Ms. Dee was there to stop her.

"Didn't the doctor say more water?"

"So if I have a glass of water, can I have a cup of coffee?"

"I would say yes, but I am not a doctor. Plus, when I was pregnant, all the things they say you can't eat or drink today, I ate and drank."

Ralynn decided it was not worth it, so she grabbed a big ole glass of water and headed out to the front porch. Waking outside, she found herself being pulled to the prayer garden again. Sitting on the rusted wrought-iron bench again, Ralynn was not sure why she had started choosing this spot, especially when the front porch furniture had been recently replaced. Ralynn did not understand why as soon as the furniture on the front of the house started to show any wear and tear, they would replace it, even though it still had life, yet the prayer garden was being unkempt. Sitting with her journal and notebook filled with all her class papers, she finally saw the metaphor as to why she had been choosing the bench that needed repair. Opening her journal, she started to write.

> This bench represents me. I am in need of repair. I fit in this garden that is in such turmoil, with weeds, dying flowers, and fallen branches.
>
> Leaves from last year's fall was now the ground cover.
>
> I was biding my time when I could leave or was I? I kept using the excuse that I was pregnant, and therefore I couldn't get a job.
>
> Sitting here today and watching the stark contrast of where I was sitting and what I could see in the distance, a new reality hit me;
>
> I was stuck.
>
> I was paralyzed with the fear that Ben would find me.
>
> Fear that I wouldn't succeed in a new life.
>
> Fear that I would just go back into the same lifecycle that was comfortable because it was what I knew.
>
> Do I have enough willpower to say no?
>
> Do I have enough willpower not to fall into another relationship?
>
> Do I have enough willpower to succeed?
>
> How do I get free from my negative attitude?
>
> How do I start to see myself worthy?
>
> I used to sit up on that porch every day. Then things changed; they

bought new furniture, and I felt more comfortable on this bench.

Lord, help me to break free from this prison that I have placed myself in.

Lord, if I start to put myself in my prison again, I will remind myself that I chose to do that and therefore I can choose to get out.

I am worthy enough to sit on that front porch in that brand-new furniture.

As she was finishing up writing in her journal she heard her name being called from the front porch. Ralynn was hoping that the doctor's office would call her back today. In the mail this morning was her insurance paperwork, and they had assigned her a doctor. She left a message and was hoping to get an appointment this week.

Now within earshot, Ms. Shaw was telling Ralynn that the doctor's office had called and wanted her to call them back ASAP. Looking at her phone she didn't have a missed call. But as soon as she was connected to the Wi-Fi, the voicemail alarm went off. Listening to the voicemail, her legs started to buckle.

This could not be true. Seriously?

Ms. Dee, who had been promoted to assistant director, and Ms. Shaw were now surrounding Ralynn as she fell to the floor sobbing.

Simultaneously Ms. Dee and Ms. Shaw asked, *"Ralynn, what is wrong?"*

Through the sobs, she tried to explain that the doctor's office made a mistake, and they wouldn't see her as a new patient. They don't take her insurance.

"How can they not take my insurance? I got it through the government. I thought they had to take me. What am I going to do? I need to find a doctor."

Ms. Shaw and Ms. Dee were now on the floor with her, holding her and letting her cry.

After Ralynn sat there trying to figure her next move, she declined calling back the doctor's office, instead she called and left Shelly a message.

Within fifteen minutes, Shelly called back to say, "You have an appointment with Dr. Smith in the morning."

Overjoyed was not even close to how Ralynn felt at that moment. It took her what seemed forever to get the insurance worked out, and no one would see her without insurance. Then fear hit Ralynn so she dialed Shelly back.

"Hello?"

"Shelly, does he know what type of insurance I have?"

"He said we will deal with all that later; right now he needs to make sure you and that baby are getting the care you need. I'll meet you at the drop-off point tomorrow at 9 a.m. Tell Ms. Dee that I will take you to lunch after your appointment, and if you want you can come back to the house for a few hours, I will take you back later."

"I would like that. I will see you tomorrow . . . and Shelly . . . thank you."

"You are welcome. Have a great rest of the night."

Able to sit down and process what just happened, Ralynn found herself laughing at what a sight it must have been to see Ms. Shaw and Ms. Dee collapsed on the vinyl kitchen floor with her. Ms. Shaw is such a classy lady who always has on a straight-cut blue skirt that falls right above her knees. Her tops are made of polyester, and she never shows her arms. It also didn't matter how hot it was; she had on nylons and pumps, but, boy, did she always leave the room smelling like roses. Ms. Dee, on the other hand, was from Chicago. She grew up on the rough side and had to fend for herself. She was on the heavier side, but you knew not to mess with her, because at 5-foot-nothing she could take you out. Then out of nowhere, her sweet side would show up, and she would hold you like a mama bear in her arms and let you cry.

It was 9 a.m., and Ms. Shelly was right on time. She had BJ with her today. His mom Jai had gotten yet another new job, and daycare was closed for in-service. Her other boys were with Jim helping around the house.

"You ready?" Shelly asked all chipper and ready to take on the day.

"Not as ready as you, but let's go."

It didn't take long to get to the doctor's office. His office was on the first floor of a medical tower, just outside of town. It wasn't anything to really write home about, but it wasn't sterile-looking either. The receptionist, who was decked out in deep purple scrubs, hair pulled back in a messy bun with an energetic personality, looked to be thirteen.

"Fill out these papers, and the doctor will see you shortly."

Ralynn's gut kept telling her something was going to go wrong. She just knew that as soon as she handed in her paperwork and insurance card, she was going to be back to square one, looking for a new doctor.

"Thank you; have a seat. It'll be just a few more minutes."

Now in panic mode while walking back to her seat, "Did she see my insurance card?"

Taking her seat, Shelly put her hand on her arm and said,

"It'll all work out."

BJ was playing contently in the playroom, and before Ralynn was called back, Shelly's sister walked in to sit with BJ while Shelly went back with her. All Ralynn could think of was "Wow, she thinks of everything. I really did not want to do this alone."

Once in the back, everything was business.

Weight.

Height.

Blood drawn.

Pee in a cup.

The nurse then had them sit in Dr. Smith's actual office, but within two minutes, he walked in and reintroduced himself to Ralynn. Without any prompting, Dr. Smith explained that he grew up very poor but that education was always placed as a high priority. He was grateful to his parents for their sacrifices and promised to give back to others. He went on to explain that he wanted Ralynn to be comfortable with him and to see him as a person who is a husband and a father of two small daughters first and then as her doctor. He then told her that the appointments will always start in his office so that she can feel comfortable talking with him in this atmosphere versus the sterile examination room. Then Dr. Smith said, "Is it okay with you if we pray first?"

With the prayer being done, Dr. Smith showed Ralynn to the exam room and said he would be back shortly. Ralynn was sitting in the exam room, wondering who this doctor really was. When she had been to doctors' offices before, it was let's get you in and out. There was no relationship building. The knock on the door made Ralynn realize she was relaxed and no longer on the verge of a panic attack.

The nurse came in and helped get Ralynn ready for the examination. Because this was her first exam, and the fact that she was about twenty-five weeks along, they needed to check many things. The appointment went well, and Ralynn and Shelly both were relieved. As they were leaving, the checkout receptionist decked out in the same dark purple scrubs and same bouncy attitude, gave Ralynn a card with all her appointments listed for the next two months. As Ralynn was about to walk out to the waiting room, the nurse told them to have an amazing day.

Ralynn walked out into the waiting room when a wave of nausea hit. She ran back to the bathroom, and the nurse who had been helping her was now holding Ralynn's hair out of the way. Another nurse walked in with ginger ale and saltines; all Ralynn could do was apologize. She was so amazed at the nurses' compassion toward her.

Reentering the waiting room, Ralynn felt that all eyes were on her, and she was embarrassed, but Shelly whispered, "You are not the first to get sick. At least you made it to the bathroom."

With all the pieces of the morning, doctor's office, hearing the heartbeat again, throwing up, and the smell of lavender, Ralynn started to cry.

"What is it?"

"I cannot believe I was going to kill my baby."

Shelly had no words. The moment didn't last too long though, as the sight of BJ asleep on Shelly's sister's lap made them both go "Aww." His peaceful look did not last long because a delivery driver walked in and the metal front doors shut with a clank.

"Eat? Eat?" BJ was clearly hungry as he put his fingers together to sign he was hungry while trying to speak. Shelly explained that he was being taught a little sign language because he was delayed in his talking.

We decided to stop for a chicken sandwich and a lemonade. We chose this particular restaurant in the chain because the playland had been built at a lower level to accommodate the older toddlers. BJ could actually go up in the tubes and down the slide. He was in heaven.

BJ had come back out to get a drink when Shelly gave him a "We will be leaving in thirty minutes warning." Ralynn couldn't believe the meltdown he had. You would have thought he was about to lose his best friend in the world. Shelly crouched down to get on BJ's level and explained we could go home now if he wanted. Just that quickly, he was back to laughing, turned around, and went back to the playland, playing with his new friends. Shelly proceeded to give BJ warnings every ten minutes. When the thirty minutes were up, we were getting everything packed up, shoes on, and we were walking out the door. Ralynn was impressed and hoped that she would be a good parent.

Spending the day with Shelly was a refreshing change. Her home was so inviting and relaxing. Ralynn decided that she was going to take advantage of the nice spring day and go out back and sit by the creek. She also decided the glider swing in the backyard had her name on it. She fell asleep swinging while listening to the water rushing through the creek that lined their property. Forgetting where she was, BJ startled her when he jumped up on the other end of it. He thought that was so funny, Ralynn not so much.

XXIV

The group at Shelly's this week was smaller than normal, even Jim and their daughter Sabrina were missing in action. They were in Texas helping Jim's folks move. There was a different feeling in the group. Ralynn, not sure what was up, decided it was just her.

"Well, ladies, you can see we are a few short tonight. I wish I could tell you it's because they all are at work. Jules and Jai are working, so we need to pray they can get their schedules changed back to Thursday evenings off. But unfortunately, Andee, who you all met last week, has chosen to leave her mom's house this week and go back to Lee's father. She called today and apologized, but he said that under no circumstance could she be a part of Thursday nights anymore. We need to pray for her and that she and Lee are safe."

After a few more announcements, Shelly said, "And tonight we are going to talk about *excuses*!"

Ouch! Where is she going with this? Excuses?

"Who makes excuses for you? Who do you make excuses for?"

Shelly kept right on talking as she was handing out the papers she had copied off for us,

"Or, what about the excuse you make for yourself, I can stop whenever I want to. It doesn't affect anyone but me. Really? Does it only affect you?"

Shelly had Ralynn's full attention as she explained how when we allow people to make excuses for us, we allow ourselves to stay in a cycle of denial. Shelly then asked us to think about our children and how our excuses affect them. Then Shelly said something that once again had Ralynn writing as fast as she could.

"Every excuse you make as to why you can't do something different in your life, affects not only you, but it affects your child as well. You are their role model, and if you can't do something different or better, how do you expect them to?"

Just when Ralynn thought Shelly was done, she gave the one-two punch.

"I know we spoke last week about dysfunctional relationships for a brief second. This week I want to go a little deeper about that and talk about codependency."

Shelly went on to explain that when we don't speak up for ourselves, we can get into relationships where we care for others and don't care for ourselves. We actually can take care of everyone else's needs to the point where we lose who we are and feel that we don't matter. She also talked about when we live in homes where there is dysfunction, codependency can become our pattern of living as a coping mechanism. She also went on to explain that when you live with someone who is an alcoholic, their demand on you for perfection is actually them covering up their shame of their addiction and transferring it on to the innocent parties of the family. She said this could be in the form of words like, "You'll never amount to anything." Shelly then talked about the demand for perfection and the "no talk rule," act as if everything is great at home.

"Ladies, the problem with all of this is that those who are being abused end up putting themselves in their own prison, thinking this is all life has to offer."

Leaving that night, Ralynn was not too sure how much more she could handle. She was grateful that Shelly had already talked a little with her about this, and how wanting a different life was easy to talk about but changing to create the different life was another story.

Starting to feel overwhelmed with the fact that Shelly would be coming to Z-House and starting to teach, Ralynn thought maybe they should cancel everything, but as soon as the thought of backing out started to creep in, she felt the same peace from the other night come over her and she heard, *"They need you to share."*

Remembering what she wrote in her journal, she was now excited that the luncheon was in just a few short days and that this class was going to be offered on site.

XXV

For the first time Ralynn realized that the more she stayed inside the house, the more depressed she got. She was grateful for the home but wanted more for the home. She was getting excited about the lady's luncheon, but something was nagging at her. Without even thinking about where she was headed, Ralynn walked out to the prayer garden to journal and pray. Coming upon the entrance she could hear the wind chimes ever so lightly. Opening the small iron gate that was being held on by only a single hinge, Ralynn wondered what happened to the visitors? Why don't people come and help? Sitting down on the black wrought-iron bench that was in desperate need of a paint job, Ralynn could have sworn she heard muffled voices. She was pretty sure it was her mind playing tricks on her because she then thought she heard them getting louder. It sounded like a guy yelling at a girl. Pushing the notion away that there really was someone out here was easy, but the memories that came flooding in were not. Ralynn got out her journal.

I remember being that girl.

Why did I become that girl?

I had always been obedient to rules.

Following the rules was what I thought would keep me safe. Following rules meant you didn't get pulled over or find yourself in jail.

But somehow following the rules had put me in a prison of my own making.

Allowing her mind to run free, a faint memory of going to church camp for the first time surfaced.

I was excited, but the only ride I could find was my mom's new boyfriend. I hated driving with him because he would start drinking as soon as he would wake up. He drank beer like it was water.

That particular day, as we drove over the railroad tracks heading out of town, a state trooper went passed us going in the opposite direction. Not exactly sure why the trooper did a U-turn with his lights on, but he pulled us over.

How he did not get a DUI or even a ticket I am still not sure. He had an open container. He had been drinking all morning, but he was the only ride I could get.

The rest of the trip was not a joyous drive. He kept staring at me in the rearview mirror, asking me, no actually demanding that I tell him what I had done to get the officer to turn around. Seriously, I was ten, and last I checked, I didn't have telepathic powers to make a police officer turn around and pull us over. But that day, somehow I had all the influence, and he was determined to make me pay for his embarrassment.

Having an "aha" moment, Ralynn got out her notebook and flipped to last night's papers. Sitting there it was like a flood of aha moments were happening. Talking to herself out loud,

"Wow, this all makes sense now."

Rereading what was written on the papers and the notes she had taken. Ralynn started writing in her journal:

He was transferring his shame on to me, because ... well . . . because my mom let him.

I pushed buttons.

I know drinking and driving was not right. I voiced my opinion.

The verbal abuse just got worse.

Unfortunately, my mom could have been the poster child for codependency.

Prison.

This prison I realized started when I was very young.

The memories were coming so fast that Ralynn was having a hard time deciphering her writing, but she knew she needed to write things down, so she could be free once and for all.

I was invited to church.

The largest denominational church in town had a bus ministry and would come pick the kids in my neighborhood up.

I was so excited to get out of the house that I made sure I was already outside playing when the bus came, so there wasn't a fear that he would change his mind and not let me go and I also didn't have to answer to where I was going.

My mom's new boyfriend had a tight leash on us. He wanted to know our every move, even if it was to go out to check the mail.

The bus was right on time, and I ran to be the first one on. The driver greeted us all with a friendly smile. This church was so beautiful. It had stained-glass windows the entire length of the sanctuary, which faced the main road. The entrance of the church reminded me of entering the castle as a guest to the Queen's ball. The rich dark mahogany trim looked amazing against the 24 x 24 off-white with dark streaks marble flooring.

I have to admit though, I was afraid that the church was going to blow up as soon as I walked through the doors. People like me didn't belong in places like this, at least that is what I heard the girls in the neighborhood say. They said that a local neighborhood pastor said that about them. And they were better than me. How did I know they were better than me? They kept telling me how much better of a person they were than me. It had to be true—why would they lie?

On Sundays we would have our own Sunday school service but then we were expected to sit in big church. Every week the pastor got up to preach in his dark-blue suit and mustard-yellow tie.

Ralynn was writing as fast as the memories were coming. She then started to remember this particular sermon. Putting her pen down, she closed her eyes as she could hear the preacher.

"Women are supposed to be submissive to their husbands."

Ralynn went back to her journal and started to write some more.

To me, just barely a teenager, what I heard him say was that women were to be at their husband's beck and call. We were to be the caretaker of the home, and when our husband asked or wanted something, the wife should jump. We as women were not to have an opinion.

Taking a break from journaling, Ralynn put her head back and allowed the sun to warm her up. She didn't realize that as she was remembering that event, her body was trembling. Why? Wanting to get to the root of that memory, she started writing again.

> What scripture did that man use?
>
> Why did he keep saying that scripture was God's word and His truth?
>
> Why did he say we needed to be obedient to it?

All of sudden, Ralynn had a flashback to the women in that church and remembered that they all felt less than and that they weren't allowed to have a voice. Journaling once again:

> Watching this church and pastor and my mom being submissive to the beatings at home, makes sense to why I became a prisoner of my own doing.

Ralynn continued to journal her thoughts with her new-found freedom from the program.

> When you are broken and hurting, you just want the hurting to stop, and you are willing to try anything. I regrettably didn't have the knowledge of the scriptures, let alone know how to study them for myself, so I just took what someone in the pulpit said as truth. I became a doormat when it came to relationships with men and quickly realized I was in prison, headed for a life sentence or even the death penalty.
>
> I want to do something different.

Continuing to write in her journal, Ralynn thought back to when she was younger.

> I would ask people how to change.
>
> With the looks I got, I thought I had two heads.
>
> Was it because I wasn't an adult yet?
>
>
> Did they think that one day I could flip a light switch and be different?
>
> Now thinking back to the class a week or so back, it made more sense.

I became like a robot on this event cycle of just letting life happen. The more this cycle did a full rotation, the worse my opinion of myself became, which resulted in worse actions. I just didn't know how to get off.

Turning to her notebook she found the cycle. Turning to a clean page in her journal she wrote:

How to get off the cycle of letting life happen and make life happen

EXPECTATION

My new expectation in life is:

WHAT?

To help others become all that they could be come.

To be whole myself.

XXVI

Ms. Shaw had decided the best day for the women of the local churches to come out was on Sunday for a late lunch or early dinner. Ralynn had enlisted Julia's help to make the food, but she was saddened when many of the women from Z-House had decided to go to their rooms when the ladies first started arriving. Trying not to dwell on that fact, Ralynn finished putting the finger sandwiches on the table. Julia had already put the fresh fruit cups at each place setting. Just as Ralynn realized she forgot to make a dessert, Shelly showed up with her famous chocolate cake. It was fresh out of the oven, and she had put it in a warming blanket, so when it was time to serve it, you thought it had just come out of the oven. The dinner portion of the meeting was filled with light-hearted conversations and laughter. To Ralynn's surprise, the women started to emerge from their rooms and joined the second portion of the meeting in the living room. Grabbing their dessert and coffee, all the women retired to the living room.

After introducing Ralynn, Ms. Shaw took a seat and let her take the meeting from there. Talking and passing out the synopsis, Ralynn explained what the proposed classes would look like. She also was very particular on what would be expected if the churches signed up to help. At the end of the meeting, Ralynn passed around a sign-up sheet with very specific places to serve. Five churches were represented, and when the paper made its way back to Ralynn, every block had been filled in. After the last lady left, Ralynn turned around, and Julia had come back out to the kitchen to help clean up. As they were talking about nothing, Julia did confide that Shelly had secretly gone back to all their rooms and persuaded them to come out and join the conversation.

After the last dish was done and Ralynn was finally walking back to her room, she pulled out her phone and texted Shelly.

"Thank you for everything, especially getting the girls to come join in. See you Thursday."

Thursday was already here, and Ralynn could not wait to see what they were going to learn in class. Walking into Jim and Shelly's house tonight though, there was no laughter or great smelling food being cooked in the kitchen. Shelly apologized but said it had been a rough week. Jim was still out on a job site working. A friend had called in a favor, so Jim was putting down ceramic in their bathroom.

"Tonight ladies, welcome to soup and sandwiches. And I hope you all know me by now to know, this is *not* what I wanted to serve you, but I just could not get it together this week. So let's grab our plates and bowls, get your kids' food, and we will let them eat downstairs tonight."

As we got settled into our dinner, Shelly started speaking.

"As you all know we are open books with you all. So to keep that line of communication open, I want to share with you what has happened in our family since we met last Thursday. I want you to see, just because a family may look good on the outside, doesn't mean they won't or don't have trouble. Most of your parenting issues right now have to do with potty-training, the terrific twos, or getting your child to actually stay dressed."

We all laughed.

"But tonight I want to share with you, what the world would call a parenting fail; we had Amber locked up this past weekend."

After Shelly picked us all up off the floor from the shock of hearing Amber was in juvenile for the weekend, we settled in to hear the rest of the story. Jim and Shelly had already shared some of the not-so-pretty parts of raising teenage girls. Amber was their strong-willed child. She was their oldest, and, boy, did they have issues. She was entering her rebellious years with full steam.

"So you all know that Jim was in Texas with Sabrina. He was helping his mom and dad. They just purchased a new home and wanted ceramic tile put in. Seeing that was the field of work that Jim was in, he agreed to go down for a long weekend and put the floor in."

Jim always joked that Sabrina was the boy he never had. She was athletic and a pure tomboy. She hung out with the boys because she said girls had too much drama. Jim and Shelly had talked about Amber's changing behavior. No one knew how bad it had gotten until it came to a head Friday night.

"With Jim out of town, Amber kept telling me she was going to spend some time with a friend who had had a baby. I didn't think anything of it. Even though she's headstrong, Amber has always had a heart for the underdog, and she allows people to take advantage of her. When Amber finally came home at 1a.m. without her car, I questioned her about her whereabouts. I found out that she had been lying to me for the entire week. After many phone calls to Jim and a friend who worked in the system, it finally blew up when Amber put her hand on her hip and said 'What! You can't charge me with anything. All I am is unruly.' And with those words, ladies, I called the non-emergency number for the sheriff's office and within a few short minutes, a deputy was in my driveway. That was at 2:30 a.m."

Seeing the genuine care in Shelly's eyes for Amber to do well in life, Ralynn found herself jealous as she wished she had had that growing up.

"Amber doesn't know how good she has it." Ralynn thought.

Shelly continued,

"With that call, the deputy came in the house, and arrested Amber—handcuffs and all. He led her down the stairs and out the door to place her in the back of the green-and-white patrol car. That was one of the hardest things I think I have ever had to face as a parent."

Now that we were all crying, Jim walked in and broke it up,

"You all, I told you to remind me to take out stock in tissue before you had a cryfest again. Why are you all crying this time? What did Shelly say this time?"

After we all stopped laughing and crying, Shelly did go on to explain that they had tried everything to get Amber to listen, and she was found to be running with a twenty-three-year-old, who happened to be her boss. Amber was determined to quit school, get her GED, and leave town. Even though Amber had heard our stories, she still wanted to choose her path. Well, her path that night was straight to jail for a weekend. Jim and Shelly said that even though that was one of the hardest things they had ever had to do, they sought wise counsel and they loved Amber enough to at least try to help change her path. Ralynn hated that they had this horrible week, but it was refreshing to know that everyone has troubles. Even the people who you would never imagine having any issues.

"So ladies, as we talked last week about excuses. I could have continued to make excuses for my daughter, which based upon the current path she was taking, Lord only knows where she would have ended up. Or as a parent, I had the right to say, enough is enough and let's get some help and see if we can change her path. Ultimately though, when she turns eighteen, all bets are off because she can walk out never to return. And that goes for any of you. You are all adults, and you have choices to make every day. One choice you make is to come here on Thursdays to learn a new way. The second choice comes when you leave out the door. Do you take what you learn and use it? Or do you use Thursday nights as a free night, and you have no intentions of changing? You are the only one who can make that choice. This week we are going to talk about our attitudes and how that affects our outlook on life."

Handing out the packets Shelly started with a poem by Walter D Wintle and Vince Lombardi. She made us all recite it out loud.

If You Believe You Can, You Can

If you think you are beaten— you are.

If you think you dare not—you don't.

If you want to win but think you can't—

It is almost a cinch you won't.

If you think you'll lose—you've lost.

For out of the world we find

That success begins with a fellow's will;

It's all in the state of mind.

Life's battles don't always go

To the stronger or the faster man;

But sooner or later the man that wins

Is the one who thinks he can.

—*Walter D. Wintle & Vince Lombardi*

Finding Hope

We spent the rest of that night talking through how our attitude or our opinion of our self really does affect how we will tackle a job. We looked at how it affects relationships.

Shelly even showed us how we can change our circumstances and future.

Ralynn was emotionally whipped by the time class was over but was finding more and more determination to do something different for herself and the baby.

XXVII

Knowing God was working on her. Ralynn wanted to know more about Him and having a relationship with Him, but it never seemed to be the right time to bring it up. Even as she walked out, she felt God telling her to ask Shelly more questions. Pushing the feelings back, she told herself she would do it later. By the time she arrived back to Z-House, the nagging would not go away. Ralynn knew she had to call and talk to Shelly and Jim in the morning about living a life of transformation. Then she felt she was to talk to Jim, seeing she looked to him as her pastor, she also decided it couldn't wait.

"Hello."

"Shelly, this is Ralynn. Is Jim home?"

"Yes he is, is everything okay?"

"Yes, I just have some questions."

"Hello."

"Jim, this is Ralynn. I want to know more about this living a life of transformation I keep seeing in my homework."

"Oh that's great, Ralynn. Which transformer would you like to be, BumbleBee or Megatron," he said with a laugh.

Giggling, Ralynn said,

"No, I want to know about living my life for Jesus."

Getting serious Jim began to explain the need for salvation, walking away from our own earthly desires, and making Jesus the Lord of our life. He told her that if she confessed Jesus as her Lord and that she believed in her heart that Christ had died for her sins, and that God had raised Him from the dead, then she would be saved. He said she needed to pray and ask Christ to take over her life. Nervously, she asked if there were specific words she needed to say. Jim told her to just share her desire to submit her life to Christ. As Ralynn began to pray with Jim over the phone, she was overcome with emotion and felt a love that she had never felt before.

As soon as Ralynn said amen, she heard Shelly in the background yelling in excitement and telling her congratulations. Before the conversation ended, Jim asked Ralynn when she would like to be baptized. She asked if there was any way to do it Thursday night with all the girls present. Without hesitation, Jim said yes.

Hanging up, she could not wait to share her news with Kia.

"Kia, I need to tell you something."

"What, you look like you are about to bust."

"I just got off the phone with Jim and Shelly, and I am going to get baptized on Thursday. I prayed and asked Jesus to forgive me and to take over my life."

"You did what?"

"I asked God to forgive me for my sins and help me every day to live differently. I wanted what Shelly and Jim have. They are different. They live different."

Kia was not impressed. She liked the classes and all, but she wasn't too sure about living a life that was self-disciplined in the matter of believing in Jesus as her Savior.

Ralynn was so excited that she wasn't sure she was going to be able to sleep, and she didn't know if Thursday would get here soon enough, but she also was sad that Kia was not excited for her. As she got ready for bed, she found herself talking out loud.

"God, please be with Kia. May she change her mind."

Crawling into bed, Ralynn then laid there and started talking again,

"God, thank you for this bed. Thank you for the things that have been given to me."

Just then the baby started to kick.

"God thank you for this baby. May everything go well. Teach me to be a good mom. May this baby grow up differently than me."

Ralynn didn't remember falling asleep but was not happy when a loud thud came from her door. Jumping out of bed, she opened the door to find Diane once again yelling at the girls to hurry up, so they could get home before their dad went to work. Diane was singing his praises. She was so excited because he called and said he found religion and things would be different. Ralynn was scared for them because summer break had just started, so they wouldn't have the safety of school for the next eight weeks.

Diane and the girls had once again left the property even with everyone begging her to stay. Once Ralynn had taken a few minutes to settle down, she grabbed her notebook and journal, and started out the front door toward the prayer garden but stopped and decided to sit in the oversized white wicker chair with the comfy cushion. Ralynn felt a heaviness for Diane's girls. She didn't know what she could do, so she started to pray for them.

"God, please keep them safe. They are just kids."

Feeling a little better and getting settled down, Ralynn felt compelled to go back and rewrite the poem they recited in class, breaking it down line-by-line and letting it speak to her.

If You Believe You Can, You Can.

It starts with my belief that I can do something different.

If you think you are beaten—you are.

I am no longer going to think that I am beaten (physically or mentally), I am not a punching bag for anyone, including myself. I will stop the negative self-talk.

If you think you dare not—you don't.

I will take chances. Not just any chances, but I will get a new board of directors to walk with me.

If you want to win but think you can't, It is almost a cinch you won't.

I will win at life because I choose to win at life. I deserve a different life, not only for me but also my little one.

If you think you'll lose—you've lost.

I have thought for a very long time that I was a lost cause, because everyone told me that. I am no longer a lost cause. Shelly has had us memorize that we were created to do good works. Now to find out what I was created to do.

For out of the world we find

That success begins with a fellow's will;

It's all in the state of mind.

Today I choose to have a better attitude and outlook. My mind will change to look at the positive and not dwell on the negative that has happened.

Life's battles don't always go

To the stronger or the faster man;

But sooner or later the man that wins

Is the one who thinks he can.

Today I choose to start my new book.

XXVIII

Monday night was finally here, and Ralynn was excited to start the classes. She knew how much they had helped her even though her circumstances hadn't changed. She was still living in Z-House. She still didn't have job. She was getting healthy on the inside, and for the first time in a long time, she was excited for the future. Ralynn was also getting eager to bring a little one into this world and to raise him or her by herself to become the man or woman that God created him or her to be.

Everything was all set and ready to go an hour before dinner was to arrive. Ralynn started getting nervous and started to doubt that the ladies would be appreciative of what Shelly was going to bring.

The tidal wave of excuses started to hit her, such as the churches won't follow through, and the girls won't come to class.

She picked up her phone to call Shelly and tell her she made a mistake and that maybe we shouldn't teach the classes here, when her phone dinged; it was a text:

"Don't let the father of lies tell you that you aren't worthy enough to teach these classes. God will use you and your obedience, even if you can't actually teach while you live there. He will use your brokenness that is being healed to reach people that I would never be able to reach because of your story. I can't wait to see how God is going to use this class for His glory."

There was a knock on the door; it was the food arriving. The ladies from the Fifth Street Church were so excited to be here. They brought a chicken spaghetti tetrazzini, and for the kids they brought corndogs and French fries. Dinner was great, and the conversations were meaningful. When it was time for class to start, a couple of the women who looked like grandmothers, excused themselves and took the kids to the toy room. They had also brought with them a storage box filled with games and crafts.

So far so good, Ralynn thought. Everything was going as planned.

The class did not go as planned though, but it did go as God planned. Shelly got up to teach and flipped the script back to Ralynn.

"Ralynn, I know this was your idea, and you had something you wanted to say tonight, didn't you?"

How does she do that? Ralynn wondered. She actually felt that she needed to talk about excuses and excuse making.

"Thank you Shelly. I really felt after the week we have had here, that what you taught on in regard to excuses is something that everyone needs to hear, and I want to share my story."

"Well then, Ralynn, why don't you share, and I will fill in or add to if I need to."

Ralynn took the floor.

"I am not sure what all your stories entail. I know we live together, but I also know we are guarded at what we say, when we say it, and with whom we talk. I want to share my story. You see I was great at making excuses as to why I deserved to be in a relationship that was not healthy and why I deserved to be the punching bag. I had learned really well to make excuses, not only for myself but also for the one who was my abuser at the time. You did hear, I said abuser at the time. I had many of them. It wasn't until I feared for my life and that I was sick and tired of being sick and tired that I wanted things to change for me."

Shelly stood up and asked a few questions.

"So, ladies, who do you make excuses for? Friends, family, boyfriends? Yourself? Next question is who makes excuses for you? Family? Friends? You see by making excuses for bad behaviors, we allow people to stay in a state of denial that the behavior is acceptable."

Shelly nodded to Ralynn to start back with her story.

"Let's take my example of making the excuses that I deserved to be in abusive relationships. By making that excuse about me, I found I gravitated toward relationships that weren't healthy. I had a lot of shame and guilt from my past, and that lent itself to believing that a relationship included abuse—sexual, emotional, verbal, and physical. Even though there were red flags all over the relationships, as soon as he said those three words, "I love you," I was forgiving him like nothing happened. I would make excuses, like I was home late or I made him mad. I knew not to ask him that question while he was watching football. And the excuses went on and on, all the while he was becoming more and more abusive. He would then tell me it was my fault that he hit me because I knew the rules to not talk while he was watching his show. I even believed the lie that I had to be intimate quickly to show the guy I loved him. I wanted to be different. I wanted new relationships to be different. I would start off saying, 'this time no sex.' This time 'no moving in.' This time you will treat me like a lady."

Shelly took back over,

"Ralynn and anyone else this is talking to, do you want to continue to live like this, or do you want to change? The challenge becomes how do we change when this is the behavior that we have seen growing up. You were told your whole life that you will never amount to anything and no one would ever love you. This pattern of living is all you know."

Ralynn jumped back in.

"Here is where it changed for me. I am going through the very same program with Shelly on Thursday nights. We were talking about codependent relationships and that, as a codependent person, you try to provide and control everything within the relationship to make sure the other person is always happy. I never addressed my own needs or desires, which set me up for continued unfulfillment in relationships. When it got bad enough, I would get out of that relationship and run into another. I never took care of me. And you see I take me wherever I go. I also thought that I had to have my life all together before I could ask Jesus to save me and transform me into a new being. Somewhere I got it in my head that because I was unworthy to be loved, Jesus couldn't genuinely love me until I was healed. Then Shelly showed me this verse in Ephesians that said that God created me as a masterpiece and for much more than what I was doing with my life. In Ephesians 2:10 it says: *"For we are God's masterpiece. He has created us anew in Christ Jesus, so we can do the good things He planned for us long ago"* (NLT)

"Wow, Ralynn, thank you for sharing." Shelly took over the conversation. "Ladies before we go any further with Ralynn's story, let's actually verbalize God's word to ourselves. Let's read out loud as a group Ephesians 2:10, but where it says we or us, say your name instead. When you do this, it makes the scriptures come to life. For Shelly is God's masterpiece. He has created Shelly anew in Christ Jesus, so that Shelly can do the good things He planned for Shelly long ago. Awesome, how did that feel?

The ladies all had smiles like something had just hit home and that maybe, just maybe, they were made for more than the lies they had bought.

Ralynn jumped back in, "I didn't realize I could change until someone showed me a different way. I would hear people say, just read your Bible or pray more. The problem was, I had a misconception about the Bible, and I definitely didn't know how to pray. So I continued in my same cycle with my same old habits. I also learned that codependency was a dysfunctional pattern of living and problem-solving developed during childhood by unrealistic family rules or behaviors. So if you looked at my past, I was a prime candidate. And I lived the statement, "See, this is why I am the way I am, and that is all there is to it." But not anymore. I know that I am worth more than that. I found out that the Bible was not just to read on Sunday and special occasions. It is the instruction manual on life I was looking for. It told me that Jesus, died for me, too, not just the person who looked like they had never sinned and their life was perfect. He wanted a relationship with me, here and now, not just in heaven. It wasn't until I started this program that I realized that I was keeping myself hostage in fear of ever changing. I kept saying I wanted something new, but I never knew where to start. Here is the hardest thing I had to come to grips with when I was shown a different way. I had to make a conscious choice to change and no longer make excuses for myself as to why it wouldn't work."

Shelly jumping back in, "Well this class is going to give you the tools so that when you say 'I am sick and tired of being sick and tired and I want to change,' you will know where to start. But it is a choice you will have to make for yourself."

The ladies started clapping and yelling *amen*. Ralynn didn't realize how excited she was. She just wanted these ladies to see they no longer needed to settle to be a statistic or someone's punching bag, and by making excuses they allow themselves to stay in their own prison.

"I also had guilt because of the things I had done. I needed to forgive myself for them just as Jesus forgave me when I asked Him to. Romans 3, verses 21–24 from the New Living Translation says: "We are made right with God by placing our faith in Jesus Christ. And this is true for everyone who believes, no matter who we are. For everyone has sinned; we all fall short of God's glorious standard. Yet God, in His grace, freely makes us right in His sight. He did this through Christ Jesus when He freed us from the penalty for our sins."

You see, until I sought and understood the forgiveness of the Father in heaven, I could never truly understand and live out forgiving myself. In these classes I learned about that, and I pray that you will want the same freedom I found. But before I got to this point, my big hangup was shame and guilt. I thought I deserved the life I was handed and that there was no way to change. I had allowed the guilt and shame to weigh me down. I thought people could see everything I had done in my yesterday, even though they had never met me. I was a prisoner of my own past and saw no future."

"Ralynn, thank you for sharing. Before we end tonight's class I want to talk about shame and guilt and how that works itself into excuses. Guilt is what I have done. By allowing ourselves to continually think because we did something bad, we need to stay in a place of 'not being worthy,' this creates many sabotaging behaviors. Do you all know what the definition of sabotage is? It is a deliberate destruction."

Piping back in, Ralynn added,

"I found that I deliberately destroyed healthy relationships because I had bought the lie that all I deserved was to be in abusive relationships."

"Remember this," Shelly jumped back into the conversation, "all abuse is not just physical or sexual, it is also verbal, emotional, and it can also be spiritual. If someone is using the Bible to shame you into living a different life or to do things that are wrong. God would never do that. He wants you to understand who He is and that He wants a relationship with you because you want it. He will never force Himself on you. Also when you accept Him as your Lord and Savior, Jim, my husband, will tell you it's not a legalistic requirement to follow what God wants, but an irresistible response because of what God has done for you, and you will desire to walk a daily life with Him. Shame and guilt have their own effects on our lives. Because of guilt and not forgiving ourselves for something in our past, we talk ourselves into thinking this is the best that life has to offer. So how do we forgive ourselves for an event or action that keeps our self-esteem and even self-confidence in this low position? Before I answer that, ladies, did you know that there is a difference between self-confidence and self-esteem? Confidence is how well you do something, like a job. But esteem is how you rate yourself on the inside, how do you feel about yourself."

Taking back over the conversation, Ralynn wanted to share her story.

"I realized after almost losing my life and finding a new future, that satan likes to keep us in this state of low self-esteem so that we will medicate ourselves. I did it through abusive relationships that looked amazing to begin with."

"Or," Shelly interjected, "you might medicate with alcohol, drugs, sex, or anything to make yourself feel better even if it is for a moment."

"Shelly, before we finish, I want to share what I learned today,"

"Okay, Go for it."

"Today as I was reading the Bible, I read my own story. It was when this lady was brought to Jesus when she was caught in the act of adultery. You can read it later in John 8, but the paraphrase is that she was brought before Jesus. The religious leaders wanted Jesus to condemn her and allow her to be killed, but Jesus said, 'All right, but let the one who has never sinned throw the first stone!'

"One by one they all left . . . Then Jesus stood up again and said to the woman, 'Where are your accusers? Didn't even one of them condemn you?'

"'No, Lord,' she said.

"And Jesus said, 'Neither do I. Go and sin no more.'

"It was then that I realized that I did not need to fear the religious leaders because they too have sin, shame, and guilt and that same Jesus that loves them and loves me just the same."

"So, ladies, what Ralynn wants you to hear is, as you are healing, don't be afraid of the religious leaders of today and what you may think they will say. The only person's opinion that matters is Jesus. What does Jesus say about you and is saying to you?"

The ladies were all very attentive, and Ralynn thought they enjoyed it. Ralynn excused herself after the last volunteer left. She thanked them profusely for coming and making this class a reality. It was quite different just going to her room afterward instead of getting into a vehicle and driving home. She was so fired up after actually teaching with Shelly that it took her a while to settle down. Watching these ladies have the same lost feeling she had when she met Shelly, she had to be reminded that this was not a sprint but a marathon. Ralynn wanted everything fixed overnight, but Shelly's words come back to her.

"You did not get into this mess overnight, so why should you be able to get it fixed overnight?"

Ralynn started to chuckle because as she was hearing Shelly's words, she also heard Jim teasing her, "She's right; she's always right."

At about 4 p.m. on Thursday, Ralynn's text alert went off. It was Shelly with a new address for tonight.

"Don't forget to bring something to get wet in and a towel."

XXIX

Kia was still not too sure about this baptism thing, but Ralynn really did not care. She just knew what she needed and wanted to do.

Kia put the address in the GPS, and it took them straight to the clubhouse of an apartment complex that was around the corner from Jim and Shelly's house. One of their partners in the ministry managed the apartments and told them anytime they needed the pool for a baptism or the clubhouse for a meeting to just call.

"Thank you, ladies, for arriving on time. We have a special treat tonight. As you can see we are not in our home but at an apartment complex pool. Ralynn called last Thursday night after class and talked with Jim about what it meant to become a Christ follower. After Ralynn prayed, she wanted to get baptized, but wanted you all to witness it. So that is why we are here. Jim, Ralynn, you ready? All right, let's all go outside to the pool."

Ralynn, Jim, and Shelly entered the pool, while the rest of the women and their children sat around the pool.

As Jim was getting ready to put a towel over her nose, he started saying

"So by the profession of your faith, I now baptize you in the name of the Father, the Son and the Holy Spirit."

Jim lowered Ralynn underwater and raised her back up. All she heard as she was coming up out of the water was shouting and applause. Even Kia was hollering and clapping.

"As a treat this week, we have a couple of food trucks out in the parking lot. You need a ticket to get your food. Nikki has them at the front door. Also, you have a second ticket for the ice cream food truck. Make sure you get your serving because if you don't, Jim will eat it all. Especially their chocolate. We will get started in here in about thirty minutes."

Everyone went outside to get dinner. The choices that night were: Taco Food Truck, Chicken and Waffles Food Truck, or BBQ Food Truck. Then, for dessert, was the most awesome homemade ice cream in all the state. Ralynn chose the butter pecan. The owner gave her a sample taste before she decided. It was rich and creamy, so she left the chocolate for Jim. As Ralynn was getting her ice cream, the owner, who was working the truck, told Ralynn how proud she was of her.

As dinner was finished, Andee stood up to apologize and tell everyone what had happened. Her boyfriend was picked up on Friday night for driving on a revoked license and because this was his third offense, he was having to sit a while in the county jail. She moved back home on Saturday.

"Andee, we are glad you are here and pray you are doing well."

"I am. And thank you for not saying, 'I told you so.'"

Shelly just gave her a hug, and that was the end of that.

"For this lesson, we are going to talk about changing a behavior, changing a lifestyle, breaking free from an addiction, or even the bondage of your past. Ladies, when people are wanting to change, break a bad habit, or even breaking an addiction, they need help.

If we try to change on our own, what happens when the temptation to just do it one more time comes along?"

Andee piped in, "Not sure you were looking for someone to actually answer that, but you go back to the person, like I did. I thought I could change him, but instead he started to change me back to my old ways and fast." Now with tears flowing, "Shelly, I am so sorry I didn't listen. I thought I could do both—be different but still stay with him."

Shelly walked over, gave Andee a one-armed hug, and kept right on talking.

"Sorry, Andee, but I already had this written, so don't think I am making this up as I go along."

We all giggled, as we read our papers.

"The temptation is to get into a bad relationship because you are lonely, so you make the excuse: Well, they aren't that bad of a person for me? Or, the temptation to visit "that place" where you know old friends are, and you use the excuse: I only did drugs once when I was there. The concern with these statements are, they can be triggers to start the negative cycle all over. Tonight we are going to look at a few scriptures and pick out main words to help us change and start a new behavior and new life changes.

Finding Hope

"For I can do everything through Christ, who gives me strength" (Philippians 4:13 NLT).

You want to change what from your life? This says *you can,* **but** with whose help?

Ladies, I know that some of you are having to make big decisions because your behavior shows you need to change . . . Well, let me just put it out there—it's how you have been able to make it when your money ran out and you still had a few weeks of the month left. Am I lying? I know more than you think I do. I do not condone this type of behavior, but each of you in your hearts needs to make a decision to do something different. I will be here to walk with you, and I will pray you want to change. But is it going to be easy? No, it is not. I am not going to make things up and say it's going to be easy, but it will be the right thing to do. I want you to see what God says: "And this same God who takes care of me will supply all your *needs* from His glorious riches, which have been given to us in Christ Jesus" (Philippians 4:19 NLT).

Did you see the promise? He will supply your *needs*! He's not promising wants or desires but *needs*. This may seem scary because changing *is* scary. The rewards, the new way of life, is well worth the change, especially if you have lost family and or friends in the process of your negative behaviors. Let's go on to see what God has next to say:

"For God has not given us a spirit of fear and timidity, but of power, love, and self-discipline" (2 Timothy 1:7 NLT).

This verse tells us a few things. If we are relying on God you will *not* have a spirit of fear, and second, you will *not* live being timid. The definition of timid is lacking self-confidence. "But God has given us also the spirit of power, love, and *self-discipline.*" Shelly raised her voice for effect. "This is the key—self-discipline. What does self-discipline mean?"

Jai was the first to speak, "It means to be in control of our self."

"Correct, and if you are in control of yourself, that will equal a new self with new behaviors. In Romans 12, verse 2, we will read from the New International Version, it says: Do not conform to the pattern of this world. To conform to the pattern of this world means your behaviors do exactly what the world says to do. The passage goes on to say, *but be transformed.* How are we supposed to be transformed? By the renewing of your mind. Do you know what it means by the renewing of your mind?"

No one said a word, so Shelly kept right on,

"You need to be transformed and the only way is to change how you see, feel, and think, and it starts with your thought process. We will look at that next week."

Ralynn loves how Shelly teaches the scripture and keeps it real. Ralynn started to think that now that she was a believer, she needed to learn how to study the scriptures for herself. She was grateful for the homework and the prompts to journal from, but she wanted to know more. Before she could talk to Jim or Shelly, Kyra was yanking on her hand heading her toward the door. Looking down at Kyra, but talking to the class, she said, "Well, good night, ladies. I guess the boss lady has spoken, and we are needing to leave."

XXX

As Ralynn was walking into the kitchen, she found herself in a better mood this week. From what she could tell, the women seemed to have enjoyed last week's lesson. A few of the women even asked her questions over the past few days. She was looking forward to the second class at Z-House.

"Just the person I want to see."

"Me?"

"Yes, Ralynn. You. Can you come into the office?"

Ralynn followed Ms. Dee into Ms. Stacy's office.

"Please take a seat."

Taking a seat, Ralynn did a double take. This was Ms. Stacy's office, but now it was filled with Ms. Dee's personal items.

"Ralynn, as you may have noticed, Ms. Stacy has not been here in the past couple of weeks."

Ralynn had to admit with everything going on in her life, she may have thought about it once that Ms. Stacy had not been around.

"She had to resign her position. Her husband got transferred out of town. So I have been promoted to assistant director, and because funds are lacking we will not be looking for a new program director."

"What does that have to do with me?"

"We will be making a formal announcement at dinner about all the changes, but I wanted to talk with you about the new class you got started last week."

"Okay? Is everything okay?"

"Sort of, but . . ."

Ralynn knew it. She was in trouble for sharing her story and for being an active part of the class.

"Ralynn, we have no problem with classes being here as long as they are not offensive to anyone."

Offensive? Ralynn was trying to think how the class was offensive.

"Ralynn, one of the volunteers went back to their husband and told them everything about Monday night. Not only does the church support this home, this particular couple does also. We are talking lots of money. Well, they said that they would stop their funding immediately if we continued letting Ms. Shelly and her program be taught onsite."

Ralynn was trying to wrap her head around what was being said as Ms. Dee continued, "Ralynn, basically they did not like the fact that you talked about living a life differently and with a personal relationship with Jesus. They are okay with the name of God being talked about but not Jesus. And they said you talked too much about the Bible being relevant to help guide you through your life. I am sorry, but we cannot have the class here any-more."

"Can we at least have Monday's class? I found a past graduate of the house, and she wants to share her story?"

"That should be fine. But after that, no more of that class; instead we will have the groups that signed up for the eight weeks bring a devotion at dinner."

Ralynn was saddened by the news. By default, she had walked into the position of helping Shelly by making sure everything was ready for that week's class. She didn't mind; it gave her something to do, now even that was being taken from her. Ralynn was getting tired living in a town that did not have a great mass transit option; it limited her abilities to find work, especially work where Ben would not come looking for her. And just when she thought things couldn't get any worse her phone rang.

"Yes this is Ralynn. Oh I see. I will be there. Thank you."

Ralynn hung up the phone and quickly texted Shelly:

New court date. Two weeks from today.

Got it on my calendar. 9 a.m.?

Yes.

I'll be there.

Thanks.

Monday evening was finally here, and it was time for class. Luckily, Ralynn had not had to tell anyone about the changes because she already had a guest speaker lined up who met the new requirements, and Shelly was going to be out of town. She also did not have to worry about the church, because it was a brand-new church to the area and was all about Jesus and helping people get back on their feet. When they came to the luncheon before they signed up, they wanted to make sure they could build relationships with the ladies who lived here and not just show up and give things away. The church, Restoration Fellowship, had just started holding services in the town adjacent to Mapleton. They not only provided the meal, they also provided babysitting, and they had five women from their church who stayed to be a part of the group.

"Good evening, I am so excited to see you all chose to come back. Ms. Shelly could not be here tonight, which was fine because we have a special treat. I know we have a few new ladies who have joined the house—welcome. As I was making phone calls I came upon the number of a previous graduate of Z-house. She happened to have tonight free and graciously agreed to come and speak to us. Please welcome Ms. Jill."

Jill had been sitting off to the side all night. She came in right after dinner was served, so the ladies did not pay much attention to her. Taking her place at the makeshift podium, an old rickety music stand, the ladies all gasped. Jill was 6 feet -tall with the six-inch heels. She probably weighed 130 pounds wet. And her outfit looked to be right out of the latest VT's catalog. As she started to speak, the ladies all had to lean in, so they could hear her because she was so soft spoken.

"First of all, Ralynn, thank you for inviting me to come back to where it all started. I have wanted to come share my story for a very long time, but I did not make it a priority to call, and for that I am sorry to all the women who have come and gone without finding a different way. I come from a single-parent home. My mom worked all the time, so I was left to fend for myself most of my life. I am grateful that she kept a roof over my head, but I wish she would have been more present in my life.

I still do not know who my father is, which created a void in my life. The abuse from my uncle started when I was six and continued until I was thirteen. I told my mom about the abuse, but my uncle was always there and had a story to tell as to why I was lying. She never believed me and still doesn't today. This abuse, the fact that no one believed me, and the absence of a father figure is what I like to call the perfect storm."

By now the ladies are on the edge of their seats not because they couldn't hear, but because they didn't want to miss a second of her talk.

"This 'perfect storm,' made me ripe for a codependent relationship. You know, those relationships where you take care of everyone else and never take care of yourself. I also regrettably found myself in relationships that were not honoring to God. I would tell people I was a Christian, but I was not honoring Him at all with my life. My son, who is now ten, is the blessing from a date rape. Why do I say he is a blessing? Because I would have never found this house and the 180 Program if I had not been pregnant. I had just found out I was pregnant, and I was contemplating suicide. I thought my life was over. No one believed me when I told them about my uncle, so I never reported the rape. I did not want to go through that shame again of being called a liar and have no one believe me.

"It was a beautiful spring day, and I was headed out of town to the bridge. I knew if I jumped from there, then I was guaranteed death, and that was better than living. As it happened Deputy Kissingly was patrolling the area when she saw me park my car and start to walk out toward the bridge. I am not sure why she stopped to talk to me that day but she did. We just sat there on the side of the road before the bridge and talked. We talked about life. We talked about goals. We talked about things we wanted to do tomorrow. After about three hours of just sitting and talking, her phone dinged. She said it was time for her shift to end.

"She stood up and reached out her hand to help me up while saying, 'I don't know about you, but I am starving for one of those burgers from Midpoint Grocery. Let's go get dinner, and we can finish talking.' I guess I forgot why I was there because without thinking I took her offer to help me up, got in her police car, and off to dinner we went. She didn't have any big words or speech. She was just a friend who cared that day. As we

Finding Hope

finished up our hamburgers and fries, she handed me her phone. She told me all I had to do was push talk if I wanted to start tomorrow on a different foot. It was the phone number to this place. After a brief conversation, Deputy Kissingly was taking me to the drop-off point. That night when I arrived here, there was laughter, cookies being baked, and a room full of women who had similar stories.

"Now that I have told you where I came from, I want to share with you how I came to be who I am today. This home and the programs they had here were amazing. I learned how to work through my past. I learned that I did not have to remain a victim of my past. I learned that my past did not define me unless I gave it permission to do so. I also learned that even though I didn't have a savings account with lots of money, I still needed to be a good steward of everything that God gave me. That included not just my finances but also anything that was donated to the home for my use. But my biggest aha moment came when I realized that I had an addiction and until I got rid of that addiction, I was still going to be a slave to my past. My addiction was not drugs. It was not alcohol. I was addicted to sex and men. I had no moral compass, but I also did not think I had anything to give this world but myself that way; that all started to change the day I chose to live here."

Now getting louder and more animated, Jill was pointing her fingers at each of us as she stated,

"Ladies, I cannot make that choice for you. This house cannot make the choice for you. These programs cannot make the choice for you. Only you can make that choice for yourself. But I will tell you, it was the best choice of my life to listen, to use all the tools they gave me, and then to act. That will be your biggest challenge. *Act*! So, where am I today? I am a successful realtor. My son is in private school. I am engaged to be married to an amazing man of God. And by the way, we have not had sex yet.

"As a matter of fact, I have not had sex since I lived here and decided I wanted to live fully for Christ. For me that meant I had to give up all sexual immorality, my addiction. Has it been hard to live a life differently? Yes! That was all I knew. They, all the volunteers and staff, walked with me slowly. They showed me a different way, not only by the classes and by being mentored, but by the way they lived. Ladies, it can be done. I am just one of the living testimonies from here. And you can be the next, if you choose to live differently."

As we started to applaud, Jill stopped us and said,

"Thank you for your kind applause, but I would much rather you save them. Your biggest thanks will be for you to be up here one day, giving your testimony about this home and the programs they brought in and how they changed your life for the better."

The ladies from Groove Community were so impressed with what they saw that night that they asked how else they could be involved, but Ralynn was conflicted because she knew that the house Jill had just spoken on was not the Z-House of today. It was just a house, and even though Ralynn had great aspirations of making it like the place Jill spoke of, funding was at the top of the list, and the classes had to go if they talked about Jesus. Giving the volunteers the obligatory "we will be in touch and thank you for coming," Ralynn found herself rushing everyone out the door, so she could go and hide.

Ralynn knew that she could not put off calling Shelly, but before she even had the chance, her text notification went off.

How'd it go? Was Jill a hit?

She was. Can you talk?

Sure. Or can you get a ride to town for coffee?

Sure. How about 11 at The Coffee Shoppe?

See you there.

XXXI

Ralynn hurried and got ready. She knew that the shuttle left for town on Tuesday at 10:30, unless someone had to go to work or into town for an appointment, so getting a ride to see Shelly was not going to be an issue.

Ralynn took off walking toward The Coffee Shoppe. The sun was beating down, and the weather reports said to expect an extremely hot summer. With the streets busier than normal, Ralynn was having to dodge not only people, but there were dogs everywhere—big dogs, small dogs, dogs in purses, yappy dogs, but the dog that caught Ralynn's attention was one whose owner was in a wheelchair. The dog didn't have on a vest nor be a breed that she had known to be trained as a service dog, but this tan scruffy dog with flopped-over ears, seemed to be ever so attentive to his owner's every move. As she watched the interactions with people and this person, it seemed he had been around for a while. Everyone knew him and stopped to say hi and pet his dog.

As she finally rounded the corner, she saw the city workers placing barricades on the sides of the roads. Ralynn had come accustomed to the city shutting down the roads for festivals or parades. But the sight of the barricades and the thought of parades made her smile. Oh, how she loved marching band. She loved learning new routines and competing. Marching band also became her solace. Her mom's boyfriends never questioned practices or Friday night games. Ralynn found herself stepping in cadence to the sound of the construction workers' hammers. Thud. Thud. Reminiscing about those times brought a smile to Ralynn's face.

But unfortunately those nice memories were then overshadowed by the next memory that included a Thud, Thud. She started remembering the time when they had moved in with her mom's boyfriend instead of him moving in with them. He had gotten angry at her mom. All Ralynn remembers is hearing the thud against her door as he threw all her mother's belongings out of their bedroom, then when she thought it had stopped and she could get some sleep, her mother came into her room and told her to

189

get dressed because they had to leave. Showing up at 3 a.m. on her aunt's doorstep was not what she had in mind when she had gone to bed that night. Lucky for her, her aunt lived in the same district, so she didn't have to miss school again.

Beeeeeepppppppppp. Beeeeeepppppppppp. The sound of a horn blaring made Ralynn jump. Shaking the memories from her head, she crossed the road and walked in the back door of The Coffee Shoppe. The smell of fresh blueberry muffins permeated the old farmhouse. Shelly was already in line when Ralynn saw her.

"What do you want? My treat?"

"Don't they make a limeade chiller? That sounds good, and it is so hot out there today."

Their regular seat was taken, plus it was so nice outside that they opted for one of the picnic tables outside. Ralynn was noticing that all the tables were made out of rough lumber that still looked like a tree trunk. She wondered where the trees had come from. Were they from the lot next door that was now becoming a boutique hotel or from a family farm? Ralynn's questions would have to wait because Shelly was on her way out from using the restroom, and her phone was actually not attached to her ear.

"So how did last night go? Sorry I couldn't be there."

"It went well. Jill has an amazing story. That is why I wanted to talk with you."

"What's up?"

Fidgeting with her cup and straw because she didn't want to hurt Shelly's feeling plus she was mad about the whole situation, Ralynn didn't know how to tell her that the classes were canceled before they even got started.

"Ralynn, what's up? You didn't just want to have coffee."

"Shelly, I am so sorry."

"Sorry for what?"

Hanging her head in shame like she had totally messed up, Ralynn just sat there for what seemed to her an eternity.

"Okay, what in the world? I miss one class, and this is what I get?"

Ralynn knew that was Shelly's way of getting her to cheer up. She lifted up her head, and with tears starting, Ralynn blurted out in a very loud voice,

"Shelly we can't have classes anymore at Z-House?"

"What? Why? What happened?"

Ralynn as calmly as she could, explained to Shelly about the church lady and pulling their funding because we talked about Jesus. Ralynn thought Shelly was going to blow a gasket, but instead she said,

"Okay, then we will get permission to hold the classes at a church instead. That way we can have more people involved. We will let Z-House be in charge on Monday nights with their dinners and mini devotions, and we will find another day and time. We will get a church to run out to . . . Wait! I got it! We will find a church that is already coming on Sunday mornings to pick up the ladies. We will see if we can use their building on Sunday mornings for a Sunday school class. That way . . ."

"Shelly we can ask, but one of the churches that sends buses on Sundays is this church, and they question the girls every week about the other churches, so they can outdo the previous week."

"Fine. Then we will find a different day and time. And if we can't have it at a church, we will start having a second group at my house. It'll be fine. So, are you ready for your ultrasound and doctor's appointment tomorrow? And do you want me to meet you and take you?"

"I completely forgot. I was so upset about the classes getting canceled and Ben's court date that I forgot. Please, can you take me?"

"Sure I will meet you in the parking lot at 9 a.m."

After Ralynn was able to get everything about the classes being canceled off her chest, the rest of her time with Shelly was talking about how to read the Bible and study it for herself. Shelly had also given her a present. It was a set of gel highlighters and a new Bible with her name engraved on the front. Ralynn thought she was going to cry again.

"Wow! I don't know what to say. Thank you."

"Well, I pray you put it to good use. Matter of fact, if you would like to be a part of an online Bible study that I do, let me know."

"What is that?"

"Right now we are in Ephesians. Every morning I will text you a passage to read. You read it, then text back what you think it means or what God is saying to you. Sometimes I might even send a prompt or two to get you thinking."

"That sounds great. Can I start tomorrow?"

"Look for my text."

Ralynn was just getting ready to pick up her phone to see what time it was when Shelly's alarm went off on hers.

"Oh, my, Ralynn, we have been sitting here for the past two hours. How did that happen? I have to go to my next meeting. Do you need a ride?"

Ralynn shook her head as she was texting.

"Okay, then I will see you tomorrow for your doctor's appointment."

Seeing Shelly run off, Ralynn found herself jealous of Jill and Shelly's life. Not that she wanted to be a realtor, but she wanted to be joyful. She wanted to be doing something with her life. Seeing The Coffee Shoppe was getting busy, Ralynn decided to hop on the bus and go to KT's. Her manager told her to stop by anytime, and a bus pass was something she never had to worry about. The city supported Z-House that way for the girls who didn't have transportation. Z-House would get everyone to the closest stop and allow the girls to utilize the transit service as much as possible.

Strolling into KT's was like walking into a previous life. Everyone was welcoming and wanted to hear how things were going. Tim made her favorite sandwich homemade chicken salad on a homemade sourdough hoagie. A freshly made dill spear complimented the lunch along with KT's famous potato salad. Thinking on the last time she was here, Ralynn was so grateful that Ben hadn't had a chance to harm anyone physically. Getting a to-go cup of strawberry lemonade, Ralynn started to get panicked that she was going to miss the bus. Anxiety was hitting her.

"Where did that come from?" Ralynn thought to herself.

It was the memory of the last night she left here and took the bus home. She was excited about the promotion. Tim had given her a cup of strawberry-lemonade to go. She couldn't wait to share her good news with Ben. But then she missed the bus. He was angry. And she thought she was going to die. Now walking at a walk-run pace to the bus stop, Ralynn started to panic. "Breathe," she kept telling herself. That was not working. "Breathe," she told herself again, but this time in a more demanding way. Still she could feel herself losing it. Then all of a sudden her phone dinged.

"Hey here is today's passage in Ephesians that we did. As you will see we are just starting. I figured why wait until tomorrow. First, before you get started, pray. Ask God to quiet your soul and to speak to you."

Ralynn didn't read the rest of the text she just started to pray.

"God please quiet this panicked feeling. God please take away this anxiety. God please help me."

By the time Ralynn was at the pick-up point she had settled down. She even got out her phone and read the rest of the text.

Hey, here is today's passage in Ephesians that we did. As you will see we are just starting. I figured why wait until tomorrow. First before you get started: pray. Ask God to quiet your soul and to speak to you.

Read Ephesians 1:1–14. Take your journal and rewrite the scripture in words that speak to you. Then text back what God said to you or what you heard.

Seeing she had a new Bible sitting right there, and she had her journal in her purse, Ralynn opened up the front of the Bible and found the page number for Ephesians.

Armed with her new highlighters and excited to do this Bible study, Ralynn found herself afraid to mark in her new Bible, to ask stupid questions, or to make a mistake.

Deciding just to read, as she finished the last verse, Ms. Debbie pulled up to collect her.

XXXII

Ralynn found herself being anxious again. She knew she wanted a healthy baby, but other than that, she didn't know if she had a preference on a boy or a girl. She was finally called back. As she stood up, Shelly didn't move.

"Come on. I am not doing this alone."

Walking back to the room, the baby was doing flips. Ralynn, holding her tummy, started to cry. She wasn't sure if they were happy tears or fear tears. Maybe a little of both.

"Ralynn, if you will step in here. And ma'am you can sit out here and wait."

"No!" Ralynn snapped. "She's coming in with me."

"Okay, please follow me."

The room was dark, and Ralynn was told to get up on the table. First, the nurse came in with a handheld machine. She turned the volume up real loud, so they could hear the baby's heartbeat.

"Yep, Real strong. I bet you are going to have a boy."

With those words Ralynn's heart sank. For the first time she guessed she really did want a girl. The tech then put a gel on Ralynn's pregnant belly. Even though it had been warmed, it was still a little cool. The tech was using the wand to move the gel so that it covered the area she was about to search for the baby. The tech was chatty and then got serious. She would move the wand then, click. Move the wand some more, then click again.

Shelly was the first to break the silence.

"Everything okay?"

"Oh, yes. I am sorry. I was making sure I got all the measurements that are needed and the pictures. So Ralynn, are you ready to find out what you are having? The baby cooperated."

Ralynn felt a tear starting to drop and fall down the side of her face. The tech turned the monitor, so she could now see everything.

"Here is a leg. Here is the heart. Look at it beating. Very strong. Everything is measuring perfectly. And let's just say this little baby does not have any extra plumbing. You are having a girl."

It was perfect. Ralynn was so happy. Shelly was crying. The tech was going through a few more pictures and then was getting ready to hit the print button when Ralynn's little girl put up her hand. Ralynn started to cry.

"Did you see that? It was like she was waving to me."

Now all three ladies were alternating between laughing and crying. When the tech was done with the ultrasound, Ralynn was taken to Dr. Smith's office. After a few minutes, he walked in with her file and what looked like a wrapped gift.

"Ralynn, everything looks great and seeing I just saw you, I don't need to do any other exams. This is for you."

He handed her the wrapped gift and an envelope. Carefully, Ralynn started to unwrap the gift. It was a photo frame that said, "My first photo" and inside the frame was the picture of her daughter waving to her. She started crying again. She then opened the envelope, it was three more photos from the ultrasound.

"Thank you."

Ralynn didn't know if it was proper, but she got up from her seat and gave Dr. Smith a hug.

"You are welcome. We will see you at your next appointment."

That night Ralynn found herself thinking about the future. She still was not excited about bringing a child back to Z-House, especially with no programing to help. She really didn't know how to parent. She was not even sure she could change a diaper. She was thankful for Sally allowing her to practice with Jessie, but she only had him for a short time, and that was so sporadic. Looking at her baby's first picture, Ralynn found herself wondering how she could have thought abortion was the only option. This little thing had been growing inside of her, and she was going to kill it.

"God, thank you. Thank you for sparing my babies life. Help me to be a good mom."

As Ralynn finished her prayer, her phone pinged.

Sorry it is late today, forgot to send before your appointment. Read Ephesians 1:15–23.

Hear: I keep asking the God of our Lord Christ the Glorious Father that He may give you the Spirit of wisdom and revelation so that you may know Him better.

May the eyes of my heart be enlightened so that hope to which He has called you, knowing that we have the same power through the Spirit of God used to raise Jesus for the dead.

Why do we not ask God for the Spirit of wisdom and revelation?

Grabbing her Bible, she turned to Ephesians and started to read. Then she texted back:

I didn't know I should ask him for wisdom and revelation.

XXXIII

Still excited about Thursday nights as she was two months ago, Ralynn couldn't believe that she had stuck it out. Not sure what class was going to hold tonight, she was anxiously waiting for Kia to get back to the house so that they wouldn't be late. Just about the time she was trying to figure out how to get Ms. Shaw or Ms. Dee to take her and Julia, Kia came flying up the driveway. Julia and Ralynn didn't waste any time, they were running out the door to meet her.

"Sorry. Jump in; let's go."

Ralynn was thrilled that Kia seemed excited to go and didn't make an excuse why she couldn't take them. They arrived just as dinner was being served. Apologizing for being late, they quickly took their seats. As Ralynn was eating, she realized how grateful she was for all that Shelly and Jim had been instilling in her and the other women. Every week they didn't let you be a victim of your past, but showed you how make changes in your life if you didn't like where you were headed. Dinner transitioned seamlessly to Shelly handing out the papers for this week's class. This is when Ralynn realized this week was no different. Shelly was talking about how thought patterns affect our lives, which in turn affect our children's lives. Not understanding what her thought pattern had to do with her unborn child, Ralynn was only partially paying attention to what Shelly was saying; instead she started to look at the diagram that was on the next page.

As Shelly was circling the word *legacy* on the diagram which she had drawn on the whiteboard, she asked,

"What legacy are you wanting to leave for your children?"

No one answered.

"Okay, ladies, let me ask it this way. If your children were taking this class when they are twenty years old, and you changed nothing about your lifestyle, what would their family map say about you? You all do remember our family maps right?"

Okay, Ralynn thought, *she has my attention now.*

Shelly went on to talk about how thoughts are just that; they are thoughts, but then she asked "Are they?" She explained that thoughts have the ability to keep you paralyzed from ever trying anything new if you allow them to hold you hostage. Shelly said that in the Bible, there was a verse that said we need to take our thoughts captive and teach them to obey Christ. She then told us the challenge, though, was when we allowed the world to speak into our thought life. She made us stop and think, what are those voices saying? She then asked us if we were hearing things like, "You will never change? You will never be good enough to do anything different than what you are doing right now. Or, are there names being associated with your reputation, like addict, whore, loser, or good-for-nothing.

Shelly then questioned us, "Why do you listen to those people?"

Even though no one was answering Shelly, Jim had gotten the tissues and placed them in the middle of the circle. How'd he know? Shelly went on, "If you allow the opinions of others to infiltrate your thoughts and you don't check them against what God has to say, then what words will you start to speak over yourself? These words, if unchecked against the truth of scripture, will create what action in your life? Now I know you have seen the word *action* in a cycle like this many times over the past couple months. So what word goes in the first blank?"

Shelly was correct we all knew that the next word was *events*, followed by *opinion*, which led to an *expectation*. But then she added that these thoughts, words, and actions became our habits, which was our go-to behavior.

"Ladies, if you do not like your go-to behavior, then we need to go back to our thoughts and see what we are saying to our self or what we are allowing others to speak over us."

Ralynn thought Shelly could have stopped right there, seeing many of the ladies were still trying to comprehend how a simple thought turned into a habit. But no, Shelly kept right on telling us that when we continue in our habits or go-to behaviors, it becomes our character or who we are.

"Do you like who you are? Are there some parts of your life that you want to change?"

Ralynn was still writing her answers to Shelly's last questions when Shelly brought it back to her first question,

"If your children were taking this class in twenty years, what would they say? Ladies, if you stay on the same course you are on today, what is the legacy you are leaving for your children? You are not in a physical prison. You are not six feet under. You have a choice today to do something different so that when your children are older, they are proud of the legacy you left them. The choice is yours!"

For the rest of that class we talked about the fact that we needed to take action if we ever wanted something different. Shelly took us to Luke 15, to the story of what we call the Prodigal Son. The son squandered his wealth away and when the money was gone, all his new friends were gone, and he was so hungry that he became a hired hand and it says, "He longed to fill his stomach with the pods that the pigs were eating, but no one gave him anything."

Shelly went on to say that in verse 17 it said, "When he came to his senses," but verse 20 says, "So he got up and went to his father."

Shelly explained that we would not wake up one day and say "Okay, today I have a different life." She told us that if we do want to do something different, then we need to make the choice today to start doing something different and as the Prodigal did—he got up and went.

Not sure where her extra passion came tonight, but Shelly was fired up and wanted us to stop and think about the consequences of our thoughts and choices before we created anymore actions in our lives.

"Ladies, I'm not sorry for getting so fired up. I see so many possibilities in all of you. And it makes me mad when you don't see it for yourself. I want you to live up to your God-given potential."

Ralynn left there fired up and couldn't wait to go back and take another look at her packet from tonight and hopefully be able to show it to Ruby and Sallie.

Pulling in, all the main lights were off. Ralynn figured that everyone had gone to their rooms. Walking through the kitchen, she found herself let down that she was right; everyone had gone to their rooms. Still fired up from class, Ralynn got out her journal and started writing:

Starting tomorrow it is a new day. I choose to no longer live according to my past. I choose to start living according to what I want for the future.

What do I want for my tomorrow?

Jeremiah 29:11 says that God has a plan for me. Okay, God, I am listening what is it?

Grabbing her notebook, Ralynn felt she should go back and look at last week's class work as it was on overcoming and being transformed into the person that God wanted her to become. Ralynn remembered that one of the scriptures said that we no longer needed to live in fear or be timid because God gave us the Spirit of self-discipline. God also asked us to no longer follow the world but to be transformed by the renewing of our mind.

Going back to her journal she wrote:

OUR THOUGHTS!

God forgive me for thinking that You can't heal me and keep me safe. God, as I start this new life allow me to see myself as You do—worthy to be called a daughter of the King, worthy to be Your daughter, and worthy to have You fight my battles.

Do not be afraid. Do not be discouraged. Follow my ways. Commit your ways to My ways and I will give You the desires of your heart.

I want to be free from the prison I have put myself in. Lord, free me today.

The spiritual gift survey said I should be a teacher, but yet I have the gifts of compassion and hospitality. God, do with me what You want.

Ralynn found herself doodling as she was daydreaming about being a teacher and helping others. Then she wrote *My GiGi's House* as she was falling asleep.

With her new commitment, she didn't want to seem unsociable but she really wanted to spend time alone with God. She had made a permanent imprint in the chair on the front porch and her comfy chair in her room was no longer so comfy now that she was in that later part of her pregnancy. Getting settled on the porch, she looked down at the clock on her phone; it was 10:10. A tear started as it reminded her of Mikki who had already come and gone from the house. She was living at Z-House when Ralynn gave her testimony but left a couple of days after Julie had spoken. Getting out her journal she started to reminisce about Mikki.

Mikki left because she thought that all life had for her was to belong to the drug dealer. Lord, she said she deserved what she got in life. She did not want to talk about You, Lord. She said You would not forgive her. She said there was too much damage done. Daddy, I saw a little girl who wanted so much to believe that God was there when her mother sold her to the drug dealer for more drugs.

Closing her eyes, Ralynn could see Mikki and her sitting on her bed, talking one night. Mikki was very direct as she was talking about how her mother would say, "If you love me you will do this for me." Ralynn started to journal again.

Lord, Mikki had lost all hope in someone she could not see, because the one who was meant to save her from harm was the one who created the most harm.

Remembering the day Mikki was walking out the door Ralynn could still hear her words: *"If this God is real, then maybe our paths will cross again, but until that time I need someone who is real. Someone that I can see and will tell me they love me and keep me safe."*

Ralynn's memories of Mikki were continuing.

Mikki would just come in and talk to Ralynn. She really didn't bond with anyone else that Ralynn knew of. Their late-night talks, even though they only lasted just over a week, consisted of her telling Ralynn so many stories. She would tell of how the newest drug dealer would come to town and her at-that-time boyfriend, would put her up for "collateral" when he didn't have enough money to purchase the drugs.

The leader would then pimp her out in his other business venture. One night, she told Ralynn that she thought she was safe because she was about six months pregnant and was starting to show more. She thought for sure he would not use her as collateral anymore and for sure she would not be pimped out. That was farthest from the truth. She found out quickly that pregnant prostitutes were worth more. Ralynn could not believe her ears. But then Mikki started crying because her boyfriend never came back to retrieve her. The abuse got worse, and then at seven months pregnant, the leader, whose street name was Crazy Z, told her to take a pill he had handed her. She knew better than to try and fake taking it because he would check her mouth himself, and she also knew the consequences of disobedience. Within a couple of hours, she had started to cramp and bleed profusely.

They rushed her to the local ER and dropped her at the door, speeding off never to be seen again. Mikki said that the doctors and nurses were not compassionate at all. They immediately drew blood and ran tests. The drugs in her system that night were off the charts, including the abortion pill.

Mikki said they were able to deliver the baby, but by the time she became coherent, the Child Protective Services social worker was waiting outside her door. It didn't matter how many times Mikki told them she did many things but drugs were not one of them, they never believed her. Mikki was told that they had a big enough case against her with the abortion pill in her system, so she signed away her parental rights to avoid prison time. Ralynn realized that Mikki had ended up in her own prison, though. Mikki then went on to tell Ralynn that she became dependent upon heroin just to make it through the day. She ended up bouncing from abuse shelter to abuse shelter when it got too bad, and if she needed to clean herself up. Mikki told her that it was 10:10 when she signed away her rights, and that time every day haunts her.

Ralynn was now crying, thinking of her. She had tried to reach out to Mikki on social media but her request had never been accepted, and it said Mikki had not seen her message either. She knew that the chances of meeting again were slim to none, but Ralynn felt drawn to reach out one more time. Ralynn got on her social media feed and typed in Mikki's name. There it was: a picture of Mikki. Her profile picture had wings superimposed on it and today's date with the saying, *"Heaven gained another angel today."*

Immediately Ralynn started to fish around on her feed and found a story. It said she been dead for a few days on the couch of a known drug dealer's apartment. Ralynn could only assume it was her newest boyfriend. Ralynn fished some more and someone had commented that "They were all so high on Meth and Cocaine, they just thought she was sleeping."

Now talking out loud to God and crying, *"But they didn't keep her safe."*

Ralynn was so mad that she got back out her journal and started to write:

> She had so much to offer.
>
> She did not see what I saw:
>
> A person created in the image of God,
>
> Someone God said was worth dying for,
>
> Someone to whom God says, I love you.
>
> God says follow Me and allow Me to transform your life into the person I created you to be.

Ralynn found herself with even more ambition to help the women who lived here for as long as she was here, even if she couldn't do it in a structured environment.

Realizing it was getting late, she put everything away so that she could get ready for class that was no longer class but was supposed to be a mini-devotional. Unfortunately, the women at New Grace were easy going about making dinner and babysitting, but not so much about leading a devotion, so Ralynn had called Shelly and she graciously came to host a talk.

Dinner once again was out of this world. For dessert you were able to choose from strawberry cheesecake or turtle cheesecake. A younger mom in the church made them for the dinner but could not attend. Ralynn found out that this woman bakes for a living, and these cheesecakes were the creamiest she had ever had. The caramel was homemade and drizzled everywhere, and the strawberry glaze, well, it had just the right sweetness and the texture was perfect so that it wasn't candied.

After the moms got their children situated, they transitioned to the couch.

"Okay, ladies, welcome. I hope you have had a great week. So we are going to change things up a little, I want to ask you a question."

Everyone sat attentive as they waited for Shelly's question.

"What do you want to talk about tonight?"

Sally was the first to speak up. "Why are you asking that? I thought we were going to go through the same program Ralynn has been going through?"

"Well, ladies, for tonight we are going to change it up. But what I will tell you, Sally We are starting a brand-new class on Saturday mornings, beginning in August."

"That's over two months away."

"You are correct, but until that time, on Monday nights we will be here every week answering your questions. So with that Sally what would you like to talk about tonight?"

"Okay, why when I say I am done with men, I find myself right back in a bad situation?"

"Good question. Does everyone agree? Should we talk about that?

Everyone was in agreement so Shelly started in.

"It's not that easy to say "I am done with men." First, the more you say you aren't going to do something, where is your focus? The focus becomes the "thing." So in this case, it is men. Your brain doesn't hear I am done with men. It hears men. So now your brain is thinking about . . ."

"*Men,*" everyone shouted and started to laugh.

"We were created by God to be in relationship. Relationships take on different forms. There is a mother–child relationship that is formed even before you take your first gulp of air. While you are "cooking" for nine to ten months, you are making a bond with your mother. Unfortunately, this bond can be great, or it can have some strains in it. If a pregnancy is amazing and the mom feels safe, there are these, what we call in layman's terms, happy drugs released, and the baby feels it. But if the mom is in a bad place and feeling threatened or in abusive situations, there are what we call bad drugs released from the fight or flight that happens in your system. So that too gets into the baby's system. As you grow up, if there are problems at home or you are not cared for especially as women, we long to have this hole filled, and even when we see red flags and warnings, the overwhelming need to be needed rises, and we plunge headfirst into the relationship."

This time Ralynn was handing out the tissues, seeing Jim hadn't come with Shelly tonight.

"Now that I have shared a little about the why and before I go any further, let me give you an example that may or may not resonate with you. You are done with guys. You are happy with just you and your kids. As a matter of fact, you have gone to the park to play. You are pushing your children on the merry-go-round. They are laughing and having a great time. You are getting tired, so you go to sit down. Then out of nowhere comes a man. He nonchalantly comes over and starts to push your children faster and faster on the merry-go- round. Your children are loving it. They are laughing, and you had not heard them laugh like that in a long time.

"You are telling the kids it is time to go and thank the man for pushing them. Now they are giving you fits because they don't want to leave. Again the man to the rescue. They listen. They obey. He says his good-byes, and the kids are now hanging on him and don't want him to go. He smiles, and you melt. You are lonely, and he just gave you a great gift. He got the kids to mind. How bad can it be? Ummmm. Real bad. You just met him. You don't know his name. Yet the loneliness, that hole, is being filled little by little.

"Now you say your goodbyes but ever so sneakily you let him know you will be back tomorrow. 'Kids we have to go. But we will be back tomorrow after I get off work.' You have just given him an invitation. I hate to say this, but until you realize this cycle you are on, you won't get off. And statistically, it will get worse and worse the longer you stay on it. I don't have a magical pill you can take. What I do have is another question and a statement. My question is this: Ladies, what expectation do you want for your life? For you? What do you want? Do you want a career? Do you need to go back to school? Now for the statement. When you keep focused on what you want for yourself, the relationships will no longer be an issue. You won't have time for them because you will be working on yourself and making your new life happen. Going back to the original statement I made, what are you thinking about?"

"The new expectation," shouted a few of the ladies.

"What are you not thinking about?"

"Men!" shouted the same few ladies.

"So, Sally, does that help you?"

"Yes, ma'am, thank you."

"Ladies, I know it is late, and we have kept the ladies from New Grace a little longer. Let's thank them again for bringing dinner, watching the kids, and joining in the discussion tonight."

Ralynn knew she still had a long way to go. As a matter of fact, as Shelly was teaching tonight, she learned once again that she needed to stay focused on what her new expectations were, so she wouldn't fall into her go-to behavior, which was a relationship. As sad as she was that Shelly had to be careful and not talk about a relationship with Jesus, she was grateful that Shelly agreed to share and to let everyone know that there will be a full class starting in August.

XXXIV

Ralynn found herself with mixed emotions as tonight was the last class at Jim and Shelly's. She felt that these weekly meetings gave her a purpose. She was learning so much and wanted to learn more. Before Shelly got started with the lesson, she was giving instructions for Sunday's graduation. On Sunday, everyone needed to be at Mapleton Christian Church for the 9 a.m. service. This church was a huge supporter of the ministry, and the one thing they like to participate in is graduation. Ralynn was excited but also scared. What if someone recognized her and called Ben? Would he show up and make a scene. Then Shelly put her mind at ease.

"Ladies, the ceremony will take place at the very end of the service. As soon as it is done, we will all leave on the bus to head to lunch at the home of the women's ministry leader. We will also bring you back after the last service is over, and everyone has left the building. Please park your vehicles at the Mini-Mart's parking lot down the street. We will use their van to transport you all there at 8:45 a.m. Sound good?"

Ralynn was pretty sure Shelly and Jim thought of everything, but even though Ralynn's mind was at ease, she still was not 100 percent sure she could make it. Shelly had that taken care of also.

"Also, ladies who live at Z-house, we have contacted Ms. Shaw, and she will be bringing you all in their van and we will make sure you get back to the pick-up point. Ladies, here is the paperwork for tonight's lesson. Make sure you have a pen to write with, and let's get started. I want you all to know how proud I am of you. Tonight's lesson is on 'Who are you listening to and do you even care?'"

Not backing off, even though it was the last week, Shelly started right in.

"Ladies, think about the TV shows and movies you watch, the radio stations you listen to, the websites you frequent, and the magazines you look at. Everything your eyes see starts to go to your mind. Remember last week when we were talking about your thoughts? Know that what we watch, read, or listen to doesn't just go in one ear and out the other; it stays in our mind—our thoughts. Then we act on it. When I was growing up, I used to watch Soap Operas. It was an alternative that I wanted to become my reality. One Friday, during the Christmas break, I had watched my favorite soap. So let me set up the whole scene for you. The whole living room was decked out for the holiday, and there was a tree in the far corner. The doorbell rings, and the young lady lets her boyfriend into the house. They get into an argument. She storms off to the corner where the tree is, and he walks over, turns her around and they kiss and make up."

As Shelly is telling this story all the ladies are like, "Aww."

"I know right . . . happily ever after. But this was all good in make believe. The problem for me as a teenager, I wanted and longed for this alternate reality. You all know my past and how my home life was not the greatest. I was longing for someone to sweep me off my feet. I wanted to be loved, no matter the consequences. Let's just say soap operas are not reality because that night, my boyfriend and I got into a fight.

It really was Christmas, and there really was a tree. But he didn't twirl me around and kiss me. He got my coat, took me home, and that was the end of our relationship."

"*Seriously?*" asked Jai.

Then Shelly explained that our life cannot be fixed in an hour TV show. She said that because we live in a society of easy fixes, we expect life to work out the way you watch in the movies or on a television show. Shelly also wanted us to understand that what we put in our minds affects not only who we are, but also our children.

She finished the class by making sure we all knew that God loved us and that until we saw ourselves as God did, we would go back to what was familiar. She explained that living a life that glorifies God is hard, especially when you may not feel worthy. She then went on to tell us a story about a woman who was not even worthy, by the world's standards, to get water from the well in town during the morning hours, she had to wait until the afternoon. Shelly went on to tell us about how on a particular afternoon this woman met a man who asked her for a drink. She tried to explain that he should not be talking to her but this man said, "If you only knew the gift God has for you and who you are speaking to, you would ask me, and I would give you living water."

The conversation went on and the woman wanted to know where to get this living water. The man then told her, "Those who drink from this well will be thirsty again. But those who drink the water I give will never be thirsty again. It becomes a fresh, bubbling spring within you. It gives you eternal life."

Shelly went on to finish the story, telling us that this woman, who is not worthy by the world's standards, wants this water, asking what she must do. The man told her to go get her husband, and she told him she didn't have a husband. The man then told her her history with men and the fact that she was living with a man not her husband now. "Ladies, this man was indeed Jesus. He wanted to make sure she was going to be truthful. He was checking her heart, and He is checking yours, too. Are you going to be truthful with Him? Who can relate to this woman? Jesus doesn't care about your past. He cares that you are truthful and want to be transformed in the way you live. Understand that satan uses our own negative self-talk and feeling unworthy to keep us in our own prison. He doesn't want you to think you are worthy of living a life that glorifies God because of your past."

Shelly then told of the story from the Bible where the guy was filled with demons. He lived in the tombs because nothing could contain him. Shelly also joked during the story that "cutting" is not something new because the Bible says this guy was doing it during Jesus's time on earth. Ralynn always loved how when Shelly was talking about the Bible, she made the scripture real. Shelly went on to read the whole story that is found in Mark 5 and shared about how Jesus came to that area. He healed the man of his demons. Jesus sent the demons into the pigs, and the pigs then ran into the Sea of Galilee. The herdsmen ran into town and told the people what had happened. Instead of being excited that Jesus was there, they were afraid and wanted Him to leave.

The man who was now healed, wanted to go with Jesus. But Jesus said, as Shelly paraphrased it, "Go back to your people and tell them all that I have done."

At this point Jim piped in, "Healed people want to follow Jesus."

Shelly then added, "It doesn't matter where you start. What matters is that as God heals you, you do as the demon-filled man did: go and tell."

Shelly went on to finish, "In the book of Matthew, Jesus comes back to that area after He has healed the man, and those same townspeople, the ones who did not want Jesus around in the first place, were now begging Him that they might even just touch His tassel to be healed. What has Jesus healed you from and is wanting you to show and tell, so others will find the same healing?"

Ralynn read the question as Shelly was reading it.

"What is God asking of you today to let go of? What is He asking you to do differently?"

Ralynn was trying to answer the questions when Shelly started talking again. "While I was teaching earlier today in the local jail, I saw this quote. It said it was attributed to Fred Smith. "You are the way you are because that's the way you want to be. If you really wanted to be any different, you would be in the process of changing right now." So ladies, what choice are you going to make today? Are you going to stay in the cycle of letting life happen, or are you going to start to make life happen?"

Ralynn could not believe it when she turned the paper over, it was the end and the last words written were:

GOD MAKES NO JUNK

As they prepared to leave, Shelly reminded them about Sunday and to be on time.

On the drive home, Kia was a little more talkative, but Julia was sullen. Ralynn was not sure if Kia wanted Ralynn to answer or if she was just talking out her feelings.

She kept mumbling things like, "but I like my life the way it is. I don't want to give up things. Why do I have to change?"

"Mama? Okay?"

"Yes, Kyra baby, I am fine. I just have a lot on my mind tonight. Did you have fun with your friends?

"Mm-hmm."

Ralynn was just about to ask Kia if she was okay, when Kia's favorite song came on. Kyra heard just the first few notes of the song and started singing at the top of her lungs,

"Gurrrll, my speaers go BOOM BOOM"

Ralynn could not believe it but Kia shut it off and started reprimanding Kyra for singing the song. Ralynn wanted to tell her it was not Kyra's fault and that she was just repeating what she was being subjected to, but she thought Kia figured that out because when they got home, she picked up her daughter and apologized for getting mad. That's when it hit her; Shelly got to Kia tonight.

Before Ralynn got to the hallway, Julia was asking if they could talk.

"Sure, do you want to come in? Or go sit back out in the living room?"

"Can we sit in here?"

"Sure, come on in."

Ralynn was pretty sure that Julia had been crying but was going to just wait until she was ready to talk before she asked if she was okay, already figuring she wasn't.

"Can we talk about what we have been learning?"

"Sure, what part?"

"Well, all of it? I want what you have. I have been watching you and do you think God will forgive me for killing my baby?"

Ralynn had to catch her breath as she looked past Julia and saw her daughter's first picture of her waving at her.

"Oh Julia, oh yes. I am so sorry. He loves you, and He wants to have a relationship with you so bad. He knows everything, and He is just waiting for you to say you want to have a relationship with Him and be forgiven for your sins."

"Ralynn, can you pray for me?"

"I can, but if you are wanting Jesus to forgive you, you have to pray that yourself."

"Right now, will you just pray for me? I am so alone. I feel so dirty. I don't know if God can really forgive me."

Taking Julia's hand, Ralynn started to pray.

"Lord be with Julia. May she feel You holding her. May she understand that You love her. May she see that she is worthy of Your love. Amen."

"Amen. Thank you, Ralynn. I feel better. We will talk in the morning."

The next morning, Julia acted like nothing had happened. Ralynn wanted to talk to her about it, but the chance never came. Ralynn figured that she would just pray for her and Kia to make decisions before it was too late.

XXXV

Sunday morning was cloudy, and it looked like rain. For many years, Ralynn had let the weather dictate her mood, but not today. Today was a first for her, she had finally accomplished this first new task in her life, finishing a program and graduating. And she was learning so much doing her Bible study by text with Shelly. Checking herself one last time in the mirror she said a quick, breathed prayer.

"Lord may we have an amazing time today. Thank you for this church and the family that is allowing us into their home today for lunch."

Walking confidently into the kitchen did her no good when Ms. Shaw was nowhere to be found, the van was gone because she allowed her old behavior to take over. She started to doubt everything.

"This cannot be happening. They promised to take us."

As of Saturday night, Kia was still not sold on the idea that she needed to participate in the graduation, but just as Ralynn turned around, Kia walked out into the kitchen with Kyra in tow. Kyra had on a beautiful pink dress. She kept complaining that the frilly lace was bothering her. Kia bent down to fix something under the dress, trying to make the dress work, but Kyra was not having it. As a matter of fact, Kyra was so animated about the itching that she had the rest of the young ladies who were sitting at the table, laughing.

"Fine, you win. No dress."

Ralynn was not sure Kyra needed her mother's permission because it was already coming up over her head as she was running away from her mother. The whole scene had some laughing so hard, they had tears, and others were holding their stomachs. Ralynn was so engrossed in this interaction, she did not hear the door open and Ms. Shaw walk in.

"Ladies, your chariot awaits."

As we pulled into the Mini-Mart to meet Shelly and Jim, the churches van was waiting for us. Within five minutes, we were all buckled in the fifteen-passenger van, driving toward the church. Ralynn felt the anxiety start. She was remembering the last time she even walked into a church building was the day she met Shelly. The closer they got to pulling in the driveway, the more her throat started to close up. The van was spinning. The laughter from the children in the van started to sound like clowns making fun of her. She couldn't breathe. She had to get out. *"Let me out!"*

The next thing Ralynn knew Shelly was sitting on the sidewalk, and she was in the back of the ambulance. *Wow, what a way to make an entrance into a new church*, Ralynn thought.

They were in the parking lot and the EMT was taking her and the baby's vitals. He asked her a few questions. She guessed her answers were sufficient because he turned his attention toward Shelly and another lady that Ralynn could only assume had come running over when the commotion started as he let her out of the back of the ambulance. Now talking to all three of the women, the EMT was giving Ralynn strict instructions because she refused to go to the hospital. Ralynn figured he wanted to make sure Shelly heard the instructions also. After telling them that he thought Ralynn had had a panic attack, he went on to reiterate that she needed to follow up with her OBGYN tomorrow. Shelly was nodding her head in agreement.

"Shelly, I am so sorry. I know I ruined everything."

"You have not ruined anything. The truth is, if you still want to go in and get your certificate of completion, we have about fifteen minutes."

"Will you go with me?"

"Yes I will be right next to you the entire time."

The closer she got to door of the church, her body started to tense, Ralynn couldn't believe how attuned to her Shelly was because she just started to whisper, "Just put one foot in front of the other. Look at me if you need to. You are doing great. These people love you very much. They want the best for you. They are not from your past. They will not judge you, I promise; I won't let them. Breathe. One foot in front of the other."

Before she knew it they were not only in the church, but in the sanctuary. Recognizing a familiar voice made her body relax. Jim was preaching. Holding Shelly's hand, she walked down front and took a seat next with the rest of the ladies. Jim was teaching from John 8. He was talking about the woman who was brought before Jesus by the religious people because she was caught in adultery. Jim explained that when you were caught in adultery back then, the custom was to be stoned to death. Jesus told the religious people that whoever was without sin could cast the first stone at her. When Jesus looked back up, no one was standing there, and Jesus asked the woman where her accusers were. She said they had left. Jim then said, Jesus told the woman, "Neither do I. Go and sin no more."

Jim continued, "Dear Church, we are all sinners in need of a Savior. These ladies that we are about to bring up on stage need your love, not your condemnation. You may have seen the ambulance when you drove in. One of our "daughters" had a massive panic attack just being driven to the church. That should never be anyone's response when they are going to be with a body of believers. So, ladies, if you would make your way up here, we want to present to you your certificates of completion. These ladies have given over two months of their time and have come over for dinner with their children. We have laughed, and we have cried. We even had a baptism a couple of weeks ago."

When Jim said that, everyone applauded. Ralynn was so glad he did not point her out.

Jim went on to explain a little about the 180 Program and what was taught each week. He explained that there was homework based in scripture and that we all have grown in our own ways. Jim then told the congregation that some of the ladies were already enrolled in college that was going to start in the fall. Again applause.

It was finally time for Jim to call the names, and Shelly presented the ladies with our certificates. Ralynn, thinking she was about to die, could not get off that stage fast enough. Her head was throbbing, and her chest was pounding.

When the pastor finally said Amen, Shelly must have seen the panic in Ralynn's face because she was at the foot of the steps so fast. Thankfully, Ralynn did not lose it. Shelly took her arm and bypassed all the well-wishers. She quickly ushered Ralynn onto the bus that was waiting. The air-conditioning was on and felt refreshing. Once again, Shelly, talking very softly, kept her focused on the future, not where they were. After about fifteen minutes, everyone was seated, and the bus took off. The pressure in her chest left immediately when the bus turned out onto the main road.

The farther away they got from the church, the better Ralynn felt. Sitting and just relaxing, taking in the scenery, Ralynn's little girl decided that it was time to wake up and do flips. Kyra was sitting next to her when all of sudden you could see her entire belly moving. Kyra started to freak out.

"Rawin, Rawin what wrong?"

Quickly moving to the seat next to her, Shelly asked, "Are you okay?"

"Yes," Ralynn said through tears and laughter.

"What is it?"

Ralynn just pointed to her belly. She was not too sure what her daughter was doing, but it felt like she was swimming, jumping, and rolling like a dolphin does in the ocean.

Now Shelly was laughing and crying. With everyone staring at her belly, her daughter must have known everyone was staring at her because now she was quiet.

"Kyra, that's my daughter. She is going to be your new friend when she gets here. Do you want to feel my belly and see if she will kick your hand?"

Kyra was reluctant but decided to put her hand on Ralynn's belly. As soon as Kyra did, her daughter kicked. It scared Kyra at first, but then she started talking to her like she was sitting right there. She was telling her new friend about all the fun things they would get to do. Ralynn hated to end that moment, but the bus was pulling up to the Green's house.

The next few hours were pure joy. The Green family treated the ladies to the most amazing pot roast dinner Ralynn had ever had. It was complete with roasted baby yellow potatoes and carrots. Mrs. Green had made homemade dinner rolls. The recipe was her mother's grandmother's. Ralynn stuffed herself so full that she just wanted to roll up in a ball and go to sleep.

Getting back on the bus, Ralynn started to feel her anxiety level rise, but that was short lived when Shelly informed everyone that they would not be going back to the church but straight to the Mini-Mart. The trip back to the parking lot was uneventful, and for that she was grateful. Ralynn thought she had created enough drama for the day. As the bus pulled into the parking lot, Ms. Debbie, the night manager, was waiting, and Ralynn was very thankful.

Finding Hope

Getting into the Z-House van, Shelly reminded Ralynn that she needed to call the OBGYN in the morning. She also offered to give her a ride if needed.

Finding relief when she was finally inside the safety of the home, the emotional roller-coaster she had been on today had done her in. Laying down thinking she was going to take a quick nap, she opened her eyes and found the clock sitting on the nightstand, reading 3:01 a.m. She rolled back over and covered up and fell back to sleep.

XXXVI

"**K**nock, knock . . . you alive in here?"

Kia was opening the door, as Ralynn was just waking up.

"I don't mean to bother you, sleeping beauty, but it is noon. Ms. Shelly just called me because she said she called you a few times, and it just went to voicemail."

"It's what time?"

"It's noon."

"Oh my, I came in here when we got home to lay down and take a nap. I guess the events of yesterday took more out of me than I thought."

Taking her phone out of her purse, she realized it was still on vibrate from church yesterday. Sure enough there were multiple texts and voicemails from Shelly.

"So you are okay?"

"Yes. Hungry but okay. I will text Shelly right now."

As soon as she hit send on the text message, Shelly was calling. She wanted to hear my voice to make sure everything really was okay. For the first time while talking with Shelly on the phone, Ralynn started to really appreciate her kindness and motherly love for her. The baby started to roll again. Ralynn also started to comprehend that she was not just pregnant but was carrying another human being who would grow up one day to be its own adult. For past few months, it was just something she was. But today she started to think about what it would be like when she entered the world. This revelation started to make her head spin. Starting to panic, she was not sure she could do this. This little human deserved better than living in a shelter. Breaking her thoughts, Shelly's voice on the other line was coming through,

"Ralynn, call the doctor and call me back when you hear from them.

Okay?"

"Yeah, sure."

Hanging up the phone she was trying to remember what she had just said yes to, when her text alert pinged.

"Call the doctor."

Ralynn was surprised that the nurse answered the phone as soon as they transferred her. After explaining what had happened, the nurse asked a few questions about how she was feeling and if the baby had been moving since then. The nurse decided it wasn't an emergency but would like to see her this week. Because Ralynn already had an appointment set for Friday, the nurse said that she would see us then.

Shelly was glad to hear that they weren't worried. Then she texted, "Hey you want to meet this week?"

"I would love to. I have a lot I want to talk to you about. Wednesday at 10 a.m. at the Coffee Shoppe?"

"That works for me."

"See you then."

While making her lunch, she realized she needed to make sure everything was on for tonight. Scarfing down her sandwich, she went in to the office to make phone calls.

An alarm when off in Ralynn's head. Wait, she said she would see me on Wednesday. Getting her phone out she texted Shelly:

Hey. You still coming tonight to facilitate?

Sorry. I can't, but isn't Tina, Chris's wife, coming tonight?

I think so.

Get her to talk. Have her tell her story.

I'll text her and tell her to be prepared.

It was finally time for dinner, and sure enough, Tina came prepared to teach with props and all. The group of ladies who came were so sweet the whole night. They loved on the kids during dinner, and almost every one of them came over to Ralynn and asked to touch her belly. She had learned to expect it, especially since Kyra thought that her new friend was already here. Every time Kyra saw Ralynn, she would run over and start talking to her belly. Ralynn was realizing that her daughter loved hearing Kyra's voice because every time Kyra started to talk, her daughter would start doing flips and kicking. Ralynn loved feeling her daughter move like that.

As dinner finished, Ralynn was getting ready to move everyone into the living room. Then Tina stood up and said, "Hey ladies, let's get the kids taken back to their room and get started in five minutes. Is that good?"

The ladies all nodded, and those with kids got them settled and came back to the living room where Tina was standing in the middle of the room now dressed like she was going to the Kentucky Derby, accented with the large-brimmed hat and white gloves.

"So, ladies, question for you. Am I the same Tina you saw at dinner?"

"Yes."

"Correct." Now taking off the hat and gloves and throwing on a t-shirt and sweatpants, she asked, "Am I the same Tina now?"

"Yes."

"Correct. I want to tell you my story. I grew up in a home where I longed to be loved. My mom and dad both were too busy for me. We didn't go to church, not even for Easter or Christmas. I had a longing to be loved. In fact, as a high schooler and even into college, I had to have a boyfriend. It didn't matter if I really liked him or not, I just didn't want to be alone. I would flirt all the time to get a guy's attention. Have you ever heard, what you get them with is what you have to do to keep them? Well I am very lucky that by the time I was in my twenties, I wasn't pregnant and only once was I in fear for my life with a guy. That lifestyle continued.

"The reason I started this lesson with changing clothes and asking if I was still the same Tina was because that is exactly what I would do. I would change clothes. I would get my hair cut. I would get my nails done. I would do anything and everything to change the outside, but not once did I think to change the inside. I continued on this cycle until I was twenty-five.

"That is when I met my husband. We met through mutual friends, and I thought he was a little weird. He wanted to talk to me and get to know me. He wanted to get to know what I wanted to do with my life. That first night he asked if he could call me. We exchanged numbers and we went home. He called me the next day and asked me out for coffee. We talked about life. We talked about the future and what we wanted in life. I never thought to ask what he did for a living, but in reality after that day, I didn't think I would hear from him again.

"We had had two dates, and he still had not kissed me or picked up on my flirting. He finally called me three days later and asked if I would like to accompany him to a work event. I said sure. He gave me the address and told me to be there before 6:30 p.m. I showed up to the address he gave me with about 200 other people. It was a youth concert. He was a youth pastor. I started laughing because I thought God had made a mistake.

"That night the energy in that place was full of life. Then Chris got up to speak. His words were not condemning, but loving. He talked about how Jesus wanted a relationship with me. Jesus wanted me to see how worthy I was of having a different outlook on who I was, not just on the outside but on the inside. And you all really know he didn't single me out personally, but because God was working on me, all I heard was my name. I left that evening more confused. I had more questions than answers.

"I also wanted to flee many times that night; now I know it was satan not wanting me to hear what Chris was saying. When the evening was over, I was so overwhelmed with emotion. I didn't know if I was coming or going. Chris must have felt my apprehension because he said we could talk tomorrow. Chris not only called first thing in the morning to check on me, he also brought lunch over so we could talk in person. Chris taught me that I didn't have to have my whole life completely put together first in order to accept Jesus.

"I needed to believe that Jesus died on the cross for my sin and that He was resurrected on the third day and ascended into heaven. I needed to pray and tell Jesus that I believed that He is the Son of God, that He died for me, and ask Him to forgive me of my sins. That afternoon I accepted Jesus as my Lord and Savior. Chris and I started to do a Bible study together so that I could learn about living my life differently. I also learned that now that I was a believer I needed to learn a new behavior and strive to please God in everything I did. The more I learned, the more I wanted to change. So, what I want to say to you is something Chris said to me many years ago:

"'Nothing you do to the outside of your body will change how you really feel about yourself. If you want to have a lasting change, it starts on the inside; and for true change to happen and to stick, that starts with a relationship with Christ.'

The ladies and I are here if you want to talk. We don't have to rush out the door. Ladies, you are worthy. Jesus died for your sins, too. He will forgive you if you just ask.

Before we end, I want to pray. Is that okay?"

Not waiting for any objection, Tina started in.

"Hey Daddy, we come before You tonight as women who were created in Your image. Some of us tonight believe that. Some in this room only see the image of who someone else has told them they are. Daddy, allow these young ladies to seek Your freedom, and may they want to choose to see Your image in the mirror. May they choose You. In the name of Your Precious Son Jesus, Amen."

Before Tina left, Sally came forward to talk with her. Ralynn was so excited but also disappointed because Tina went to Sally's room, so she had to wait until they came out to hear what happened. Ralynn waited impatiently. Finally, at 10pm they emerged from Sally's room. Sally was crying. Tina was crying.

"Ralynn, won't you welcome Sally to the family."

Ralynn started to cry. She wanted to text Shelly, but it was 10 p.m., so she opted to wait until morning.

"We will see you Sunday morning. The van will be here to pick up anyone who wants to come to church and see Sally get baptized."

Ralynn wanted so badly to go, but after last week's episode at church, she wasn't too sure that would be in everyone's best interest. Before she turned in for the night, Kia came in her room. She said that she had been thinking about what she already learned and what she was learning again. She wasn't ready to go as far as baptism, but she did want to start living a life more on purpose. Ralynn was excited to hear that, seeing Kyra was already imitating so much of what Kia allowed her to see and hear.

XXXVII

Just like a creature of habit, Shelly was sitting in the same spot when Ralynn walked into the Coffee Shoppe.

"Shelly, thank you for meeting me. I want to talk through what happened on Sunday and also to ask you a few questions."

"Okay, I am listening."

"I have never had that happen before. I have never felt like I couldn't breathe. The heaviness in my chest. It was . . . well, I thought I was dying. I don't want to feel that way. Can you help me?"

"I don't know much about anxiety or panic attacks. So I do not want to steer you wrong, but there is a clinic for children that has a counseling section to the ministry. Hold on let me call them right now."

Getting her phone out, she dialed the number.

"Hello, yes this is Shelly. I have a question for you. Do you all take adult patients in the counseling department? Oh, I see. Do you know another place that would take government insurance? Christ-centered and sees adults? Oh really . . . Okay. Yes, please I would love the number. Thanks. Yes, you too. Bye."

Putting her phone down, she slid the piece of paper with the phone number on it over to Ralynn.

"They do not take adult patients. They did, however, give us the number to a place that doesn't take insurance but sees patients, and the price is based upon your income. That is the number I gave you there. Now if you want a non-Christian group that your insurance covers, then call Middlestone. They are a government agency, so there will be no talk of God or Jesus. The choice is yours."

"Well, seeing I do not have any income, I guess my only choice is Middlestone. Do you have their number?"

"I do. It is 555–2233. If you are only going there because of finances, at least call Haven Counseling and ask them if there was anything they may be able to help with. Don't just settle because of your financial situation right now."

After an awkward pause, Ralynn broke the silence with her real reason for wanting to meet.

"Shelly, you know I need a job. You know I am pregnant. Shelly, I need to start today changing everything that I thought I knew about life. Will you help me? I do not want my daughter to end up just another statistic. I want her to have a much better life than I did."

Shelly just sat there. Ralynn wasn't sure if she blew her away by all her requests or the fact that she was serious about doing life different for her and her daughter. Ralynn could tell the wheels were turning in Shelly's brain. She started writing things down on a piece of paper that was blank except for Ralynn's name at the top, the date and the letters ILP.

"Shelly what is ILP?"

"It stands for Individualized Life Plan. You remember in class when we talked about a ten-year goal and also our weekly goals? This paper is going to be something we work through together, and I will bring it to all of our meetings. What you write down will be our starting place. We will look at where you want to be spiritually, in education, your personal goals, for work or a career, and in relationships with others."

Shelly turned to the next page and asked Ralynn two questions.

"Ralynn, how do you see yourself? And when you were younger, what did you always want to do?"

Those were hard questions, and she had to think for a moment.

"You know, Shelly, I am not sure I ever thought much about tomorrow when I was younger. For the most part, I just wanted today to end, so I would be one day closer to being old enough to leave and finally be out on my own."

"Great answer. Do you know why?"

Shrugging her shoulders, Shelly continued. "Because you are being truthful. You didn't come up with some elaborate dream that was not real. By telling me the truth, you are being real to yourself, and we will be able to help you better. So I bet you have a hard time thinking about the ten- year goal?"

"How'd you know that? For as long as I can remember, I stopped trying to accomplish anything. Based on what I learned about myself in the classes, every time I wanted to go after something like tryout for cheerleading or even the soccer team, I was told that I couldn't. It would never work, or I would never make the team. So I quit dreaming and trying. I think that was when I started to live just to end that day alive and turn eighteen, so I could move out."

Shelly handed her the paper to fill out the rest of the questions. It was a lot harder than she thought. She had to stop and ask herself, "Where do I really want to be in the future when it comes to: spiritual goals, education goals, personal goals, work/career goals, and relational goals." Before the time ended, Shelly asked how Monday night had gone. All of a sudden, Ralynn realized she had completely forgotten to call her and tell her about Sally. After filling Shelly in, Ralynn asked Shelly if she would go to Chris's church on Sunday morning with her. She really wanted to support Sally. Shelly told her that she would meet her there, and maybe Jim and the girls might come. Ralynn was really hoping they would. But for now she needed to get back to the pickup point before she missed her ride.

XXXVIII

When Ralynn got back to Z-House, a letter had arrived for her. It was from Ruby. She had moved out in a huff one weekend over not having anything to do. At least that is what she had told Ralynn was her reasoning at the time. Ralynn found out that Ruby had met a guy online and had it all arranged for him to pick her up. They were in love and were going to live happily ever after. In this first letter, she shared how the guy she had met online was actually wanted in North Dakota on aggravated burglary and assault charges, being pressed by his now ex-wife.

When he was finally caught, Ruby, being naïve and in love, asked no questions when they were pulled over, and he handed her a black zipper bag. He said, "If you love me, you will tell the police that the bag is yours, and if you don't, you know what will happen when I get out and find you." Her letter went on to say that she knew his threats were always followed through on, so she took the fall for the drugs. To top it off, they were pulled over in a school zone. Luckily, she went on to say that the investigators knew she was not selling nor was this hers but because she swore it was her bag they gave her a sentence of eleven months and twenty-nine days to be served in the local jail. She did say though that if she got a job in the jail and had good behavior she could cut her time in half.

That first letter about killed Ralynn, and she didn't think it could get any worse. Then then the second letter arrived the very next day. This letter was so dark. Ruby had given up on herself, and you could hear it. Ralynn knew Ruby was worth more than she saw in herself, but never being in jail herself, she didn't know what to do. Ralynn decided to write her back and answer her questions, but then she would share what she had learned by going to Shelly's every Thursday night.

Ruby,

I hope you will read this letter with the love I have for you. I wish your life had turned out differently, but for whatever reason you are in our local jail. I want to share something I learned while I was attending Ms. Shelly's Thursday night dinners. She quoted Fred Smith. She told us that she had seen it over the pay phone in a jail cell one day when she went to speak.

You are the way you are because that's the way you want to be. If you really wanted to be any different, you would be in the process of changing right now.

That week's lesson was on choices, and how every day, the choices we make affect our tomorrow. So if we wanted to be something different tomorrow, we needed to start with today.

Shelly also told us about Jim Collins, the author of *Good to Great*. He talks in his book about how businesses are like a bus. On this bus, they have all these people on it, but to have a successful business, you have to have the right people in the right seats. Shelly says that those we allow to ride our buses affect us. And if they are toxic (poisonous, up to death) or dysfunctional (not functioning properly), they can guide and direct us right past a road-closed sign where the bridge is out, and we end up at the bottom of a ravine. Shelly then told us we needed to slam on the brakes and kick everyone off. Then proceed to the next stop sign and pick up new people. Those people are the ones who believe in you and will urge you to become all that God created you to be.

Ruby, I want to be one of those people when you get out. I want you to see that you are worth more than what men have told you. Worth more than the voices of your past are telling you. Ms. Shelly told us all the time that we should not let our excuses become the reality of our tomorrow. Do you want to do something different, Ruby? Are you ready to see yourself as God sees you? I hope you will write back, Ruby. God loves you, and I want you to see that.

Love,

Ralynn

Keeping with her word, Shelly and the whole family showed up for Sally's baptism. Ralynn really enjoyed the church service. She loved the way Chris preached. He was so personable. He reminded her of Jim. During service, Ralynn leaned over to Shelly and said, "I feel welcomed here. I want to come back."

Shelly just squeezed her hand and smiled.

To Ralynn's surprise Ruby wrote back that very next week. She was thrilled that Ralynn was willing to walk with her and show her something different. But even more exciting was the fact that a new class was starting in the local jail, and she signed up. She wasn't sure what it was exactly because everything was new, but the counselor had told the ladies that it was going to be unlike anything they had ever been to.

Letters were exchanged back and forth, and Ruby was getting excited to start the new class and had found out that Ralynn's Ms. Shelly was going to be the teacher. Ralynn could not believe what she was reading when Ruby's latest letter had arrived.

Ralynn,

Ms. Shelly said she was going to start up classes at her house again so that those of us who want to continue in the program can do so out in the free world. I am so excited. I have learned so much. And yes, she taught on the bus analogy. Will you be on my new board of directors?

Ruby

Things at Z-House had been going really well. Because the women of the local churches had been more involved, even more churches had signed up to get involved. The men's group from 8th Avenue Church of Christ, came out to the house for three weeks in a row and trimmed trees, cleaned up the flower beds, and mulched. They even sanded down the wrought-iron furniture and spray painted it so that it looked brand new. Some of the men even took it upon themselves to fix all the fencing and gate around the prayer garden. The outside was starting to take shape again, and it looked amazing.

XXXIX

Ralynn could not wait for the weekend to hurry up and be over. Dr. Smith had already given her soon-to-be-born daughter her eviction notice, and Monday morning was it. Ralynn had her instructions to be at the hospital by 6 a.m. to start the induction process. Sitting in her room, she was caught off guard when Ms. Dee had asked her to drive to the store with her. Ralynn was excited to get out for a few minutes and get a few things for the hospital stay. She was oblivious when Ms. Dee drove right past the store and turned onto the road that Shelly lived on. Pulling into Shelly's driveway,

"Ralynn, could you go get a package from Shelly for me?"

Ralynn knocked on the door, and Shelly yelled for her to come in. As she walked up, actually waddled up the stairs to the kitchen where Shelly was standing, everyone yelled,

"Surprise!"

Ralynn was surprised as she looked around and saw that the house was full of women, not just from Z-House, but weekly volunteers and the ladies who had graduated with her from the 180 Program.

The afternoon was so amazing, with food, cake, and games. And as Ralynn finally finished opening the last gift, she was pretty sure that her baby girl did not have a tangible need in the world.

The afternoon came to an end, and Ralynn realized she was getting more and more anxious for 6 a.m. She absolutely loved Dr. Smith. She was sad that he would be moving away to Michigan after the first of the year to be close to his wife's family. Remembering back to her first appointment, she thought about the fact that he never judged her. Not once. At every appointment before she went into the exam room, he would have her wait for him in his office, he would pray with her and for her and for the baby. During the first couple of appointments, she remembered he would ask,

"Are you sure you are going to keep the baby?

Then he would proceed to tell her about families that were waiting patiently for a child but could not conceive. He told her that they would make great parents if she chose adoption. His prayers were always asking God to speak to her heart about the decision of adoption, to allowing her to be the best mom and to always follow Christ in all that she did in raising her gift from God, this child.

Starting to yawn, Ralynn crawled into bed; she was excited that tomorrow she would meet her daughter.

While Ralynn was waiting patiently for Shelly to pick her up at 5:30 a.m., Ms. Dee and Ms. Shaw walked in to say goodbye. As grateful as Ralynn was for everything Z-House had done for her, she was looking forward to having Shelly and Jim help her for a few days to acclimate to being a mom.

The ride to the hospital was a quiet one except for the radio playing. Shelly had on the local Christian radio station, and Ralynn found herself singing as a praise and worship song came on. She knew her soon-to-be-born daughter liked it also because she was just doing what felt like flips. Just as they were about to pull in to the hospital, Ralynn started to feel funny, like she was going to throw up. She had been having pains but didn't think anything about it.

"Shelly, I think I just peed my pants."

Ralynn didn't really understand what Shelly was doing, but she parked in the emergency turn around and quickly ran in. Before Ralynn could get out, an orderly and wheelchair were coming out the sliding doors, making a beeline for her door.

"Shelly, I thought we were supposed to go to the maternity floor, not the ER?"

Trying to get out of the van, the pain that had been just a nuisance was now so intense that she couldn't move. She was looking at the orderly, trying to catch her breath, but she figured he must have done this before because he grabbed her arm and swung her around and put her in the wheelchair. Then he quickly navigated the back hallways to get her to the maternity floor.

Labor was intense, and Ralynn knew she needed to apologize to Shelly for shouting, yelling, and for squeezing her hand off. After eight hours, her little bundle of joy came into the world, weighing six pounds and having a set of lungs on her. As they handed her to Ralynn, all she could think was, *"Can we put her back in? I am not ready to be a mom? Put her back in; this has to be a mistake. How can I feed her and clothe her? I have a hard enough time getting ready myself. Put her back in."*

But then the nurse put her on Ralynn's chest, and she melted. Whispering in her ear, Ralynn vowed that nothing or no one would ever hurt my little girl. *Never!*

Shelly leaned in, "What's her name?"

"Missy. Not Melissa or Lisa but Missy."

The tears started flowing again, but this time it was because she was so happy.

The next forty-eight hours, Ralynn was occupied with filling out the packet of paperwork that was left by the hospital's social worker. The first thing was a tri-fold colorful brochure with Dolly Parton's picture on it, introducing Imagination Library. By filling out Missy's information, she would receive a free book every month until she was five. Ralynn stopped for a moment, taking in Missy sleeping and remembering what Shelly had talked about in their parenting class: "Reading and talking to your baby increases their vocabulary by 300 words over their peers who have no one that reads or talk with them."

Then it came to filling out the birth certificate, which was the hardest. She never told Ben she was pregnant, and he quit bothering her after his second arrest. Ralynn was so thankful that he had finally let her be because she really thought he was going to kill her that night at KT's. Ralynn did hear though, through the rumor mill that he was living with his old girl-friend and her kids. Ralynn found herself saying a quick prayer for the girlfriend and her kids that she may find her self-worth sooner than later and walk away from Ben before it was too late.

Looking into Missy's little face as she now lay asleep on her lap, she chose to say she was uncertain who her father was. As she was finishing up the Social Security paperwork, someone knocked on the door. It was Kim, a friend of Jim and Shelly's. She had a goodie bag for Ralynn. Pulling out diapers and wipes for Missy, Ralynn was ecstatic when she found a milkshake from the ice cream truck. The rest of the bag was filled with every kind of chocolate bar and every kind of chip. Ralynn was starving for some junk food and was forever grateful. Kim stayed for just a few moments but excused herself when the nurse walked in with the discharge papers.

As the nurse was finishing up explaining everything and had started for the door, the room phone started to ring. It was the front desk asking if it was okay for the Waddells to come back. A few minutes later Jim and Shelly walked in, ready to load Missy and her up to take them to their home for a few days. While packing up Missy, Ralynn realized what the major piece missing in the home was. The house had cooking classes. They had seminars on how to dress for success. Groups came in and taught interviewing skills and resume writing.

They even had a parenting class, but what was missing was the actual application on how to change a diaper, how to make a bottle, and how to get a baby on a schedule. All the things that you learn as you go, but if you come from a background of trauma and dysfunction, having the learning curve tilted in your favor with little things like learning how to actually care for another human being, that would be huge.

"Ralynn, earth to Ralynn. You okay?"

"Sorry, I was just thinking about a part of the house that is missing. It's that piece you are taking the time to show me."

Jim loaded up all Ralynn and Missy's things onto the cart, and Shelly was pushing Ralynn down the hallway when the nurse stopped them. "We can't release her until we see the car seat actually buckled in the vehicle."

Jim, a few steps ahead, turned and said, "I will meet you all in the front of the hospital—in the patient pick-up/drop-off area."

Getting loaded into the van, Ralynn noticed that there were more gifts with her name and or Missy's name on them. There was also a pack-n-play and stroller. Overwhelmed with gratitude, Ralynn started to cry.

XXXX

The first couple of days were rough. Ralynn realized she was not prepared to be a mom. Yes, Sally let her practice with Jessie before she had Missy, but it was different when you're responsible for them twenty-four hours a day, seven days a week. Shelly never raised her voice as she was teaching Ralynn on how to be a parent, and for that Ralynn was thankful. As the days turned to weeks, Ralynn was proud of herself because she was finally getting into a routine with Missy. Her six-week checkup had gone well, and she was ready to find a job and put Missy in daycare, with the hopes of getting a place of her own.

Then it happened. Missy would not stop crying. Ralynn was so tired. She just wanted to sleep. She started to raise her voice toward Missy. She just wanted Missy to sleep. Those next few weeks were pretty dark. Ralynn was pretty sure if Shelly had not been there Missy would have ended up being taken from her. Once again, Ralynn was not prepared for all it took to be a mom, and to make matters worse, she could not call Rita because she was still living in her own dysfunction.

Things with Missy had finally gotten back into a routine, she was sleeping and eating and was an all-around happy baby. The time had finally come for Ralynn to start her job. Again she was grateful for Shelly's help because even with all the programs and help from the government, she was not able to find an affordable daycare for Missy. Shelly agreed to watch Missy, and Ralynn was so thankful. For the first month, Shelly not only watched Missy, but she also drove Ralynn back and forth to work. The bus system did not run to Shelly's house, nor did it run to the area where Ralynn was working.

After about two months of work, Ralynn would try to get rides home, so Shelly didn't have to get out in rush-hour traffic to get her. She knew it was a burden on Shelly, and she did not know how she would ever repay Jim and Shelly for everything. As she was walking up to the house, Jim drove in. He was not in his truck but in a SUV. Ralynn was trying to figure out what happened when Shelly came running out the front door with Missy and told her to follow her. Jim got out of the SUV and handed Shelly the keys.

"Did you tell her?"

Shelly, shaking her head started to squeal with excitement. "Ralynn," handing her the keys, "Here is your new vehicle."

Ralynn was not comprehending what was being said. "Excuse me?"

"Ralynn," Jim jumped in, "We had a donor call today because they heard about all your success, and they had an extra vehicle. They wanted to donate it to you."

Now in tears, Ralynn could not believe what Jim was saying.

"Mine?"

"Yes, Ralynn, yours. The only thing you have to do is pay for title and tags and get insurance."

Shelly had been hinting to Ralynn about donors and how sometimes they will donate vehicles, so Ralynn had already been saving money. By Friday morning, Ralynn was driving herself to work. She could not believe the freedom she felt. She also could not believe that someone had chosen her to have the vehicle.

Even though great things were happening, Ralynn was starting to question being Missy's mom. Maybe Missy would be better off if she gave her up for adoption. Maybe she was not meant to be a parent. Ralynn was finding it more and more difficult to bond with Missy. She loved her, but she just was having a hard time being a mom, and anytime Missy would not sleep or get fussy, Ralynn's fuse was getting shorter and shorter. She was thankful when Shelly stepped in. Shelly had seen the signs and that her demeanor had changed over the past few weeks. She gave Ralynn a number for a counselor and support group that dealt with postpartum depression. Ralynn found it so freeing to know she was not going crazy and that she could overcome this also.

Finding Hope

Ralynn and Missy stayed with Jim and Shelly longer than she wanted. She knew that God had her there, though, so she could continue to grow, not only as a person but also a mom. Missy had just had her second birthday, and the day was finally here. Missy and Ralynn were moving into their very own apartment. With the help of the budgeting class, she was ready to go it alone. She had been at her job long enough that she had already gotten a few raises for her production and could afford rent. Ralynn was grateful to be on her own, but she didn't have much of anything to fill the apartment. Missy had a pack-n-play still to sleep in and Jim's sister had donated a sleeper sofa. Jim and Shelly had just brought the sofa in and placed it along the long wall when people from all over started knocking on the door. Unbeknownst to Ralynn, Kim, who had become like an aunt to Missy, had made a few phone calls and before nightfall, the little 960 square feet apartment was a home.

Pictures were hung, dishes washed and put away, and the refrigerator was stocked. There were gift cards to gas stations, grocery stores, and restaurants to get Ralynn over the hump of being on her own and without any government assistance. Her last raise had put her over the threshold of getting any help from the government—no more Aid to Families with Dependent Children and food stamps, but she was okay with that because she was going to look forward to what the future held.

To Be Continued

Ralynn had been in her apartment now for just over two years. She didn't have to work that beautiful Friday morning, which she was thankful for because it had started to snow. Rush hour and snow in Tennessee don't mix. She had opted to keep Missy at home with her also, so when the text message went off saying schools and daycares were going to be closing early, she was happy they were already tucked safely in their apartment.

Ralynn decided she should turn on the television just to check the situation, seeing she was supposed to meet with a group of women that night. She had gotten involved in a mom's group at a local church. Ralynn could not believe her luck when she found out that all the children were around Missy's age. Ralynn found something she never knew was missing in her life: community.

As she was surfing channels a news cast headline caught her attention so she paused for a moment on that channel: *"Local social worker attacked."*

Ralynn could not believe what she was seeing on the news. The name Shelly Waddell was placed prominently under this women sitting in a chair. Ralynn did not recognize the person they were showing on the clip. After what seemed like an eternity, the commercials were done, and the news was back on. There she was, sitting in her chair. She was badly beaten. She looked helpless sitting there. Ralynn wanted to run to her but what could she do? What could anyone do?

Just then her phone rang, and the caller ID said Shelly Waddell.

About the Author

In 1985 Meredith found herself with an unplanned pregnancy. She was a freshman in college and in love with a young man she had started dating a few months earlier. She will tell you that she was very fortunate to have a mom who chose life in 1966 and a bonus mom, who at the time, was very involved in the Right to Life movement. Meredith clearly remembers the nurse at the college clinic asking, "Would you like the number to the abortion clinic?"

Meredith married that young man, Rob Kendall, in 1985 and just five months later, they welcomed their firstborn daughter into this world. Today they have three strong daughters with good-looking husbands and her grandchildren are above average.

In 1986, Rob and Meredith took in their first young mom who found herself in an unplanned pregnancy. They did not have much themselves and actually were the recipients of a box of USDA food every month, but they had an extra bed and a safe, tiny two-bedroom apartment.

Over the years, Meredith felt called to help women overcome their struggles and become all they were created to be. She knew they just needed a coach like she had found in her husband Rob. He has always been her biggest cheerleader even when she reverted back into her self-sabotaging behaviors.

For the past fifteen years Meredith has been on the frontlines of ministry and is the survivor of a gang attack in 2011. Since that time she has struggled with PTSD and other stress-related illnesses. Rob and Meredith founded Advancing the Gospel (AtG) in 2003 and is the author of the 180 Program, which is a series of life-recovery Bible studies used in churches, prisons, and recovery centers throughout the United States.

To learn more about The 180 Program, please visit www.The180program.org

To reach Meredith for a speaking engagement, email her at meredith@the180program.org

Finding Hope

The characters in *My GiGi's House* are purely fictional, but the program, *The 180 Program*, is a life-recovery curriculum that was written after Rob and Meredith Kendall walked away from very successful careers to follow a calling on their life to empower single mothers who found themselves caught in abuse, addiction or negative cycles of life. On the following pages you will find a sampling of the curriculum.

At the time this book was written the curriculum consists of:

New Beginnings

Parenting 180

Budgeting 180

Relationships 180

Leadership

Career Readiness

The New Beginnings and the Career Readiness are also available in Spanish.

Also available is Refocus, which is the non-faith based New Beginnings, and Job Skills.

A teen program is also available and includes:

Teen Leadership

Teen Bible Study called My Plan His Plan

Teen Refocus

To learn more about the curriculum, go to:
www.the180program.org

The New Beginnings is an 8-week life-recovery study. It can be done in a group with a facilitator or used one on one. There are videos that complement the book. The videos were taped at CTN in Nashville, and are 28 minutes in length.

Have you ever asked yourself, "why do I keep doing the same thing over and over?"

In this 8- weeks we will look at your family map and all the characteristics of those who influenced you during your formative years. What most don't realize that how you were parented or who your parents allowed to speak into your lives, shaped your ability to deal with the stresses of life. Some of the things we "caught" growing up weren't so bad, but then others may have set us on a path of personal destruction.

Many do not realize that words that are spoken over us as children to start with and into our adult years if we have not learned who we want to be, allow others "expectations" to become our realities. As time goes on, it gets harder and harder to get off this cycle called "letting life happen."

The challenge is how do we rewrite our story? Or as Ms. Shelly in the book says, "Write a New Book, with a different ending?"

It starts today by saying, enough is enough and I am sick and tire of being sick and tired.

Are you ready to become all that God created you to be?

Our prayer is that you will find purpose, dignity and value as you let go of the shame and guilt of the past and allow God to create in you a clean heart.

Leadership:

This 8-week study helps you look into the scriptures and also other leaders good and bad to learn from their mistakes. This study is more about asking God to show you and to mold you into the leader He created you to be. Not everyone will be a CEO of a company or an Entrepreneur, but we are all called to be the leaders of our home and even if you don't have the title manager at work now, it is always good to be prepared for that promotion.

Parenting 180

Parenting 180 is not about spanking or learning how to discipline. It is a 6-week study that looks at you the parent. It starts with a very serious question:

If I asked your child who was grown to use adjectives like,

Kind
Mean
Addicted
Alcoholic
Religious
Hypocritical
Caring
Etc......

What would they say about you?

Most parenting is not about learning how to discipline; it is about becoming the best role model for your child. You need to be the one that when they become an adult, they want to be just like you.

During this study we look at different types of parenting. We look at who we allow to speak into our children's lives and that doesn't just include people.

Have you ever heard the saying, "Your actions speak so loudly I can't hear your words?"

Most of parenting is not taught it is caught. So what do you want your children to "catch?"

Budgeting:

We want to help you have a dollar left over at the end of the month. This budget takes into account food stamps and aid to families with dependent children. It also takes into account paying people for rides and using the public transportation. Our prayer is that you will learn how to become self-sufficient.

Finding Hope

Relationships:

In this 8 week study we look at many things that effect a relationship. We start by looking at our relationship with God, because we need to know who we are before we can be in a successful relationship with others. Emotions how do they enhance and take away from a relationship. Then we look at words like:

Self-Control
Anger
Rage
Shame
Guilt
Co-Dependency

We will also look at abuse and ask the question "why do we let people have so much control over OUR lives?"

Career Readiness:

In 2013, the ministry that Rob and Meredith Kendall founded bought a restaurant. It was a pizzeria. The premise of the pizzeria was to hire those who felt they could not get a job elsewhere because of their past, or to hire teenagers who were just entering the workforce and give them a chance to learn the skills needed to survive in a career later on.

After having the pizzeria for two years, it was apparent that even though they had a job's program, it needed to be revamped to include teaching the applicant how to become the "bill of goods" they sold us during the interview. We quickly learned that most could get someone to do a great looking resume and even teach them the correct answers. What they did not teach and therefore what Career Readiness teaches is how do you actually become the person you say you are in the interview.

This program has helped many become successful in their careers as they started to look at what they did before and after work very much affected their work ethic and performance.

Breaking the Broken
www.breakingthebroken.com

The model of Ministry that Rob and Meredith used is called Restorative Justice. It is not about throwing money at a situation, but about restoring someone back to purpose, value and dignity. This takes time and is done through relationships.

Rob wrote a book called Breaking the Broken: Debunking the Myth of Social Justice. In his book he not only shares how he came upon a one-year sabbatical, but what God showed him during that year when it came to a Biblical way of serving those the world would call "the least of these."

Relationships are messy and they don't always turn out like you would hope. Everyone you walk with in life has a free will and sometimes, evil wins. But as I, Meredith like to say, "If you aren't 6-feet under, you still have a choice to do something different with today."

CPSIA information can be obtained
at www.ICGtesting.com
Printed in the USA
FFHW011946220519
52581230-58043FF

9 781949 572476